GLIMMER TRAIN STORIES

COVER ART
Backyard Boat, Ohio, *by Jane Zwinger*

PUBLISHED QUARTERLY
in spring, summer, fall, and winter by Glimmer Train Press, Inc.
1211 NW Glisan Street, Suite 207, Portland, Oregon 97209-3054
Telephone: 503/221-0836 Facsimile: 503/221-0837
www.glimmertrain.org

PRINTED IN U.S.A.
Indexed in *The American Humanities Index*.
Member of the Council of Literary Magazines and Presses

Glimmer Train (ISSN #1055-7520), registered in U.S. Patent and Trademark Office, is published quarterly, $36 per year in the U.S., by Glimmer Train Press, Inc., Suite 207, 1211 NW Glisan, Portland, OR 97209. Periodicals postage paid at Portland, OR, and additional mailing offices. POSTMASTER: Send address changes to Glimmer Train Press, P.O. Box 3000, Denville, NJ 07834-9929.

ISSN # 1055-7520, **ISBN # 1-59553-008-8**, CPDA BIPAD # 79021

DISTRIBUTION: Bookstores can purchase *Glimmer Train Stories* through these distributors:
DEMCO, Inc., 4810 Forest Run Road, Madison, WI 53707 ph: 800/356-1200
Ingram Periodicals, 1226 Heil Quaker Blvd., LaVergne, TN 37086
Peribo PTY Ltd., 58 Beaumont Rd., Mt. Kuring-Gai, NSW 2080, AUSTRALIA
Source Interlink, 27500 Riverview Center Blvd., Suite 400, Bonita Sprints, FL 36134
Ubiquity, 607 Degraw St., Brooklyn, NY 11217

SUBSCRIPTION SVCS: EBSCO, Divine, Blackwell's UK

Coretta Scott King in Atlanta, 1969.
Photo credit: Flip Schulke/Corbis

April 27, 1927 – January 30, 2006

We dedicate this issue to Coretta Scott King,
a steady champion of human rights.

Susan & Linda

PAST CONTRIBUTING AUTHORS AND ARTISTS

Many of issues 1 through 58 are available for thirteen dollars each.

Robert A. Abel • David Abrams • Linsey Abrams • Steve Adams • Diane King Akers • Daniel Alarcón • Susan Alenick • Rosemary Altea • Julia Alvarez • Brian Ames • A. Manette Ansay • Margaret Atwood • Dalia Azim • Kevin Bacon • Michael Bahler • Doreen Baingana • Aida Baker • Russell Banks • Brad Barkley • Andrea Barrett • Kyle Ann Bates • Richard Bausch • Robert Bausch • Charles Baxter • Ann Beattie • Barbara Bechtold • Cathie Beck • Jeff Becker • Janet Belding • Sallie Bingham • Kristen Birchett • Melanie Bishop • James Carlos Blake • Corinne Demas Bliss • Valerie Block • Joan Bohorfoush • Matt Bondurant • Robin Bradford • Harold Brodkey • Oliver Broudy • Danit Brown • Kurt McGinnis Brown • Paul Brownfield • Ayşe Papatya Bucak • Judy Budnitz • Susanna Bullock • Christopher Bundy • Jenny A. Burkholder • Evan Burton • Robert Olen Butler • Michael Byers • Christine Byl • Gerard Byrne • Jack Cady • Annie Callan • Kevin Canty • Peter Carey • Ioanna Carlsen • Ron Carlson • H.G. Carroll • David Cates • Brian Champeau • Vikram Chandra • Diane Chang • Mike Chasar • Xiaofei Chen • Yunny Chen • Robert Chibka • Chieh Chieng • Carolyn Chute • George Makana Clark • Dennis Clemmens • Aaron Cohen • Robert Cohen • Evan S. Connell • Joan Connor • Ellen Cooney • Rand Richards Cooper • Lydia E. Copeland • Michelle Coppedge • Rita D. Costello • Wendy Counsil • Doug Crandell • M. Allen Cunningham • Ronald F. Currie Jr. • William J. Cyr • Quinn Dalton • Bilal Dardai • Tristan Davies • C.V. Davis • Laurence de Looze • Toi Derricotte • Janet Desaulniers • Tiziana di Marina • Junot Díaz • Stephen Dixon • Matthew Doherty • Leslie Dormen • Michael Dorris • Siobhan Dowd • Greg Downs • Eugenie Doyle • Tiffany Drever • Alan Arthur Drew • Andre Dubus • Andre Dubus III • Stuart Dybek • Wayne Dyer • Melodie S. Edwards • Ron Egatz • Barbara Eiswerth • Mary Relindes Ellis • Sherry Ellis • Susan Engberg • Lin Enger • James English • Tony Eprile • Louise Erdrich • Zoë Evamy • Nomi Eve • George Fahey • Edward Falco • Anthony Farrington • Merrill Feitell • J. M. Ferguson Jr. • Lisa Fetchko • Joseph Flanagan • Charlotte Forbes • Susan Fox • Michael Frank • Pete Fromm • Abby Frucht • Daniel Gabriel • Avital Gad-Cykman • Ernest Gaines • Tess Gallagher • Louis Gallo • Elizabeth Gallu • Kent Gardien • Ellen Gilchrist • Allyson Goldin • Mary Gordon • Peter Gordon • Elizabeth Graver • Lisa Graley • Jo-Ann Graziano • Andrew Sean Greer • Gail Greiner • John Griesemer • Zoë Griffith-Jones • Paul Griner • Aaron Gwyn • L.B. Haas • Patricia Hampl • Christian Hansen • Ann Harleman • Elizabeth Logan Harris • Marina Harris • Erin Hart • Kent Haruf • Daniel Hayes • David Haynes • Daniel Hecht • Ursula Hegi • Amy Hempel • Joshua Henkin • Cristina Henríquez • David Hicks • Andee Hochman • Alice Hoffman • Jack Holland • Noy Holland • Travis Holland • Lucy Honig • Ann Hood • Linda Hornbuckle • David Huddle • Sandra Hunter • Siri Hustvedt • Quang Huynh • Frances Hwang • Leo Hwang • Catherine Ryan Hyde • Stewart David Ikeda • Lawson Fusao Inada • Elizabeth Inness-Brown • Debra Innocenti • Bruce Jacobson • Andrea Jeyaveeran • Ha Jin • Charles Johnson • Leslie Johnson • Sarah Anne Johnson • Wayne Johnson • Allen Morris Jones • Nalini Jones • Thom Jones • Cyril Jones-Kellet • Elizabeth Judd • Tom Miller Juvik • Jiri Kajanë • Anita Shah Kapadia • Hester Kaplan • Wayne Karlin • Amy Karr • Ariana-Sophia Kartsonis • Andrew Kass • Kate Kasten • Tom Kealey • David Kear • Andrea King Kelly • Jenny Kennedy • Thomas E. Kennedy • Tim Keppel • Jamaica Kincaid • Lily King • Maina wa Kinyatti • Carolyn Kizer • Carrie Knowles • Clark E. Knowles • N.S. Köenings • Jonathan Kooker • David Koon • Karen Kovacik • Jake Kreilkamp • Erika Krouse • Marilyn Krysl • Frances Kuffel • Evan Kuhlman • Mandy Dawn Kuntz • Anatoly Kurchatkin • Victoria Lancelotta • Rattawut Lapcharoensap • Jenni Lapidus • Doug Lawson • Don Lee • Frances Lefkowitz • Peter Lefcourt • Jon Leon • Doris Lessing • Jennifer Levasseur • Debra Levy • Janice Levy • Yiyun Li • Christine Liotta • Rosina Lippi-Green • David Long • Nathan Long • Salvatore Diego Lopez • Melissa Lowver • William Luvaas • Barry Lyga • David H. Lynn • Richard Lyons • Bruce Machart • Jeff MacNelly • R. Kevin Maler • Kelly Malone • Paul Mandelbaum • George Manner • Jana Martin • Lee Martin • Valerie Martin • Juan Martinez • Daniel Mason • Alice Mattison • Bruce McAllister • Jane McCafferty • Judith McClain • Cammie McGovern • Cate McGowan • Eileen McGuire • Susan McInnis • Gregory McNamee • Jenny Drake McPhee • Amalia Melis • Askold Melnyczuk • Susan Messer • Frank Michel • Paul Michel • Nancy Middleton • Alyce Miller • Katherine Min • Mary McGarry Morris • Ted Morrissey • Mary Morrissy • Bernard Mulligan • Abdelrahman Munif • Manuel Muñoz • Karen Munro • Paula Nangle • Kent Nelson • Randy F. Nelson • Lucia Nevai • Thisbe Nissen • Miriam Novogrodsky • Sigrid Nunez • N. Nye • Ron Nyren • Joyce Carol Oates • Tim O'Brien • Vana O'Brien • Mary O'Dell • Chris Offutt • Jennifer Oh • Laura Oliver • Felicia Olivera • Jimmy Olsen • Thomas O'Malley • Stewart O'Nan • Elizabeth Oness • Gina Oschner • Karen Outen • Mary Overton • Patricia Page • Ann Pancake • Peter Parsons • Roy Parvin • Karenmary Penn • Susan Perabo • Dawn Karima Pettigrew • Constance Pierce • William Pierce • Angela Pneuman • Steven Polansky • John Prendergast • Jessica Printz • Melissa Pritchard • E. Annie Proulx • Eric Puchner • Kevin Rabalais • Jonathan Raban • George Rabasa • Margo Rabb • Mark Rader • Paul Rawlins • Yosefa Raz • Karen Regen-Tuero • Frederick Reiken • Nancy Reisman • Yelizaveta P. Renfro • Linda Reynolds • Kurt Rheinheimer • Anne Rice • Michelle Richmond • Alberto Ríos • Roxana Robinson • Anya Robyak • Susan Jackson Rodgers • Andrew Roe • Paulette Roeske • Stan Rogal • Carol Roh-Spaulding • Frank Ronan • Julie Rose • Elizabeth Rosen • Janice Rosenberg • Jane Rosenzweig • Karen Sagstetter • Kiran Kaur Saini • Mark Salzman • Mark Sanders • Carl Schaffer • R. K. Scher • Robert Schirmer • Libby Schmais • Natalie Schoen • Adam Schuitema • Jim Schumock • Lynn Sharon Schwartz • Barbara Scot • Peter Selgin • Amy Selwyn • Catherine Seto • Bob Shacochis • Evelyn Sharenov • Sally Shivnan • Daryl Siegel • Ami Silber • Al Sim • George Singleton • Floyd Skloot • Brian Slattery • Roland Sodowsky • Scott Southwick • R. Clifton Spargo • Gregory Spatz • Brent Spencer • L.M. Spencer • Lara Stapleton • Lori Ann Stephens • Barbara Stevens • John Stinson • George Stolz • William Styron • Virgil Suárez • Karen Swenson • Liz Szabla • Shimon Tanaka • Mika Tanner • Lois Taylor • Paul Theroux • Abigail Thomas • Randolph Thomas • Joyce Thompson • Patrick Tierney • Aaron Tillman • Tamara B. Titus • Andrew Toos • Pauls Toutonghi • Vu Tran • Patricia Traxler • Jessica Treadway • Doug Trevor • William Trevor • Rob Trucks • Kathryn Trueblood • Jennifer Tseng • Carol Turner • Christine Turner • Kathleen Tyau • Michael Upchurch • Lee Upton • Gerard Varni • Katherine Vaz • A. J. Verdelle • Daniel Villasenor • Robert Vivian • Sergio Gabriel Waisman • Daniel Wallace • Ren Wanding • Eric Wasserman • Mary Yukari Waters • Jonathan Wei • Jamie Weisman • Lance Weller • Ed Weyhing • J. Patrice Whetsell • Joan Wickersham • Lex Williford • Gary Wilson • Robin Winick • Mark Wisniewski • Terry Wolverton • Monica Wood • Christopher Woods • Leslie A. Wootten • wormser • Celia Wren • Callie Wright • Calvin Wright • Brennen Wysong • June Unjoo Yang • Nancy Zafris • Silas Zobal • Jane Zwinger

CONTENTS

Here I am with my mother's first cousin, Basil. At one time he had been a sailor, and though you can't see it in this picture, he had a tattoo of an anchor on his arm. I was fascinated with him, so much so that I fashioned a cigar out of modeling clay so he and I could sit around, a couple of old salts, enjoying a smoke.

Lee Martin's most recent books are *The Bright Forever* (Shaye Areheart Books), and *Turning Bones*, part of the American Lives Series at the University of Nebraska Press. He is also the author of *Quakertown* (Dutton, 2001), *From Our House* (Dutton, 2000), and *The Least You Need to Know* (Sarabande Books, 1996). He directs the MFA program in Creative Writing at Ohio State University.

SEA DOGS

Lee Martin

Lee Martin

I warn you; nothing much is going to happen. But the little that will begins one evening toward dusk when my neighbor, Buddy Pope, strides across the grass, a casserole dish held between his hands. I see him through the kitchen window where I'm opening a can of Natural Balance Duck and Potato for my basset hound, Stump, and I reach to switch off the light, but, too late, Buddy has spotted me—I can tell by the way he lifts the casserole dish higher, extends it with his oven-mitt-covered hands—and I have no choice but to wave at him and then go out into my backyard and open the gate.

"Ahoy, neighbor." A former Navy man, this is the way he talks. "Time for mess." He bows his head over the casserole dish and sniffs. "Andouille jambalaya," he says. "Permission requested to come aboard, sir."

It's October, and the leaves have started to fall. Here in our small town in southern Illinois, we can burn them on Saturdays, air quality and the ozone layer be damned. We rake our leaves to the sides of our streets or onto our backyard gardens and set them to burn. The air smells of the must and the smoke the way it has this time of year as long as I can recall, nearly sixty years since I was a kid in Rat Town, that mess of tumble-down houses in the lowlands where each spring the creek still rises and comes up to the doorsteps. I'm glad to be safe and dry here in Orchard Heights, this modest gathering of ranch homes on streets with names like Apple Blossom and Cherry Blossom and Peach Tree.

Glimmer Train Stories, Issue 59, Summer 2006

Buddy thinks he knows my life—me, Sam Brady, a bachelor all my sixty-five years—and I wish I could believe that he does. He thinks he knows it because his dear wife, Bess, is now six months gone, and he imagines that we share the misery of men living alone. "You and me," he said once not long after she died. He laid his hand on my shoulder. "Jesus, Sammy. We're a pair."

But my life is not his. I'd tell him this if I had the heart. I'd tell him I have no idea what it is to love someone all that time—nearly forty years he and Bess were married—and to lose them one day without warning. An aneurysm in her brain. "Buddy, my head hurts," she said, and then the next instant, she fell to the kitchen floor, already gone. All my adult life I've lived alone, except for the dogs, the latest being Stump, who stands now at the screen door waiting for his Duck and Potato.

"He gets contentious," I tell Buddy. Nothing could be further from the truth; like all basset hounds, Stump is long on patience, steadfast with his devotion, mild tempered, and affectionate—a perfect companion. His nose is up against the storm-door glass. His velvety ears hang in loose folds, their ends curling slightly inward. He stares at me with his sad-ass eyes. "Stump," I say to Buddy. "He puts the hurt in me if he doesn't get his grub."

"Don't we all." Buddy lifts the casserole dish toward my nose. "Sailor, don't we all."

So what can I do but let him into my house and tell him to set the casserole dish on the range? He tells me exactly how he made it, and I know what's coming next. "I could give you the recipe." He snaps his fingers. "Or you could come on down to the senior center—that's the ticket—and, Sammy, you could learn to do for yourself."

It's not the first time he's asked. He's learned to cook by joining a widowers' group—Seasoned Chefs—and every Wednesday evening he goes downtown to the senior center and works up a new dish. Good for him. I mean it. Here's to every sad-sack SOB getting on with his life. But me? The truth is I don't much know how to be around people anymore. The past thirty-eight years, before I retired, I worked for, and finally owned, a custodial service. When I was a young man the boss would send me out somewhere—Sherman's Department Store, the IGA Foodliner, Loy's Skating Rink—and I'd spend the night hours, after all the customers and the workers had gone, stripping and waxing floors. Later, when I was the owner, I kept that job for myself. I even took jobs out of town—as far away as Paducah and Cape Girardeau—just for the pleasure of all that time on the road, all that quiet and no one else around.

"Sorry, Buddy. No can do." For a moment, I'm tempted—I'll admit that—but then I think of myself trying to make conversation with all those men, widowers who have a genuine right to their loneliness, and I can't imagine it. Stump is bumping his nose into the back of my leg. I get down on a knee and scratch his ears. I let him sniff my face, give me a lick. I stare into those sad eyes. "I'm about to get busy," I say to Buddy.

"Busy?" He stands with his hands on his hips. He still has on his oven mitts and he looks…well, if you want the truth…he looks like a man afraid of his own hands, and I feel guilty for disappointing him. "Sammy," he says, but I cut him off before he can launch into what I know will be another attempt to persuade me not to be so much of a loner.

"Winter's coming," I tell him. "I've got to build Stump a new house."

"What's wrong with the one he's got?"

"Oh, it won't do," I say, still looking into Stump's eyes. "Nope, not at all. Not for a dog like this."

Some nights, I tell it to him—the old Stumper. He gets down on his belly by my chair, and I let my hand trail over his head. I say it to him again, the old story. I tell him about Dewey Finn, a boy who lived across the alley from me in Rat Town. Dewey Finn. He called me sweetheart. "Sammy, sweetheart," he said once. "You're a pal." We were twelve; we thought we'd be friends forever. Then one night, Dewey took my hand. That was all. We were walking down the alley, and he took my hand and held it while we walked and neither of us said a word. Sometimes I close my eyes and dream myself back to that night.

I feel the heat of his skin; I can still call to mind the way that alley in Rat Town seemed all at once a frightening and wonderful place. I had no words for it, the way I felt. All I could do was go on into my house and sit there alone in the dark and try to tell myself I wasn't the boy Dewey thought I was, wasn't like him, wasn't his sweetheart. At my back door, he'd leaned over and kissed me on the lips, and I'd let him. "Sammy, sweetheart," he'd said, and then he'd slipped off into the dark.

I wouldn't say a word to him after that night. I put him out of my life, scared to death because he knew the inside of me, knew it before I did. It was a wrong thing to be, a boy who liked other boys the way he was supposed to like girls. I knew that, growing up in Rat Town, where men, when they wanted to get mean with someone, called him a cocksucker, a queer, asked him who he was corn holing. You have to understand. I would have done anything not to have been the boy Dewey somehow knew I was. So when a group of older boys cornered me one night in an alley uptown and said they'd heard that Dewey and I were kissey-kissey friends, I said no, it wasn't true, not about me, said it was Dewey who was like that. "Queer," I said, the way I'd heard it said so many times in our town.

It wasn't long before he was dead, his head smashed with a tire iron, a knife taken to his privates. When the police came to ask me if I knew anything about who might have done it, I said no, I was sorry, but I didn't. And that was pretty much the end of it. Though there was talk about who was responsible, no one ever got called to account. No one ever had to answer for the murder of Dewey Finn.

After that, I didn't want much to do with people or anything they had to offer. Now, when Stump looks at me with those sad eyes, I imagine that even he knows how guilty I am. He has no choice, though, but to tolerate me. He's a dog, and there are things he wants—his Duck and Potato, a house to keep him warm in winter and out of the rain in spring and the sun in summer—and he knows I'm the only one he's got who can offer him food and shelter, and, if he'll permit me to call it this, love.

• • •

I start with a picture in my head—a kids' playhouse I saw once years ago in a backyard in a town I was passing through on my way to somewhere else. I'd never seen anything like it—that house—made in the shape of a sailing ship: hull and deck and mast and crow's nest, something out of *Peter Pan* or *Mutiny on the Bounty*. What a sight, this ship. All for the sake of a kid—some lucky kid. I had to pull over to the curb, had to sit there and talk myself out of going into that backyard, walking past the playhouse up to the real house, a house of brick and bay windows. I wanted to put my face up to one of those windows, just for the chance to get a glimpse of the miraculous life I imagined going on inside.

Sometimes now I take Stump out for a walk at night, and we slip through the dark, past houses all lit up. I see people's lives going on: mothers rocking babies; an old man in an arched doorway, leaning over to kiss his wife; a woman wiping her hands on a dish towel; a teenage girl dancing to music. Sometimes I'll hear someone laughing, a television playing, a voice calling out, *Sweetie, hurry. You've got to see this. My God, what a hoot.*

We keep moving. Stump's toenails click on the sidewalk. My hand holds tight to his leash. I carry a plastic bread wrapper in my jacket pocket because eventually he'll do his business in someone's yard, and I'll pick it up, the way any good neighbor would.

"You've got it all wrong," Buddy says to me one afternoon when he comes to watch me in the backyard with my lumber and saws and hammer and nails. I've caught him on certain afternoons peeking out his window, and now he's finally come to tell me exactly what he thinks. I'm nailing together the hull, overlapping the planks the way you would a clapboard house. "That's a clinker hull," he says. "Now, sailor, how in the hell are you going to cut cannon ports in a clinker hull? What you want is a carvel hull, the planks all flush and even. Then you'll be in business."

"Cannon ports?" I stop driving nails. The air, after all that *pop, pop, pop*, clears out, and I watch a lone maple leaf come drifting down, twirling and then floating, until it finally settles on Stump who's sleeping in the sun. "Why would I want cannon ports?"

Buddy narrows his eyes, sets his jaw, tips back his head. "Sailor," he says, "what if Seaman Stump suffers an enemy attack?" Then he gives me a wink, and it almost breaks my heart because I know he's telling me he's lonely. I know he's asking me to please play along. What he wants more than anything now is to help me build this ship, to have my company to help him pass the hours.

Stump is lolled over on his side, the maple leaf stuck to his white belly, but he doesn't know it. His legs are up in the air, and one of them twitches, the only sign that he might have felt that leaf at all, but he keeps snoozing, belly full, warming in the sun.

"Buddy," I say, and I say this in all earnestness, careful not to hurt his feelings. "I've never known Stump to be the fighting kind."

"Sailor," Buddy says, "do you want to be authentic or not?"

"A carvel hull," I say, imagining the two of us working together.

"Let me grab my carpenter's apron," he says, and apparently I want to be authentic because I don't stop him, and the next thing I know we're pulling off the planks and starting over.

While we work, he tells me stories of the earliest shipbuilders—the Egyptians and the Chinese—the ones who knew that to build a sailing vessel was a matter of faith. They could make it watertight—hull and keel and prow—and then set it to launch with no guarantee that it would ever return to port. The gods that ruled the seas might, at any instant, take a whim to dash a ship against an outcropping of rocks, or spin it topsy-turvy with giant waves, or the winds might get fickle and carry it so far from course it would never be able to right itself. So the builders carved eyes into the ships' bows so they might better find their way. Later these eye goddesses evolved into Christian figureheads meant to ward off whatever invisible demons waited to besiege seafarers.

Buddy stands across from me, marking lengths of plank for the deck. "I always thought Bess was looking out for me." He lays a two-by-four between two sawhorses, measures with his tape, and then draws a mark with his thick, flat carpenter's pencil. "She was my friend. My first mate, I always called her. Sammy, do you remember that?"

I'm at my table saw cutting the planks that he's marked, and just before I bring the blade down, I say, "I do, Buddy. I surely do. You were her Popeye; she was your Olive Oyl."

The saw whines, its blade slicing through wood. Sawdust sifts down to coat the toe of my boot. The scent of freshly cut pine sharpens the air. When I raise the saw blade, and its shrill noise falls back, I see that Buddy has laid down his pencil, and he's bowed his head. His carpenter's apron, its strings tied too loosely, sags from his hips. His hands grip the two-by-four, and it looks as if he can barely hold himself up.

"Buddy?" I say.

He snaps up his head, and what I see in his eyes surprises me. I know that somehow I've hurt him.

"How can you say something like that?" he asks, his voice smaller than I've ever heard it. "Make a joke like that? Popeye and Olive Oyl… a cartoon, for Pete's sake. Jesus, Sammy. I'm talking about Bess and me. I'm talking about people who meant something to each other. Forty years together. But, of course, you wouldn't know anything about that, would you?"

All along, I've been wanting to tell him this—when it comes to love and what we've lost, he and I are not the same; he's owned an abundance I'll never know—but now that the moment is here, what I feel inside, instead of the relief that I'd imagined, is a misery, because Buddy knows without a doubt that I'm a man who resents his life, thinks himself unworthy of anyone's affection, and now the greatest gesture of love I can manage is to build this ship, this fancy house for my dog. I can't even tell Buddy I'm sorry, and finally he picks up the two-by-four he's marked and hands it to me. Without a word, we go back to work, and for just that instant I get a sense of what it must have been like for him and Bess—all the times they must have hurt each other, all the compromises they made for the sake of love.

I like to think of the old shipbuilders and their faith. I imagine them fitting the timbers together, raising up the castles and masts. Day after day of this work, their methods tried and true, a mastery learned over time.

Now, here we are, Buddy and I, each afraid to admit that we've reached the age where our circumstances—widower and bachelor—sweep us, scared to death, into our last years.

"She took care of me," Buddy says. "Bess." His voice is so small I can choose not to hear it if I prefer. But I do hear it. I hear the way it quivers. I take it inside me, knowing that later, in the night, when Stump has fallen asleep by my chair, and the house is still, I'll remember the way Buddy said her name, "Bess," and I'll recall, as I do now, how night after night, all summer, I used to hear her laugh coming from their house. "Buddy, you kill me," she said one night as Stump and I passed by, and she said it in a way that told me that whatever Buddy had done, it delighted her. She was sitting in a chair by the living room's picture window. She tossed back her head, threw up her hands as she laughed. I stood in the dark and watched her, this petite woman who tap danced in the community talent show, who still wore Buddy's high-school class ring on a gold chain around her neck, who could look at me—yes, even me—with a smile that made me believe she'd been waiting years for me to come along, and I thought, *My God, she's an angel.*

So the next afternoon, when Buddy brings me a chicken curry and again asks me to come with him to the senior center for his Seasoned Chefs cooking lesson, I feel so bad about hurting him with my Popeye and Olive Oyl remark that I tell him I will.

The Seasoned Chefs wear cooks' aprons—the kind that tie around the neck and at the small of the back, only these aprons aren't white. They're egg-yolk orange with black script letters that say, Real Men Do It In The Kitchen.

They're milling around, helping one another tie their aprons, chatting about the new coffee house uptown where you can buy espressos and cappuccinos and herbal teas—even cucumber-infused water if that's your pleasure. "Cucumber water," a man says, and shakes his head, amazed.

It's easy to pretend that our town is a different place than it was when we were all young. We have that coffeehouse, and the Arcadia Theater, where I used to watch Rock Hudson pictures from the balcony. When he was a teenager, he spent summers here on his uncle's farm.

Once—this was much later, when he was a star—I saw him drinking a root-beer float at Tresslers' lunch counter. Anyway, the Arcadia now has three screens. At Christmas there's a spectacular light display at the city park, and cooking classes like this one for men who suddenly find themselves on their own. When you get down to it, though, nothing much has changed about the way we treat one another. I see the same graffiti about queers and fags spray painted on the railroad trestle south of town, or scratched into the paint on the restroom wall in the city park; I hear young boys calling each other those names. From time to time, even after all these years, I'll hear the name, Dewey Finn. I'll be at the IGA Foodliner, or the Town and Country Lanes where I sometimes bowl a few lines—it can happen anywhere in our town—and I'll hear someone say, *That boy. That Dewey Finn. They cut his nuts out. You know. He was that way.*

I can't help but envy the Seasoned Chefs and the easy way they move among one another, knotting aprons, patting backs. Ask anyone who lives alone. Ask them what it's like to go days, months, sometimes years, and have no one to touch them, not even a finger grazing a wrist, a hand brushing across a shoulder. A hug? Some people would pay money for that. Trust me, there are these people in the world, more than you probably want to know.

The teacher, a woman our age with rouged cheeks and hair dyed blond, is setting out mixing bowls and sauce pans and measuring cups, laying out whisks and ladles and spatulas and stirring spoons.

"That's Vera." Buddy slips an apron over my head and helps me tie it. "She's got that household-hints program on the radio. *Very Vera.* You ever catch it? If you need to know anything—how to get barbecue sauces out of a good shirt, how to make refrigerator pickles—you can just call her up and ask."

"Have you ever done those things?" I ask him.

"Not yet. But I could if I ever wanted to." He leans close to me and whispers. "Sometimes, I phone up her show and ask her a question just to hear her talk—you know, right to me."

Vera claps her hands together and tells us it's time to learn her special recipe for chili con carne. She does a little Flamenco stomp. She snaps her fingers over her head, and the Seasoned Chefs—"Ready, boys?" she asks—gather around her.

I work with Buddy. "Stick with me, Sammy," he says, "and everything will be ship-shape."

We listen to Vera as she shows us how to brown the ground beef. "Stir it over a low flame," she says. "Don't let it stick to the pan."

"That's a snap," Buddy tells me, and we get to work.

It's easy, this cooking. I stir the beef while Buddy opens a can of tomato juice. We're getting everything ready: beef and juice and kidney beans. We gather the seasonings: cayenne pepper, chili powder, salt, and then Vera's secret ingredient—just a squeeze of lime juice. "Oh, that's zesty," I hear one of the men say, and the other Seasoned Chefs agree. *Yes, that's zesty. A little squeeze. That's very Vera.*

I don't mind saying I'm caught up in it all: the satisfying aroma of beef sizzling and browning, the men's high spirits, Vera's heels tapping over the tile floor and her bright voice cheering us on: "Follow the recipe so you won't make a mess-of-me."

Once, she even stops and pats my back. "That's lovely," she says. "That's wonderful. Buddy, you've brought us a ringer."

For some reason, I get a picture of Stump in the backyard, carrying around that rubber horseshoe he likes to gnaw on. He's probably dropped it on the step, the way he often does when I'm out of the house. I find it there when I come home, and old Stump, sitting beside it, waiting for me to open the door and let him in.

It's a silly story, this one I'm telling. A story about a man and his dog and a fancy house that looks like a ship, and this cooking class where men like Buddy Pope can feel, for a few hours, that they might just manage to chart and navigate the rest of their days.

Me? I wish I could trust this feeling I have, this thing rising up in me I can only call joy. I want Vera's hand to linger on my back. I want to say to her, *I caused a boy's death. My friend. Because of me, he died. How do I live with that? What do you advise?* I want to say it to her because at this moment, when she's telling me that what I'm doing is lovely, she's touching me in a way I haven't felt for years, her hand rubbing slow, gentle circles on my back.

But, of course, I can't say any of this to her. I can only smile and thank her, as I do the other Seasoned Chefs before I leave—*Thank you for letting me join you. Thank you for your conversation*—and Buddy when he drops me off at home—*Thank you for inviting me.*

"Sammy," he says. "Forget about it. We're neighbors."

He insists I take our leftover chili con carne, freshly sealed in one of Bess's Tupperware bowls he knew to bring.

This politeness, I think, as I step through my gate. Yes, the rubber horseshoe is on the step, and yes, Stump is waiting. This courtesy, I tell myself as I unlock the door and hold it open so Stump can waddle into the house. This is as much as I can hope for; this is what I have.

So Buddy and I finish Stump's house—even though I've spent weeks drawing up the plans, pleasant days at the public library studying how to build the curved hull, the castle tower, the stern wheel, the crow's nest; spent nights imagining the hours in the afternoon sun, Stump dozing on the grass while I measured and sawed, cutting the lengths and angles just so. How good it would be to work in that autumn sun, to feel its warmth on my face, across my back, to coax the ship along, plank by plank, no thought of the time passing, the light shortening as we moved toward winter.

And it is that way, the days Buddy and I spend together. We work, for the most part, without talking, falling into a comfortable rhythm of measuring and sawing and nailing. We design a drawbridge so Stump can waddle up to the top deck—the *promenade*, Buddy insists I call it—with as much dignity as a basset hound can manage. We cut a hatch into the deck, equip it with a rubberized pet door so Stump, when he takes a notion, can nose his way through and follow a gangway down into the hull. He can go below. I catch on to the sailor's lingo. Pretty soon, I'm talking about fore and aft, bow and stern, port and starboard. "Steady as she goes," I say to Buddy as we raise the mast tower, and he says to me, "That's it. Now you're getting your legs."

I let him cut the cannon ports in the hull and rig them with hinged shutters that we can prop open or close. Stump, when he's below deck, sticks his face out a cannon port and sniffs the air. "Ahoy," I say to him, and he barks.

Then, one day toward evening, we're finished. For a moment, we stand in the last of daylight, admiring our work, and, pleased as I am, already I miss the way the hours have so pleasantly unfolded with Buddy.

"I've got a surprise," he says. "It's over at the house. I'll be right back."

While he's gone, Stump sniffs around the perimeter of the ship, and I imagine he's trying to make up his mind about such a thing.

Then, Buddy's back, and he has a flag. "Vera stitched it for me," he says. He unfolds it, and I see that it's a Jolly Roger of sorts, only instead of a skull, there's Stump's face, and below it the crossbones are Milk Bone dog biscuits.

"Not too authentic," I can't resist saying to Buddy.

"Well," he says, "who's to notice except us old sea dogs?"

He gets up on deck with a stepladder and hangs the flag from the mast tower. Then he comes back to where I'm standing, and we put our hands on our hips and tip back our heads to study that flag furling and popping in the wind.

Stump lifts a leg and pees on the stern.

"Looks like he's christened it," Buddy says with a laugh. "Now all it needs is a name."

I don't even give it a thought. "How about we call her *The Bess*?"

For a long time, Buddy doesn't say a word. He just keeps looking up at that flag. His eyes close for an instant. Then he opens them and says, "If that's what you want."

"It is," I tell him.

And that's it. That's the whole story. I told you, it's not much. But you have to understand what it is to be me—a man who has always been afraid of himself. You have to move with me through the light, nearly gone now, to fetch a can of red paint from my basement, to hand a brush to Buddy Pope and have him take it, his eyes meeting mine, both of us unashamed of how sentimental this all is. You have to know what it is to watch him kneel down along the prow of that ship—the house of Stump—and to watch him with such care paint the first stroke, the bristles of the brush folding back with a slow, steady grace, the motion of his hand tender and sure; to think of Dewey Finn and how he took my hand that time in Rat Town; to know that this—this gift I make to Buddy—isn't forgiveness, but as close as I can come on this evening near to winter, as close as I'll ever come here on dry land.

A picture with my grandfather, just minutes before I knocked out my front tooth falling up the stairs. That same year, I broke my arm falling down the stairs. Eight subsequent years of ballet lessons did little to improve the grace of a skinny, knobby-kneed kid intent on running pell-mell at *the world. My mother's warning every time I took three and four stairs at a time? "Slow down!" Even today, my knees and elbows and hips are always bruised, though it is my husband, who in patient exasperation, asks, "Are you okay?"*

Kerry Neville Bakken's collection of stories, *Necessary Lies*, won the G. S. Sharat Chandra Prize for Short Fiction and will be published by University of Missouri-Kansas City's BkMk Press in 2006. Her stories and essays have most recently appeared in *Story Quarterly*, the *Texas Review*, and *Shorewords: A Collection of American Women's Coastal Writings*. She is the recipient of the Associated Writing Program's Intro Journals Award for Fiction and the Henfield/Transatlantic Review Fellowship in Fiction. She is an Assistant Professor of English at Allegheny College in Meadville, Pennsylvania, where she lives with her husband and two children.

THE EFFECTS OF LIGHT

Kerry Neville Bakken

All material in nature, the mountains and the streams and the air and we, are made of light which has been spent, and this crumpled mass called material casts a shadow, and this shadow belongs to light.

—Louis I. Kahn

The air conditioning quit hours ago, so like dogs we stick our faces out the cracked windows of the bus, panting into the wind. Too many times we have had to stop at dingy gas stations for little cups of coffee, cigarettes, and greasy spanakopita. Or for pile-ups of goats glaring in the middle of the road, jangling their bells in admonition. Or once for the driver to take a slow deliberate piss into a field of yellow wildflowers. I admired his swagger as he reboarded the bus, shrugging, still working on his belt buckle.

Sarah emphatically did not. "Disgusting," she said. All afternoon she has been staring into hills shaggy with cypress trees, then at the cliffs, the edges of Mount Zas, and the sea. Her long blond hair is clipped up in an unbrushed tangle, her neck and cheeks flushed, sunburned. She looks lovely and alone, as if she's been traveling forever, like one of those colonial heroines lollygagging about India or Morocco, churning up the copper dust with her heavy skirts. Though Sarah is with me here, it is right that she appears as if she is not: we are divorcing. I no longer have a claim.

The rest of the passengers, the Greeks, have kept their curtains drawn against the sharp sunlight. Not Sarah. Of all people Sarah should know better. She, the expert on the effects of light, her life's work, wandering from one small-town museum or historic mansion to another, calculating the sun's cumulative damage on textiles and watercolors, bleached sideboards and yellowed draperies. Now, though, her fingers curl and flex in the light as if she is trying to palm its energy, store it up.

I take up two seats, one for my ass, one for my leg. The widows on the bus *tsk tsk* my indolence, my American gall, then see the gangly crutches propped against the window, perhaps even notice my face blanch and tighten as the bus jounces over ruts. Do they hear the sharp intake of breath and turn, as Sarah does at a particularly bad spot of the road, when my spine and knee and ankle summon up the fall once again down all those flights of stairs, the breaks, the unnatural angle of repose? I grit my teeth. All I can do is ride it out.

Sarah says, "All of that out there is broom."

"Broom?" I ask.

"Those yellow flowers. They're supposed to smell like honey."

A guidebook is propped open in her lap, notes scratched in the margin, things starred and underlined.

"Planning the Post-Suicide Deluxe Tour?" I ask.

She shuts it quickly, gripping it tight between her hands. *Greek Islands 2003.* Both current and specific. I try to imagine her wandering the travel aisle of some mega-bookstore, squatting before the Greece section. Sarah likes to arm herself with odd facts and statistics: broom and honey. It is her way to make sense of what she does not yet know.

"Jack, let me be clear," she says. "I'm here to help you get through this, to manage with the getting around. But I'm not yours all the time. You know that, right? This is not a save-our-marriage-through-shared-devastation vacation. This doesn't make us not end."

Again, the bus dips into some foot-deep pothole and I wince. My leg aches as if I'd crabbed these miles bare-kneed on stones like a medieval penitent. Sarah relents, pats the top of her smooth knee.

I swing my leg over and prop it on hers. The muscles hang loose from my calf and thigh. Her fingers settle like birds where my bones and ligaments are anchored together by pins and screws. "It will be okay," she says, and taps a gentle rhythm. Then her hands, on second thought, fly suddenly away.

We both know it will not. Not for Kate. Not for me. For Sarah, yes.

I imagine that, in addition to the guidebook, there is also a journal she will fill with pressed flowers and neat columns of strange local specialties she will try once and once only (goat balls; sheep innards; unpronounceable, unidentifiable grilled meats). In her suitcase, I can imagine a rubber-banded stash of index cards listing obscure Byzantine shrines huddled in remote towns, their peeling frescoes and cracked icons, their collapsed barrel rooftops and empty windows, swallows roosting on the crossbeams, shitting all over what is left of the impassive, sun-bleached Madonnas. And of course, she will jot off postcards, carefully worded—*Jack is doing as well as can be expected.* Which is to say, not okay.

My sister, Kate, is dead, by her own hand. The administrator in Athens, Ms. Maria Nikolaides, a stern woman who mentioned that her BA was from some business college in Indiana, said that I did not have to come all the way to Greece for the body and a suitcase of papers and clothes. Greece was a modern country. An EU country. Greece could certainly handle the respectful and efficient transport of a body and a suitcase.

"After all," she said, "Greece is the EU industry standard in international waterway shipping!"

There were certain documents and authorizations needed before aforementioned body and effects could be released, but she would see that everything was handled with the utmost proficiency.

"She's my sister," I said. "Her name is Kate. She's not a fucking body."

"Excuse me, sir, but I'm reminding you I received my BA in Indiana at Lakeland Business Institute, and I know such words, so I'm pleasing you to not use such words."

There was silence.

"Of course, sir," she continued, "there are things better accomplished by a live person. But, sir, I give you the EU promise and satisfaction that the body and the suitcase will arise at your doorstep in perfect condition."

The last time I saw Kate, the live person arise: Kennedy Airport, security gate, her red hair cropped close to her skull, a blue jewel glinting in the side of her nose, a stiff leather backpack slung over her shoulders. I don't know what she had in there except, of course, her medications, which I'd bought since I had the money and she had no insurance. Three hundred and sixty capsules that, taken in sufficient quantity, stop a body's heart and brain, dreams and breath.

At twenty-seven Kate was already exhausted, and as she turned to wave, I thought there was something final and empty in her smile, though Greece and its promise of light and lightness still waited for her beyond that metal detector and the dour security agent, beyond the boorish pat-down she was subjected to due to the alarm she triggered. Of course, that finality in her smile is only my retrospective knowledge. But still the alarm sounded, the wand whined as it passed back and forth over her body.

I should have called Kate back. That's what you do when you love someone, even when you're exhausted, even when they exhaust you. But I was relieved to see her go. Final blueprints were due on an eight-bedroom house in East Hampton for an unnecessarily wealthy young couple. I'd been stalling, drawing one tedious, rambling, shingled cottage after another, concentrating my efforts on getting Sarah out of her sister's sixth-floor walk-up, off the pull-out loveseat, and back into our one-bedroom, doormanned, elevatored apartment. The couple was about to pull the project from the firm—they, too, were bored by what I'd been giving them, though that was what they initially wanted. So three days and nights on speed and no sleep equaled one clean, vacant, long-windowed Philip C. Johnson rip-off, and one swooning couple liberated from the Glen Plaids and inherited pearls. I, however, was spent, and stumbled over to the walk-up, determined to bring Sarah back home, to make it right between us again.

It was as simple as this: four flights up I tripped, fell all the way back down.

We arrive at Moutsouna in the late haze of dusk, the very last passengers on the bus, and are deposited at the entrance to the town square, which sits on a sandy bay. It is as Kate described in one of her letters: three old men at the kafenio, spinning their koboloi, smoking, drinking coffee and ouzo. Blue doors. Pots of red geraniums. Cats. Too many cats winding their tails around chair legs, mewling over fish guts. And dogs splayed out under trees, wrecked from the heat, from too many puppies sucking their teats.

Sarah is at a loss. Her guidebook has not prepared her for this. There are no helpful women pointing the way, offering cold water and a bathroom. Only these old men eyeing her green shorts and my leg with suspicion. After all, the last foreigner through these parts may have been Kate, who'd gone and made an American mess of herself. And here we are with our matching red American Tourister suitcases, wedding presents that had traveled with us to Thailand, Italy, St. Lucia. After this final trip together, we'd divide the pieces: would she get the weekender and I the garment bag? Would they ever meet unexpectedly on the tarmac, bump into each other on the baggage carousel? Hello, former life; hello, lost love.

But here we are now, side by side. The cripple and his in-name-only wife with their matched luggage. An American Spectacle.

It is rough going over the gravel with all eyes on me, waiting to see if the crutches will skid out, if I'll land on my ass. Sarah holds her breath. She knows if I fall it will be days before I'll be able to get up again, and more murky days on Percoset. This is how close to the bone I am cutting it with this trip. But there was—is—no one else to come. Our parents are both long gone. I am the live person. I am the person who can arise. I am now, or soon will be, a family of one.

I stop short of the table, breathing hard already. "Excuse me," I say, to no one in particular. "Hello. Pension Anna?" I don't know if they will know English. I don't know Greek except what I'd heard repeated in my sister's letters. I don't know what is rude or respectful here. So I decide to keep it short, keep my distance. Fewer words, fewer opportunities for misunderstanding.

All the men exhale at once. Are they male Fates knitting their smoke together in tacit agreement to send us in the wrong direction? Hell? They are impenetrable and unperturbed.

"Pension Anna?" I say, trying a different inflection. Silence again. From inside the kafenio someone is shouting, and then techno music blares briefly from a radio. Someone yells and it goes quiet, then something that I take to be Greek news comes on.

Sarah shouts out, "Please, Pension Anna?" She walks over to the table. The men startle and laugh, reveal yawning gaps where there should be teeth. The one in the middle reaches over and pats her hand.

"Anna," he says, and points left, down the road along the bay, then makes a snake-like motion with his hand and a clicking noise with his mouth. This can only mean far. Very far.

"Taxi?" Sarah asks, and points back to me. They all look again, appraising my leg, the crutches, the sheen of sweat on my face. I look away to the sea, back to our red suitcases, so solemn and absurd in the middle of the dusty road. Construction cones. Bowling pins ready to be knocked down.

The men speak loudly, arguing perhaps, though what they say is, of course, unintelligible to us. They are deciding upon a course of action. Pick our pockets? Rape Sarah? Nothing seems impossible in this evening half-light.

Sarah waits, fists clenched at her side, exhausted by all of this negotiation. The man in the middle jumps up, disappears inside the kafenio, and returns with a young man, bare chested and hairy, swinging a sharp knife. His hair is shorn and his nose juts sharply from his face, giving the impression that he is all hard angles. A heavy gold cross hangs from his neck on a thick chain.

He wipes the knife across the seat of his jeans but doesn't offer to shake our hands. "Amerikanee eehsay? I am Nikos. I give you ride to Anna." His English is good, if halting. "Let me wash first. I clean the fish for tonight so I stink. Maybe you come and eat some like Katerina. You come for Katerina, nai?"

I shrug, uncertain. It is English, but it means nothing. I glance at Sarah. Perhaps she caught something? But she is leaning against one of the rickety wooden chairs, eyes closed, tears streaking her face. A scrawny tabby circles her feet, mewing for scraps. Its orange tail, a strange, lopped stump, twitches back and forth.

Nikos stamps his foot. "Ssshttt," he says. The cat streaks off, disappears beneath an overturned boat that is pulled up onto the beach. He looks away, then clears his voice and says again, "You come for Kate? Katerina? Kate? Katerina?" He reaches his hand out and rests it on Sarah's shoulder, forgetting that it is rank with fish.

I startle. Her name is a flower unfolding again and again in his mouth. She sounds alive, waiting for us somewhere, sitting on a hot stone beach, flicking a fat ant from her shoulder, turning her face to the sun, her skin brown and freckled, spitting olive pits into the sea.

Sarah turns and is suddenly, momentarily surprised that the hand on her shoulder is not mine, but Nikos's. Her smile is at once filled with gratitude. She rests her hand on his.

He steps back, nods, and says he will wash up, that we must sit and have something to drink. Two tall glasses of cold water, two tall iced coffees—*frappes* he calls them—two small crescent cookies that taste of anise. The *frappe* is bitter and strong with at least three inches of thick foam floating on top. Sarah gulps her water in one long swallow, leaves the coffee, and walks the few yards down to the empty beach.

Dingy lounge chairs speckled in bird shit are stacked in four squat columns; umbrellas are piled in an enormous heap like a strange mass of red and white striped insects, wings tucked under, encrusted in salt. A fat gull skitters across the sand and hops up onto the overturned boat. It digs its long yellow beak furiously into gray feathers, ruffling up mites, then flaps its wings once and settles in, impassively surveying the scene. Does anyone pay five Euros for the sun bed? Does anyone come here, to the end of the road?

Sarah kicks off her sneakers, shakes her hair free, and strides into the water. She reaches down, brings up handfuls of pebbles, and hurls them away. Further out, water laps her calves, thighs, then her green shorts. When she turns and waves, her hand brushing the sky, I know she is not asking me to hobble down and join her. She is merely checking in, making sure I haven't toppled from the rickety chair and brained myself on the stony patio. Before I can think to wave back, she is under water, swimming furiously, quickly away.

The gull gives no notice, though the old men are suddenly quiet.

When she surfaces, her hair hangs in dark skeins across her face.

It has been a long day, and, despite the guidebook, she loved Kate, took better care of her, perhaps, than me. Sarah had been the one to find the psychiatrist. Had been the one to check her into the hospital. And check her back in again.

And when Kate stopped taking her medication for the tenth or twentieth time, when she said she was sure she was well? When she disappeared and finally called from some godforsaken rat-ass town in Florida without any money, asking for help?

At the time, my attention was tied up in a dark Lower East Side loft: another young, moneyed couple wanted the place gutted to its bones, reconceived into something fabulous, something shimmering, worthy of a spread in *Architectural Digest*. What that something fabulous was? Nobody yet knew, but it had to be fabulous and fast. So Sarah was the one who went down to Fort Lauderdale and found Kate holed up in a dank room in one of those awful trucker motels. Apparently she met some guy in a bar in the city; they were tired of all the gray slush, all the shit of New York, and so she got in his car, they drove south, and when he got tired of her, he left. Sarah had been the one who had suggested the recuperative month in Greece, imagining an olive grove, peaches, blue sky, the buoyancy of salt water, light. Elements not present in a New York City winter. A rest cure. So this trip, this task, this penance is difficult for her in ways I cannot know.

They load me into the bed of a pick-up along with two sacks of potatoes, a box of onions, a case of water, four bottles of wine, and a stinky dog, Argos, with matted orange fur. Sarah tries to make me comfortable, but will not look me in the eye when she closes the truck-bed gate.

"I'm going to sit up front," she says, combing her fingers through her wet hair, catching them in the knots. "I'll try to keep him from going too fast. Nice and easy over the bumps." Her legs are marbled in dried salt, her shorts still wet.

The dog leans against my shoulder for the entire ride out. Every now and then he licks my ear. I scratch his head, feel little lumps that I take for ticks. He thumps his tail in appreciation. Suddenly, he vaults over the side of the truck and I watch him bound off down the beach, his enormous balls swinging against his hind legs. He is chasing some sort of stalky brown bird that he will never catch. The bird hops along the shoreline, teasing him, letting him get close, then quickly, legs up, skims the water's surface. The dog still runs, still follows. Such ease, those lanky legs, those joints in perfect, hinged movement. It is beautiful to watch his failure.

I lean my head against the cab, feel the murmuring of their voices inside. What can they have to talk about? What can she understand?

Where is the octopus? The secret swimming cove? The ancient ruin?

I could tell her she need not look far. The ruin is here. Right here.

There was the first letter from Kate:

Jack,

Outside the village, there is this little house where I live on the beach with a pale green doorway fringed by the dark vines of grape leaves. Kyria Anna's home. In her garden, under the purple sweet of lilacs, a marble man sleeps. One of the kouroi of Naxos. "He is old," she whispers to me, "three thousand years old." His fingers are worn by the wind. His nose is flattened by rain. His thighs, once full, are now thin. Kyria Anna whispers, afraid her voice might rouse his heavy stone lids, that the man might wake and discover his trouble. "What trouble?" I ask. It seems a perfect place to sleep and sleep. She pulled back the low-lying limbs of the lilac. Those long-ago hands, which had coaxed life from that marble, had abandoned him, left him without legs, left him to the unformed bone of marble. Worn down now by countless seasons of mud and rain, by her hands pruning lilacs, skimming his rigid hips. I fell by his side and wept into my hands. What an unnatural, unbearable sleep. Kyria Anna stroked my hair, understanding my grief.

This place is beautiful, but I see too much here. Sarah would understand the damage all this light can do.

The dog is paddling in the sea now. I watch as Argos disappears beneath the water, then reappears again, paddles in a circle, around and around, pawing like a child after some errant beach ball, then back underwater, and then he is out of sight entirely. Fishing? Pleasure paddle? Or some trick to relieve the ticks and the smear of rash across his belly?

Inexplicably, the dog gets there before we do, already snoozing on the portico. Pension Anna is surrounded by a rose-trellised garden that stretches out toward the beach and nothing else. The hand-painted sign rocks in the breeze. I smell salt, sea, roses, something cooking, meat, olive oil. Nikos has gone on inside, carrying the sacks of food for his mother. This is what Sarah has discovered. He lives behind the kafenio, his kafenio, and his mother here.

"Jack," she says, "he knew Kate. She used to walk to the kafenio every afternoon, all the way from here, and drink retsina, and she would sit at the same little table and cry. The old men called her crazy."

"He told you all this?"

"His English isn't as bad as you think. He has cousins in Astoria who visit every summer. Let's get settled." She hefts a bag on each shoulder and marches up the gravel walk, determined to get on with our evening and the next day

It is stupid, of course. I need never have left New York. I could have sent Francis X. Cleary Funeral Home to Kennedy Airport to collect Kate. I could have had her personal effects shipped to my apartment. Alternately, Sarah and I need never have moved beyond the air-conditioned splendor of the Hyatt Regency Athens. We could have dealt with Ms. Maria Nikolaides with her Indiana BA, signed the papers in the hotel bar, gotten smashed on those iceless gin and tonics, then taken the elevator to our rooms on the eighth floor. Kate was already waiting for us at the Athens airport. She is still waiting for us there in cold storage. We are taking a three-day detour to see what she saw before she died.

What did Kate see here? There are no trees, no fragrant groves of olives or almonds. Only a desert meeting the blue sea, dunes sprouting scrub pine, prickly pear, a few fishing boats in the distance aimlessly drifting on glass.

"Germans," Kyria Anna says later that evening when she comes to our room offering a tray of little plates of food: olives dressed in oregano and oil, sliced tomatoes, a hunk of feta, meatballs, bread, a small carafe of yeasty wine, a bowl of cherries. Argos waits in the doorway, whining. "That's why my husband built here. Nothing around. Nowhere. They come for sun and stay for summer. Germans don't like crowds or clothes, just their, how do you say," she points to her chest and arms, "their body cooking, and wrinkles, and titties to their knees." She laughs. "They come in three weeks." She ticks off the time on her fingers.

"But what do you think?" she continues. "Katerina say you build big houses in America. What do you think of what my husband build?"

"He did fine. This should stand the test of time," I say, though already I can feel the room is not level, which may be just a matter of the foundation sinking unevenly over time.

She looks at me slyly, then laughs. "You not see the cracks on the wall outside? Nikos is always fixing. You look tomorrow then you tell me what builder my husband is. He was a teacher first, of mathematics. Not builder."

I can see why Kate liked her. She is a generous, direct woman, though dressed, as all the widows in Greece seem still to be, in black. Like a magpie, she chatters on, inspecting us, hovering in the room, adjusting the covers around the edges of the twin beds, counting the utensils and the pots and pans in the economical kitchenette, swatting a moth dead.

"Your sister," she finally says, and shakes her head, "she was too much alone. She was cursed with it. And you?" she says, tilting her head toward my leg.

"I fell," I say. "Far."

Sarah laughs.

Kyria Anna does, too. "Katerina say you fell to rock bottom. Now I see what she mean."

"I'm getting better," I say. "I won't need these forever." I send the crutches clattering to the floor.

"Kalinikta," Kyria Anna says, then she is gone, back out into the inscrutable night with all those stars.

We eat like two year olds, oil dripping down our chins, using our fingers. We have no napkins, just wipe with the backs of our hands, licking off the excess with our tongues. Laugh too much.

"She's lovely," I say, remembering her shuffled hop into the air, the fruitless clap of her hand for the moth, the way she wet her thumb and rubbed at some nonexistent stain on the whitewashed wall.

Sarah chews thoughtfully on bread, swallows. "When I was signing in, she was watching you through the window, one hand worrying a bit of lace she'd pulled from her pocket, the other rubbing at her eyes."

"Kate liked to write about her. She said she made her feel safe."

> Kyria Anna has the ugliest toes I've ever seen. Nails yellow and twisted, they poke through her black stockings that she wears even in the deadliest heat. Even when she's out back in her garden watering her endless rows of tomato plants. They are also the most beautiful toes I have ever seen.

We sleep soundly under the ticking of a fan, beside the wash of the tide even in our hard twin beds. We have arrived at Kate's end. It is no starting point. Our map divulges no roads, there are no penciled-in *x*'s, no hieroglyphs hinting some dirt path.

I dream not of my real fall, not my real fucked-up fall down all those flights of stairs, but a dream fall with Kate. (Oh Kate! My heart leaps. You are alive!) I dream of falling with Kate. Kate and I stumbling over rusty spikes of barbed wire. We slip suddenly down the loose shale of a bald cliff nettled with briar, tangled thyme, tumble over the crumbling foundations of some long forgotten house. The only sound is our slipping, rocks skidding and clacking, then nothing.

I wake to light through the cracks in the shutters, the sheet tangled around my legs. Across the room in the other narrow bed, Sarah's body is a graceful curve and dip under the sheet; it makes a steady rise and fall. I fall back sweating to the pillow, grateful that she is here. Olives and oregano are in my mouth, under my tongue. Our suitcases stand as we left them at attention against the wall. We never even bothered to unpack, to undress, to brush teeth, to speak, finally, of Kate. Two days to get on with it before returning to Athens.

Kyria Anna is singing while hanging the wash, a great tub of sheets and towels she wrings out by hand then clips up to the line. I find her out back, in her black dress, black stockings, and slippers. Already the laundry line holds twenty feet of voluminous white underwear and thick-strapped bras, dresses and housecoats and slips, though mostly what hangs there are clothes belonging to Nikos.

"Kalimera, Jack," she says. "You sleep good?"

"Good morning," I say and check my watch. Six-thirty.

"Katerina always up with the birds, too. Then fly with the birds into hills. She climb the big rocks." She turns and waves her hand in the direction of the hills, which give way to rock shears. "She go all day. I say take care. Dogs. Gypsies. They curse you. You get...how you say?" She twirls her finger in the air.

"Dizzy?" I say.

"Yes," she says, then points to her ankle. "She comes back one day and walk like this." She staggers down a row of tomatoes, dragging her foot along the ground, then stops, raises her hands in apology.

"It's okay," I say. "This isn't forever. What happened?"

"She not say. Her eye, her..." She points to her ankle.

"Ankle," I say.

"Ankle," she says. "Blood. It all big with blood. Maybe she fall." She twists a towel and water spills to the ground. She looks at me, studies my face, as I study hers, and nods. I know what she will say. "Maybe she jump off rock."

I walk the garden rows, the vines heavy with tomatoes, eggplant, and squash. How does anything grow here? I can't imagine rain. I lean on the crutches, study the rocks above the hills, and imagine Kate, eyes closed, taking one of her crazy leaps.

A pink-flowered bathing suit, zinc oxide smeared across her nose. I am dog paddling in the deep end of the pool at Wykygyl Country Club, embarrassed at babysitting my little sister while our parents play golf, but so be it. In revenge, I have dared her: "Jump off the high dive, Kate." She will do it. Really, she has no choice. She climbs the ladder, her knobby legs shivering, and stands forever on the edge, contemplating the fall between the solid here of the pebbly board beneath her feet and the forever of below. "Chicken," I yell. And with that, she bends her knees and hurls herself, all flailing arms and legs, into the air. Suddenly, I can see she is not ready for this, will belly flop, strike bottom, smack concrete. She will, I know with terrifying certainty, die.

I dive under. I cannot find her.

She has already broken the surface, hooting and hollering, climbing back up the ladder, is on the edge of the diving board. "Kiss my ass, Jack," she shouts, turns, points to her bottom, and jumps in again, backwards this time.

Argos trots over, a mangled rabbit in his mouth. With a final regal shake, he dumps it at my feet. There is no blood, just the limp brown body, neck wrenched at the odd angle, dark eyes open, unblinking. He is panting, has given good chase, his breath hot and heavy on my leg. "Good boy," I say, though I am not at all sure of this. I scratch his head, then look back up to the hills, the rocks, then the sky. What is it that writers and painters are always saying about Greece? The effects of light. The glorious effects of light. But the delirious, deleterious effects, too.

Last letter from Kate:

Jack:

I wander at will up here. If there are no-trespassing signs, I can't read them. It is quite literally all Greek to me. Besides, I long to trespass, to be where I shouldn't. I won't lie and say I am well, but I am at home with

> these rocks and stars and sea. You would be, too, I think. I wander at will up in the hills. I lay on rocks like some pagan, lolling about, watch ants in procession, stare down the goats, keep my pockets weighted with stones to throw at terrifying dogs. I found a little chapel. The door was open. A Madonna with sad eyes hung next to the altar. On the floor, boxes of thin beeswax candles and matches. I closed the door and lit the candles one by one. One hundred, two hundred? I lost count. I knelt and prayed, my knees and feet numb, but I kept at it until all the candles burned down to the quick, smoked out. How long was I there? Hours, days, years? I pricked my finger on a thorn and left a thumbprint of blood over the chapel door when I left. Do you understand?

Kate was not crazy. She didn't magic-marker walls with miniscule letters; she didn't receive signals from aliens through her silver fillings. She had an understandable, controllable disease. That's what her doctors said. Bipolar disorder. Completely manageable with the right cocktail of drugs, they assured, their black pens scratching notes on her charts. Disorder equals disarray, muddle, unrest. But also suggesting its opposite. The mind's house can be made orderly, restful, safe for habitation again.

I don't pretend to understand how Kate felt either sick or well. It was easier to love her when she was well, than when sick. But that does not mean I loved her any less, that I did not jump out of bed at three in the morning when she called, her voice small and desperate: "Please, Jack. Please help me." That I did not chase down the first empty cab, running after it like a maniac, half dressed, wild with fear that my decision not to call someone else was the wrong decision.

It does not mean that I was not angry, unbearably angry at her for what she did to her thin arms and legs, her hollow stomach and tiny, sad breasts, those razor cuts, those cross-hatchings, all that blood. It does not mean that I did not turn and run into that ugly kitchen and puke into the sink full of dishes.

But Kate was my sister and I was her brother-knight, charged with her safekeeping. I splashed my face with water, gargled, and walked back into that bedroom. I scooped her from the floor and stood with her in the shower in the bright fluorescent lights, sponging down all that damage. Nothing too deep, nothing that couldn't be butterfly-bandaged, nothing that wouldn't eventually heal. Except what we both would always carry inside of us: not her naked body and all that blood, not even the scars that would remain in thin, white splinters across her thighs, her arms, and stomach, but this: love is horrifying, holds us hostage, requires us always to answer the phone, to make the drive, to wash the blood from the body, to look at each other clearly under the light and not flinch, not look away.

We eat yogurt, honey, and peaches for breakfast. Sarah reads the guidebook.

"You don't need that," I say. "There are ruins right here. An ancient statue out back that Kate wrote to me about. And up in the hills, some sort of chapel you can walk to in a few hours' time. There's a Madonna icon, probably in disrepair."

She reaches across the table for my hand. It is unexpected. "I'm thinking I might stay on. Not here. But when we get back to Athens, if you're doing okay and think you can manage the flight back, I might try some other islands." Her voice trails off. She lets go of my hand and bites into a peach.

Is she looking at me, or sideways to the sea, to another shore, another breakfast of peaches and honey with another man? Perhaps *Greek Islands 2003* has been annotated beyond Naxos since our flight over. Where might a soon-to-be-single, thirty-something woman go? Her dark sunglasses make her impenetrable this morning, something maybe she finds necessary since we haven't shared a bedroom in over a year. Such close proximity to the past, to love that is over, is disturbing, upending the fragile balance of days and nights.

"Do what you want," I say. "We're under no obligation to each other anymore." Who is this person sitting here? Who can think about island hopping when there is still Kate, still all these strangers who speak her name, and summon her up out of this bright and empty sky?

She wipes her mouth with the back of her hand. "There are monasteries and churches all over the place, and so much in deterioration, so much in need of help. I might be able to get some research done. I might even do some good while I'm here."

Sarah stands, braces herself against the iron railing, and hocks the peach pit from her mouth. It clatters, like a stone, against the concrete walk. She says, "Because all I can do now is think that this is the place where Kate killed herself. Right here. Maybe in my bed, maybe in yours. And we did nothing to stop her. We just packed her off to die alone."

How do we do good here?

It is late morning. We make our way down the path behind the pension toward the kouros, Kate's sleeping statue. I shuffle behind Sarah and Kyria Anna, amused by their aimless chatter, their wandering back and forth across the path as Kyria Anna points to this and that flower, rattling off a fast string of Greek names. Sarah nods, tries to pronounce what is unpronounceable on a first try. Every few minutes we pause, wipe dust from our eyes with a damp lace-edged handkerchief. Suddenly we stop beneath an olive tree, swapping swigs of water from a plastic jug. Kyria Anna sits on the ground, stretches her legs out, and kicks off her slippers. Sarah plucks a red poppy and tucks it behind her ear. I rest my crutches against the tree, lean into the trunk, look up through the silvery green leaves to the sky. Around us, the shrill rattle of cicadas.

Kyria Anna wags her finger. "I not show him to everyone. Not to the Germans and their titties," she says. "Not to Greeks. Not to government. You show, you lose. Too many tourists. No quiet then. Then I become bus stop." She points over a little rise. "He is there. Over the stone wall. Behind the trees. Lemons. Lilacs. He is there. You go. I stay and sleep a little." She scuttles up against the trunk and closes her eyes. Her toes, I notice, poke through her stockings. They are ugly, beautiful.

Of course, I can't climb over a four-foot stone wall and Sarah can't hoist me over. What more would I need to see anyway? Kate showed him to me. Sarah fills in the gaps and comes running back, her hands filled with lilac bundles, pockets crammed with lemons, three bee stings on her thigh. She is yelping.

"What did you do?" I ask. "Pilfer the treasury and fuck the god?"

"Shut up," she says. "Just help me over."

Kyria Anna mixes up a mud paste and spreads it on the three swollen lumps. Sarah sighs. Kate would not have been pleased at such ransacking of her marble man, though I am at such a thought: Sarah tramping up over the block of marble, snapping off the lilac branches, shaking the lemon tree, satisfied only when she hears the thump of lemons hitting him squarely in the face. What use is he to her, this half-finished man, this lump of marble, this legless thing? Did she straddle him, spit in his face, make him eat crow?

Nikos has come to take us for a swim. I point stupidly to my leg, as if he hasn't noticed.

He smiles. "It's okay. Water is flat where we go. No waves. You sit. It will be good for the leg. You see."

Is he even a day over twenty-five? Maybe he just looks young, with that chest, those arms, and those barrel legs that lift sacks of potatoes, that heave wheelbarrows of cement up the gravel drive to Kyria Anna's expanding patio, that can, I imagine, flip a woman onto her back, make her sigh with pleasure. He has brought three masks, two snorkels, and one float. He and Sarah will hunt octopus while I bob around. He says he can catch an octopus with his hands and a piece of stocking.

"What do you mean 'stocking'?" I say.

"You know," Sarah says, "pantyhose." Apparently something else they found to talk about in the tiny cab of the pick-up.

Once again, I am propped up in the bed of the pick-up with Argos, who curls up next to my feet, head on my crutches, and sleeps. In order to get to the cove, we head inland, pass fields of truck-sized rocks, then fields of recently harvested potatoes heaped in piles like collections of shrunken heads. And pens of goats, always goats with little crumbling goat herder's huts. No level used to build these. Just stones and mud, a bit of straw and dung, a good eye, and necessity. Like a monk's cell. Something Kate would have liked, too. The narrow bed, the square table beneath the window, the stone jug filled with cold water, the hard bread and sharp cheese, the trill of birds, the warm flood of light through the window.

Our hermit's camp we'd built one summer was nothing more than a piece of plywood and tarp stocked with a cooler of Coke and peanut-butter sandwiches. Our parents were divorcing. Not, I should add, amicably. Our father had become an extraordinary drunk; once he showed up at the house, waving around his hunting rifle, threatening to kill us all. My mother was off on the golf course, in her pink seersucker skirt. They were monstrous. So Kate and I hid out in our hermit's camp in the woods just beyond the neat fencing of our suburban development with our stockpile of books, our ammo of candy bars, in our platoon of two.

When does it sour? When does the bleating of the goats sound like betrayal? When does the morning sun begin to burn? I rub my knees, shift weight, ease the pressure, though nothing seems to work. Argos woofs in companionable complaint. I pull my cap over my eyes, try to sleep.

Of course the cove is beautiful. We are standing at the side of the road looking down the narrow dirt path into the water. The only way down. It is the fall from my dream. Nikos looks stupid and uncomfortable. Obviously, he forgot about the descent. Sarah stands there chewing her lip, twisting the ties of her sarong. Argos, fleet footed, is already down the path, barking at us from below. I can tell from the way his paws kick up the ground that it is not sand, but a beach of pebbles, brilliant white in this blaze of sun. Above, the fat bees circle us, buzz our ears, then dive into tall red flowers, lapping nectar; they emerge dusty and incandescent. No one speaks. There is only Argos's desperate bark and the endless hum of the heat.

"Fuck it," I say. "We came all the way out here. You'll just have to carry me."

I can see this surprises Sarah. Nikos, who does not know me, does not know to be surprised. He squats. "Get on," he says, and I hug my arms around his neck.

We proceed carefully, too carefully I want to say to him, as we are never in any danger of slipping. His balance is too perfect. He could balance an elephant, a tiger, and ten acrobats on his back, or a jumble of five sons and daughters. Every now and then I swing my head around to look at Sarah whose lips are curled back in the flat smile of fear. The snorkel gear hangs around her neck and plastic lunch bags dangle from each hand like weights. Her body jogs forward and backward, heels skidding out under her, sending bits and pieces of cliff our way. She is afraid for me and watches for the tiny rocks and sticks that threaten Nikos's way, my way, forgetting to watch her own. More than once she swears.

At the bottom Nikos wants to run back up to fetch my crutches. It is pointless, I tell him. They'll just sink right in. Before he can argue, my T-shirt and sandals are off and I am already crab-crawling in the water, Argos close behind, his nose bumping my head, mistaking me for kin. I don't mind.

When I turn back, Sarah is shaking her head, laughing, and if she is shocked, refuses to show it, because she has stripped off her bikini top. A challenge. Briefly, I look away. What is the etiquette of divorce, even one proceeding as amicably as ours? When your-soon-to-be-ex-wife is standing half-naked before you, do you look away? And when you look back, how long can you look? Can you, dare you, resurrect the memory of what once was? Her breasts against your chest, in your hands, in your mouth? When I look back Sarah's breasts are a thick smear of white sunscreen. Her thighs show the red welts of the bees.

Nikos tosses her the tins of anchovies and dolmades from the plastic bag. "Wind," he says, "put it on top of the clothes." He blows up the float and brings it to me, then points toward the far end of the cove, a half mile or so away. "We'll swim out. But you use this," he says, and hands me a mask, "just hang head over into water. Be happy." He smiles, spits in the mask, then dunks it underwater. "That's what I say to Katerina. Be happy." He rubs the mask clean with his fingers, pulls it down over his eyes, and hands it over. "There. You see good now. Twenty twenty. Argos will stay for companion. Just be careful of urchins. If you are so lucky to step on one, you must pee on you."

"Nikos," I say, "I can't step on one. I can't walk. I could only fall on one. Which would mean I'd had an accident. And you mean unlucky. Not lucky."

"Unlucky, yes." He waves his hands. "Do not say accident. You will be fine. But is good to know in case you step on urchin. You pee on you." He holds an imaginary and extraordinarily large penis in his hands and pretends to pee on the bottom of his foot that he has raised into the air. He jumps up and down, shouting, "Ouch! Ouch! Ouch!" He glances over at Sarah to see if she is watching this idiotic bit of pantomime.

She is, and is laughing, but then suddenly is worried. "You won't go out far, will you, Jack? Not so deep that you can't sit up if you fall?" She jams a water bottle down into the rocks beside me, underwater, to keep it cool and close.

"I'm not some invalid. Go," I order. "Kiddie pool, water wings, and Argos the Lifeguard. What else could I need?"

They cast their bodies, bellies down, into the water, skimming the surface like skipped stones. I reach for Sarah's foot, not to stop her, just to tell her to be careful, but she shimmers away. For several minutes I follow the pair of orange snorkel tubes pushing through the surface like periscopes. If only I could see what is happening beneath: toe striking thigh, hand grazing nipple, breath quickening. The surface is unbearably still, and they move discreetly, proficiently, feet churning like waterwheels, hunting their octopus.

Argos paddles in, trots to shore, and ceremoniously licks my knees. I pour out handfuls of water from the bottle. He laps gratefully, then retreats to the shade of a rocky overhang, collapsing into sleep.

What is there to see in all this blue? The cheap plastic mask puddles water, obscures vision. Hollowed rocks become ancient cups; corroded cans become bronze figurines. I am startled to realize that indeed I am looking for fossils, for shards of amphora, bits of pottery that I am not just bobbing about in the sea, but hunting, too. In the shallows, the stony floor spills a prism of sedimentary colors: gold, copper, obsidian. Further out, along the rocky edges of the cove, sea urchins flower in prickly colonies. One false move and a spiny blossom could snap off. I tense, grip the edges of the float. My body is ill suited for such delicate maneuvering, kicking as I can only with my one leg. I back paddle, steering the bulky float away from the rocks, from bumping into anything that might prick a hole.

Cautiously, I roll to my back, dangle my legs in the water, shut my eyes to the sun. There is no shutting out the sun, though; it swims against my eyelids, itches against the salt on my skin. I doze. Five minutes? A half hour? The float doesn't seem to move, though suddenly I am beached and there is an old man standing above me, chattering at me, and I am waving my hands at him. What am I supposed to say?

"No, no Greek. American," I say, groggy with sun and sleep. Argos is at my side, barking. In warning? I don't know how to read him yet.

The man stops his chatter, smiles. He is holding baskets in each hand and squats down.

I sit up, swing my legs out in front of me. I would like to stand, but can't. I would like to explain this to him, but can't. So I just sit there like some dumb lazy American, some polio victim. Obviously, he is going to show me what he has in his baskets. Shrunken heads? I think of those mounds of potatoes. Bloody goat balls? He pulls back a cloth. Something white, spongy. Brain? I've never seen intestines, but maybe that.

"Tiree," he says.

I try a friendly shrug.

He pulls a knife from his pocket, dunks it in the water, carves off a piece of whatever it is, and hands it over to me. Seeing as how there is no way to refuse, I eat.

Cheese.

He wants me to buy his cheese. I turn the pockets of my swimsuit inside out. I have no money. This time he shrugs, pats my head. "Okay," he tries. He takes out the round of cheese, wraps it in paper, and sets it beside me. "Yassas," he says, and heads back up the cliff, whistling the whole way, though I can see it strains his muscles. The angle is steep. Rocks tumble, bounce back down to the bottom.

I unwrap the cheese, break off two hunks. One for Argos, one for me. Damn you, Kate. How could you leave all this?

They return triumphant. Nikos has an octopus crammed down inside the stocking that he has tied around his wrist. Sarah is exuberant. She tells me he has turned its head inside out.

"We grill octopus for goodbye dinner tonight," Nikos says.

She ties her bikini top back on then joins me at the edge of the sea. We watch Nikos as he scrubs, then smashes the octopus against the rocks.

I point to the path. "I know Nikos is strong, but that path is harder going up. I watched someone do it."

Her hand is on my knee. "I won't let him drop you," she says.

Kyria Anna hangs the octopus on the laundry line to dry. "You look good," she says. "Better with sun. Maybe you stay?"

Is this how Kate succumbed? One month that became two, then three, then forever?

She pins up another tentacle. "You think of your sister. You not cursed like her. You sad. Your sister dead. Your leg not right. You get over it. But Katerina? She sad always. Morning and night. She cry into the yogurt. She cry into the sea. She cry for fleas on Argos."

I unpin the towels from the line. They are dry, stiff, sun baked. Kyria Anna swats me away.

"Tst, tst," she scolds.

"Let me help," I say. "I need something to do." I am close to tears. I could not save my sister. Nothing I could do could save my sister. I had my apartment, emptied of Sarah, a living-room couch, books and companionship, enough room. Both of us had been hobbled in some way, leveled by what life had thrown, what we had been unable to bear. But I sent her away to a beautiful, lonely place to die. The rest cure that was no hermit's camp, no bunker of two.

Kyria Anna must see something of this in my face. She hands over the laundry basket.

Sarah and I rest under the ticking of the fan. We have eaten with Kyria Anna and Nikos. Grilled octopus in lemon and oregano, meatballs, potatoes, tomatoes still warm from the sun, and wine that tastes of this soil. We leave for the port tomorrow afternoon. Nikos has offered to drive us. The bed of the truck over the stop and go of the bus. An easy choice. He will set up a mattress for me and, of course, Argos will be my faithful companion. Nikos promises, even at a careful pace, the ride will be much more efficient. Two and one half hours versus the five it takes the bus.

I have, I think, made my peace with Kate here, seen most of what she would have wanted me to see.

"Sarah, can I ask you something?"

She turns over, waiting.

"Would you try to find that chapel tomorrow? I'm sure Nikos would know where it is. He'd walk with you."

She breathes out. "That's it?"

"What else is there?"

"I don't want to sleep with him, Jack. You know, don't you?"

"Know what?"

"He was sleeping with Kate. He was in a sort of love with her. He found her and she was still alive. At least I think that's what he said. But you know, it's a big island, and the nearest hospital is so far away, and he didn't know what pills she'd taken, and he made it to the hospital, to the port, in an hour and a half. At night, Jack. Just think, at night, in that goddamn truck, with Kate lying in the back, Kyria Anna holding on to her and the truck for dear life, and who knows, Argos probably back there, too, all of them praying, and Nikos speeding on these fucking roads in the middle of the night. By the time he gets to the hospital she's gone. Or maybe he just thought she was still alive. He loved her, so maybe he was just hoping he felt something at her throat jump against his hand."

I am listening to Sarah say this, listening to her voice rise and rise, and I know that Kate was dead by the time Nikos and Kyria Anna found her. Kate jumping off the high dive. She'd vault herself wholeheartedly into that forever. Damn her for almost killing those who loved her, for those who would vault themselves down dark, mountain roads, who would hold her body to theirs, whispering prayers, who would perhaps lick her feet, her ear, in search of some response.

And what would Sarah and Nikos find, what would anyone find up at that chapel? The nubs of candles? Melted puddles of beeswax? A rusty stain above the chapel door? Gone probably, or soon would be, scoured clean by the autumn rains. As we will be. Though for now, we stay, hunt octopus and hang it out to dry in the glorious sun. Or tour another island, meet someone new, save a painting from the ravages of light. Learn how to walk again, how to swim in the salty sea. Dream of birds and rabbits, of a world without ticks and rashes, wake only to stretch and bark and run.

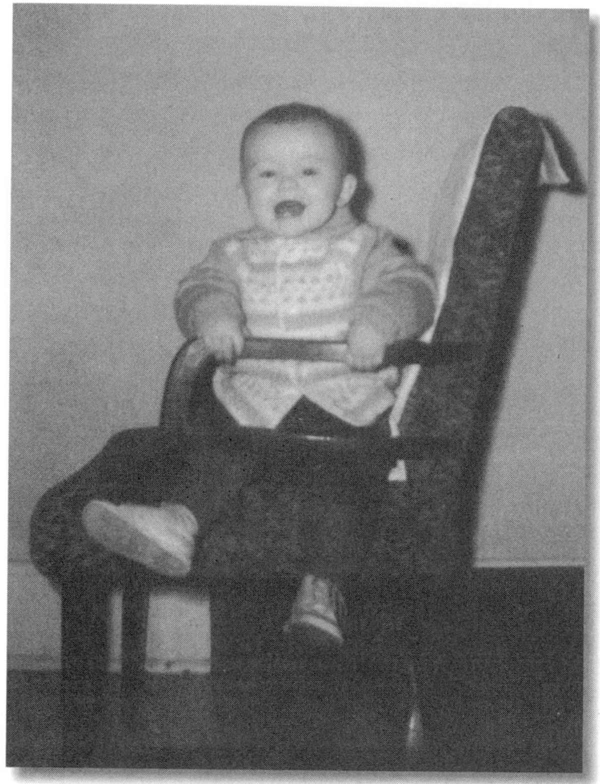

One year old and already I'm facing the "wrong" direction.

Robert Schirmer's short-story collection *Living with Strangers* won the Bobst Award for Emerging Writers and was published by NYU Press. He's been the recipient of an O. Henry Award and a Pushcart Prize, as well as fellowships from the Chesterfield Film Company's Writer's Film Project and the Sewanee Writers' Conference. "Fag Killer" is his second story to appear in *Glimmer Train*.

FAG KILLER

Robert Schirmer

Robert Schirmer

Iris McGregor had three sons and they were all gay except possibly for her youngest, Eddie, who had not declared himself yet, so when the police found the body of another murdered gay man tossed in some brush in an empty lot outside town, she grew disquieted. The second murder suggested the first had not been just a case of a man who happened to be gay who'd been killed, but that gay men were the specific targets. Both dead men's skulls had been crushed with heavy stones, or so the police speculated, and Iris had no reason to doubt them. Her oldest, Reed, had been serving on the St. Justin's police force for several years and already earned a couple commendations for bravery.

She'd been raising her sons for twenty-five years in St. Justin, Wisconsin, a small-sized city on the bank of the Mississippi River, known more for its desirable waterfront views than for explosions of homophobic violence. As news of the killings began to dominate the local news, Iris found herself worrying about Christian in particular. He was eighteen, set to start college in the fall, and her most visibly vulnerable son. Christian (and the irony of the name was not lost on her) was delicately built and effeminate, with pale skin, gray flat lips, a bony chest, and a voice that gave the impression he was always somewhat out of breath.

He was *on the surface*, or so Reed had once noted with an affectionate laugh, the very cliché of a gay man, a Midwestern version of a young John Waters or Quentin Crisp. Even as a baby, Christian was the son who had rejected her breasts, preferring manmade formula to the milk her glands naturally secreted for his benefit. Although Christian's effeminacy had disappointed Iris at first, in time her disappointment had given way to concern that he would stand out as prey for the bullies and hate mongers that stalked most schools, pushing and punching and bloodying whatever misfit was breathing within arm's reach. Just how much Christian had or had not been tortured by his classmates, Iris never knew, but he remained levelheaded and calm throughout most of those years, and never once showed an inclination to act like anyone other than who he was—an unashamed gay male, interested more in history and the fanatical consolidation of power that had led to the persecutions of Jews, Poles, and homosexuals in Hitler's Third Reich, than in whatever persecution he was inadvertently generating around him. His friends were other "losers" around school, and he cared for them openly and without apology, although most were less intelligent or focused than he was. It was this—Christian's steely stubbornness, his willful self-possession—that Iris considered his most masculine trait.

Still, with the town now gripped by a wave of inexplicable violence, she developed a fear of Christian going out after dark. "How about you invite some of your friends over," she proposed one evening while Christian was in the living room raiding the laundry basket for a fresh shirt. "I'll play Houdini Mom and disappear into my bedroom. You could have the run of the house."

"Then there's Eddie," Christian reminded her.

"Oh, Eddie. But he's hardly ever around, is he?" She couldn't pinpoint why she wasn't worried about Eddie roaming the night streets. Although he was only fifteen, he seemed less touchable. And he was a wrestler. He knew body slams and choke holds.

"He hates us," Christian said, tossing his arms into a T-shirt and slipping it over his head. Then he stared at it on him, already having second thoughts.

"Us, what do you mean, us?"

"Not you and me, Mom. Me and my loser friends."

It was true that Christian and Eddie had never been close. Eddie hung around with a tougher crowd, other members of the wrestling team, and Christian was a frank embarrassment to him. "That's his natural machismo talking," Iris said. "Don't take it personally. That's just his loser mother's opinion, of course." She giggled, charmed by her own glibness.

Christian positioned his pale slender feet into a pair of flip-flops. Iris couldn't help but feel a little envious; her son's feet were more attractive than her own. "I have to go out tonight," he said. "We have tickets to hear the Intimate Thrashers at Oyster."

He didn't mention who "we" was, and Iris didn't ask. The world seemed impossibly large to her then, crowded with billions of men and women she didn't and could never know, any number of whom might be harboring secret hatreds and ugly rages. "You need to be careful," she warned him.

"I know," Christian said carelessly. "A fag killer's on the loose, I know, Mom."

Fag killer. A ragged shadow crept to mind with a hand hewn out of marble. "Stick together then," she said. "Hang out in a group."

After Christian left for Oyster and the Intimate Thrashers, she phoned Reed. "You're the police, couldn't you follow him now and then, just to make sure he's okay?"

"Follow him?" In his apartment across town, Reed held the phone receiver cradled under his chin while he prepared to butter a slice of toast. But he was out of butter, so he just shoved the toast dry into his mouth. Dry toast; was that where his life was stuck at, dry toast? He stared at his police shirt and badge draped over a chair. More and more, he was beginning to wonder exactly what that uniform meant to him.

"I mean unofficially," Iris said. "No one would have to know. We could just be vigilant, you and I."

"You have a very homespun perception of the police, Mom."

"I'm not saying you have to follow him nonstop, or even openly. Just from time to time. You're a cop, honey. Be stealthy. Stay far enough away so Christian won't know you're tailing him."

"I haven't agreed to this," he said.

Yet in bed that night, with the sultry heat pressing down around him, making Reed glad, for once, that he was sleeping alone, he thought about what his mother had said. He remembered the jeering taunts he'd heard leveled at Christian over the years, the sidelong mocking glances he'd sometimes sensed, sometimes actually seen, from other men shaking their heads at his brother in a restaurant or at a mall. Occasionally a group of girls would scowl or smile knowingly, discounting Christian because he so clearly would never find them attractive. Reed hadn't mentioned to his mother that, just last week, on his way home from an evening shift at the station, he'd stopped at an ATM and spotted, on the wall facing the alley of the building next door, a spray-painted message: *Christian McGregor is a faggot*. Reed's heart had begun to accelerate, but what could he do? He drove to a nearby convenience store and bought some cleanser, washcloths, and a hard-bristle scrub brush. For a long while he stood hunched in the shadows of the alley, madly trying to scrub the words off the wall, aching for his brother—then mad as hell, not at Christian for being unable to hide who he was, because why should he hide, but just angry at the perpetrators, the faceless vocal enemy he couldn't silence. *Christian McGregor is a faggot*: how long had this judgment been muddying up the wall?

His brother Christian. Once, less than a year after their father had died, when Reed was a teenager and Christian a small boy, Reed had watched Christian faint into a fire. His mother had been in the house tending Eddie, still a baby then, while Christian was assigned to Reed's care. Reed had been burning a heap of fragrant dead leaves in the backyard, daydreaming about nothing much, when Christian moved too close to the flame, inhaled a sulfuric lungful of smoke, and passed out. Reed's response had been so sudden, so automatic, as he yanked Christian out of the flames the child was collapsing into, that Christian wasn't even singed. "What a smoky boy you smell like!" his mother had said later, as she lifted Christian into her arms and carried him into the house, sniffing his shirt and neck and spiky hair. Somehow during the rescue Reed's hand *had* burned, but he kept this a secret from his mother, as he kept the whole incident a secret. His was not a conspicuous burn, but nonetheless left a tiny permanent uprising of scar against the knuckles of his right hand that, as an adult, he glanced at from time to time as a welcome reminder of...he couldn't be sure what.

Reed scrubbed the wall until his scarred hand tightened up, but he couldn't erase the obscenity—which was what he considered the words: obscenity. He returned to the store and purchased a can of black spray paint. "Forgot something?" the cashier asked, but he shrugged and didn't trust her smile. Her lips were tinted with black gloss, roughly the same color as the spray paint, and she seemed able to smell the cleanser on him. He returned to the alley and altered the message so it now read: *Christ is 4 faggots.* After he was finished he admired the handiwork, his breath quickening, for if he were caught at this it might endanger his job. At the same time he was inwardly convinced he would not be discovered, for the darkness concealed him, and he was right to protect his brother in this way. He didn't care if his new message might offend Christians, or that it scarcely made sense as now written. The Bible seemed remote to him, an archaic document that was just complicating matters. But his mother still attended church every Sunday, and Reed had been raised to believe in a higher power even when that power, if it existed at all, often seemed as angry and unseen as the person who had painted his brother's name across the wall. In the end Reed sprayed over his own words, blotting out the entire message, so all that remained was a black stinking cloud of paint swirling over the wall like a Hiroshima mushroom cloud.

Reed kicked around in his bed for some time, unable to get comfortable in the heat, his mother's words echoing back to him: *You're the police. Be stealthy.* When he finally drifted off to sleep, he envisioned Christian's prostrate body in a field of tall weeds, his head broken open, blood matting down his brillo-spiked hair, all of him, the death of him, gleaming in moonlight. The image was so powerful, so singularly disturbing, that the next night, when Iris dropped a hint that Christian had gone to a 7:30 movie with friends at the cineplex, Reed found himself parked in the movie theater's back parking lot, waiting for the boys to emerge. Once people began flooding out the doors, Reed watched while Christian and his two friends, both male, strolled to the friend's car, speaking animatedly and tossing pebbles at one another. His brother seemed happy, Reed saw with mild surprise, or looked happier than Reed could remember himself feeling over the past weeks. Reed drove behind them for several blocks; parked along the side of the road, out of sight, while they stopped at a convenience store for a twelve pack of beer; followed them to a video store; and finally back to the house of one of the boys. He waited until the three were safely inside before he drove away.

He undressed for bed and phoned Alex, his ex-lover, on a whim. "We don't have to pretend we've never known each other," he said.

There was a long silence on the other end. "Officer Reed," Alex said.

"Is it a crime to keep in touch?"

He could hear Alex breathing on the other end. "No crime, officer," he said with a smile in his voice. "No such crime that I know of."

Reed didn't know that Eddie had been the one who had spray-painted the slur against Christian on the side of the building. Eddie had done this the previous Saturday night with a couple of guys from the wrestling team, Danny and Bruce, after they'd downed several beers and a couple of shots of whiskey for good measure. Danny and Bruce were a year older than Eddie, and he knew they had problems with him because his brother was Christian McGregor, *The Flame Christian McGregor.* Probably they had their suspicions about him as well—guilt by brotherly association—even though Eddie was afforded some respect because his wrestling record for pins far outweighed his losses; how could they *not*, in some sense, respect his power?

Danny and Bruce had egged Eddie into the vandalism, roughhousing around until he relented and agreed that Christian disgusted him as much as he did them. His head spinning with drink, Eddie had stood in the alley, thinking of how much his brother weighed him down, Christian's persecution always coming back at him. He'd had enough, definitely enough. So Eddie took the spray can that Danny handed him and spelled out his brother's name, attaching that name to *faggot* with a zealousness that also left him feeling vaguely sick, digging deep as he was into some personal inner darkness. The boys jumped into their car and crammed themselves into the front seat when a different car pulled up to the ATM machine, headlights sweeping toward them, briefly illuminating them before plunging them back into darkness.

They drove around town and quaffed a couple more beers, which had grown lukewarm in the heat. They clapped Eddie on the back and slung their arms around his neck, praising him for being *criminal*. For a moment Eddie coasted on a wave of giddy comradeship, sitting between his two friends, but when he clapped Danny on the shoulder in return, Danny pulled away with a tense mocking smile on his face.

Soon things began to turn darker. Bruce remembered Greg Averill owned a farm on the edge of town. Averill was a math teacher at their high school who had given Danny and Bruce each a *D* in geometry, which had nearly affected their eligibility for next year's wrestling squad. "Isn't he maybe queer, too?" Danny asked. "Man, they're everywhere. Greg, what a fag name."

Eddie had no real interest in going to Averill's place—he'd gotten a *C+* in algebra—but he had no way home otherwise, so he rode with them out to the farm. Bruce wanted to piss on the mailbox, or maybe bust a window, or they could use the remainder of the spray paint for a message on the lawn that would make Averill think twice before he failed or fucked anyone again. Danny said no, that was uninspired. "That fag killer's raised the stakes," he said. "He's upped the ante, my friend."

How they ended up in the pasture leading to the barn on the edge of Averill's property, Eddie couldn't say. Everything seemed to be disjointed and moving too fast. The smell of the spray paint still burned in his nostrils, and his brother's name vibrated in his head, *Christian, Christian*. He was beginning to think Danny and Bruce meant to torch the barn. They were standing beside the barn, in fact, contemplating its enormous wall, when they saw a lamb sleeping on a hump of grass near the door, apparently having been locked out. Danny chortled and staggered over to it, and somehow the animal was in his arms. They carried it about a hundred yards until they were out of the pasture and had stepped into a line of trees. The animal had fully awoken and began to bleat. It was a strange lamb with a shrunken back hoof and a gnarl of black wool on its head. "What the hell?" Bruce said. "This is a goddamned fucking lamb."

Danny shrugged. The animal seemed to mock them now, growing panicked by their agitated movements and the smell of spray paint and alcohol. A hot wind surged past and blew their own drunken breath back into their faces. The lamb kicked at Danny's arm so that he lost hold and dropped it. Bruce fell on top of the lamb and wrestled it while Danny's hand closed around a stone and struck at the black spot at the animal's head. Bruce chose his own stone and struck at it, too. Danny held out his stone to Eddie, an offering. Eddie shook his head no. The blood and violence stunned him.

At last the animal lay broken and still at their feet. Eddie threw up in some brush, the fumes of the spray paint having moved into his brain now, poisoning him. He was sick of it all, who his brothers were and who his friends were. A lamb—Christ, they'd murdered a lamb! Danny shook his head, dazed, and jumped to his feet. He jeered at Eddie, an edge of drunken uneasiness in his voice as he stared down at his shirt, flecked with lamb's blood. He said this was *sport*, nothing more, because it was only a goddamned lamb, and they didn't have souls in the first place. All of the four-leggeds didn't have souls, everyone knew that. The fear they'd seen in the animal's eyes, the desperate will to live, had been just a primal bestial thing.

But Bruce was spooked now, with Eddie sick and the cursed lamb dead at their feet. He suggested they get rid of the carcass and then motivate their asses home.

The boys moved further into the trees. Danny lay the dead animal down and kicked some dirt over it. "He wouldn't even take a shot with us," he said, looking squarely at Eddie. "McGregor—Mc*Greg*or—wouldn't even take a shot."

Back at the car they removed their bloodied shirts before they climbed inside. Eddie removed his, too. His shirt was clean, which made it worthless to him now. He tried to sit in the front again, but Danny shoved him into the backseat.

Bruce drove them back toward town because Danny was "too far gone" and wouldn't be able to keep the car from weaving into the other lane or off the road altogether. The car was steamy, but they didn't bother to open their windows, as if that might expose their crimes somehow. The stink of their sweat and their guilt began to swell in the car, a masculine odor that Eddie, alone in the backseat, thought would make him sick, until he realized dimly that he was breathing the smell in willingly. He couldn't stop himself. His two friends sat hot and restless in the front seat and he wanted in that moment to be sitting up there between them. This was such an unwelcome thought, so *Christian* a thought, that Eddie grabbed the empty paper bag in which they'd been carrying the beers and vomited into it.

"Christ," Danny said. "Would you cut the goddamned vomitous puking? This is my old man's car."

Once in town they stopped in back of Benton's Automotive to toss their bloodied shirts into a dumpster. Bruce had the idea to burn the shirts as a final anarchic protest, and Eddie would have gladly taken part in that ritual. All his vomiting was sobering him up quickly; his own unbloodied shirt now repulsed him. He was bothered that he'd thrown up about the lamb; what had he been thinking? That would cost him in the long run. But Danny had turned sensible by then and said, "No, a flame would attract a cop to the scene, or," and he looked at Eddie, "this jerk's brother."

Eddie liked Reed in almost equal proportion to how much he hated Christian, but he said nothing in his brother's defense. They opened a bag of half-rotted food that was already inside the dumpster, dropped the shirts into the bag, and drove away.

"I hear that cop brother of yours is a faggot, too," Danny said, not bothering to turn and make eye contact with Eddie as he spoke. "That true, Mc*Greg*or?"

Eddie stared at the strip of raw sunburn on the back of Danny's cleanly shaven neck. "Fuck you," he said.

"You wish," Danny said. The boys in front laughed and shook their heads in understanding, then fell back into silence.

They dropped Eddie off first. They didn't bother to say goodbye, just backed out of the driveway and drove in the opposite direction from where their homes were. Bare-chested, chilled, Eddie sneaked into the house and walked upstairs to his room. He passed Christian's room with a loathing that rose from somewhere deep inside him up into his mouth and tasted like tin. When had loathing taken the taste of tin? He brushed his teeth twice to rid his mouth of the taste. This was his life and he was stuck in the molasses center of it. The animal snorts of Christian's snoring trailed him down the hall to his own room.

When a third man was found dead, this time along the riverbank only a mile from her home, Iris's uneasiness turned to tangible fear. The murder presented an additional puzzle for the police. The morning news announced the most recent gay murder victim as twenty-two-year-old college graduate Ronald Temple. But the young man's sobbing mother appeared on the news later in the day, dabbing at her eyes with some throttled tissue, and insisted that her son had not been gay. "The girls loved him," she said. "He was just a normal boy like anyone. He didn't deserve this."

The head of the police force appeared on a live televised news conference to reassure the citizens of St. Justin that every officer was dedicated to uncovering the identity of this killer, this "cowardly scourge of a man." The lieutenant was flanked by several officers, including Reed, who stood to the left nearly out of the camera's range. Iris thrilled seeing him—*So handsome*, she thought, and then, in a rush, *so alive*. But her joy dimmed a little when she noticed that Reed seemed the only one who doubted the lieutenant's bravado.

A reporter asked the lieutenant if they had any idea why this man had targeted gay men for death, or if the most recent victim had been gay at all. "Our sources indicate the young man was gay, so we're proceeding on that assumption," the lieutenant said. A different reporter asked why the police trusted these sources over the claims of the victim's own mother. "This isn't the time to go into that," the lieutenant said. "But if he wasn't, then it's a real shocker, isn't it? That you can be murdered for what you are only suspected of being?" His voice shook with indignation. Iris, still watching Reed's face in the background, unable *not* to watch his face, sensed from his expression that he didn't much care for the lieutenant's answer, yet she'd missed what it was the lieutenant had said wrong. She felt thick witted and slow, a mental lurch blind to subtext and inference.

That night she sat in bed trying to read, but her eyes strayed off the page and she stared around the room instead. Something seemed out of place, yet everything was arranged precisely as it had been twenty-five years ago when Carl was still alive and leaving his damp towels strewn across the floor. Now it seemed wrong that she hadn't moved things around after all this time; a lack of preparedness, maybe, or was it a lack of vision? Vision, vigilance—what she needed to be doing, she decided, was paying more attention to things.

And what she noticed in the following days was a tension building in the persistent heat that had settled over the town like a muggy blanket. Her next-door neighbor, Mr. Jackman, kept his water sprinkler running for hours most afternoons. Occasionally the sprinkler would jerk out of its mannerly rotation, as if it had developed a malevolent will of its own, and shoot streams of water over her bushes and against the side of her house. This, too, seemed a part of what was building out of the heat and the headlines, out of the very fabric of the town, an agitation rising from the earth. Iris could feel it rising. Once Mrs. Jackman came over to the house unexpectedly and sat at the kitchen table with Iris for lemonade and a crumb cake. "What do you think of my husband?" she asked Iris. She was a mildly disheveled woman with blunt scratches down both wrists and dreamy eyes that made her look never fully awake. "Do you think he's a kind man, or even a perceptive one?"

The question put Iris at a loss. Mr. Jackman had always treated her with respect, yet he never struck her as being especially kind or perceptive, and Mrs. Jackman had gotten those scratches from somewhere. After a long pause Mrs. Jackman said, "I see," and stood up without touching her square of crumb cake. "Well you'd be wrong."

At the hospital business office where Iris worked, faces started standing out more, mostly men's faces—their darting eyes and tight mouths, perspiring foreheads and firmly set jaws. Always the thought came to her: *Could this be the one the police are looking for? Or this one?* What about that broker in the well-tailored suit who admitted to her, in a low voice so as not to broadcast his shame, that he was actually a little worried about his hospital bill, given that his wife's cancer treatments were so phenomenally high, and he'd just lost considerable money in bad property investments, and didn't want to have to take out a second mortgage on the house. Or what about the young bearded man who waved a neatly Xeroxed copy of his hospital bill in Iris's face, insisting that he couldn't pay his bills, absolutely would *not* pay. He didn't have insurance, and look at some of the charges. How much was he being charged for that stinking aspirin that had no more cured his headaches than a handful of placebos? How much for that ill-fitting pair of slippers he hadn't even requested? It was all craziness, this hospital; was the world itself going crazy, spun off its axis, moving toward some grand chaos? At last he took a deep breath, composed himself, and walked meekly out of her office.

Occasionally young couples from the university would pass by Iris's house on their way from the river promenade, and was it her imagination, or were too many of them tugging at their lover's arm, or yelling or crying or both, their bodies knotted and tense? The national headlines she scanned from time to time suggested things weren't so different outside of St. Justin—droughts, power shortages, random attacks on lovers and strangers. A young Kentucky man had been tethered to the fender of a car, his arms bound, mockingly, in a lover's knot, then dragged half a mile until he was dead for trying to make a "pass" at two men in a bar. When Iris first read this story, she sneaked into the backyard and tossed the paper into the Jackman's garbage bin so her boys wouldn't stumble upon it. But she couldn't possibly keep them from hearing about the Kentucky man. The news refused to remain silent.

And what was she to make of the occasional graffiti she noticed sprayed on bathroom walls or the sides of cement walls in parking garages: *Nigger, spick, bitch, faggot.* Who was writing this stuff? St. Justin was not an urban wasteland. Iris had the uneasy sense the world was revealing itself in too much detail, prodding her to catch up on what she'd missed. Even her clothes seemed to fit her wrong these days, hanging loose with unflattering bulges in the hips and shoulders.

She left work a couple hours early one Friday afternoon, pleading a headache, which was only a mild fabrication. A dull pain pressed behind her eyes, threatening to break open into something she could only hope would be insight, but now it was just pain. She drove home, walked upstairs, and heard an unfamiliar stirring in Christian's room that she couldn't place. She entered without knocking and found him lying on the bed in his underwear beside a freckled boy who was also in his underwear.

They didn't appear to be doing anything more than holding each other and pecking softly at the other's mouth, but Iris gasped as if someone had set a lighted match to her hair. "Put some clothes on!" she cried, although this was not what she'd meant to say.

"Too hot," Christian said dryly. The boy yanked a sheet over himself, but Christian remained nonplussed. "Sorry if we scared you," he said.

"No, no, I'm not scared, of course not." She meant to avert her eyes, but somehow could not.

"We thought, you know, you were still at work."

The boy looked embarrassed, in danger of bolting, but Christian's arm around his bare shoulder stayed him.

"Headache," Iris said and rubbed her temples, mostly for show. She smiled, closed the door, and walked to her own room, unable to banish from her mind the image of Christian with a lover, their skinny bodies and colorless skin. She'd never walked in on any of her sons in the middle of an intimate moment. Of course she knew he was gay, but she'd always imagined in a non-practicing way. Reed was an active gay man, and she adored Alex, and was happy he and Reed were back in touch, even if only in a temporary basis, but Christian... She didn't know what to make of it. Actually, she both liked knowing that Christian had sexual needs and simultaneously feared that this would single him out even more, up his gay-visibility quotient somehow, increase the chance someone might want to harm him.

She stepped out of her dress. When had it become so baggy and over-stretched? Last week she'd noticed that the elastic was shot in one of her skirts. She hadn't dwelled on it then, because it hadn't seemed worth further examination; only now, with the boys' muffled voices drifting to her from down the hall, strumming at her own loneliness, it dawned on her that Christian might be responsible. She waited a moment for the thought to settle. She lay the offending dress down on the bed, stepped into a pair of shorts, slipped on a flowered blouse, then lay on top of the bed and stared with a peculiar longing at her own empty dress. Possibly dressing in her clothes—the only female clothes on hand—was part of some intimate private ritual that Christian and his friend played together, which culminated in the two of them making out on Christian's bed. Of course, Christian was so lean, she was more likely to stretch out *his* clothes, but then again, men's bodies were deceptive, muscular even when they didn't appear that way.

Iris didn't consider that Eddie might be wearing her clothes, and he was so cagey and covert about his actions, he gave her no reason to suspect him. Privately he couldn't believe he had started doing this. He was not frequent about it, because Christian was often in the house while their mother was at work, lying on the sofa squinting into a book or maybe philosophizing into the phone with a friend who Eddie found just as maddening as he found his brother. During these times when they were alone, Eddie and Christian rarely spoke, and when they made direct eye contact, usually inadvertently, Christian's expression implied he knew how Eddie felt about him, and neither respected it nor cared to sway his brother's opinion one way or another.

The compulsion overtook Eddie when he was alone in the house, usually on one of those afternoons when Christian left to work at the copying center downtown. Or that's how Eddie came to think of his own behavior, as a compulsion steeling into his blood, a different man's impulses and drives. Often he was staring at the TV—music videos, hip hop, burning down the house—or else rifling through some of his mother's magazines that were spread across the coffee table. So many of the magazines devoted full-page ads to semi-dressed men and women together, their nude tanned limbs entwined, sometimes stretched out over two pages: pouting lips, mysterious heavy-lidded eyes, erotic underclothes. Eddie couldn't stop staring at the photographs, of the men as well as the women, even when they began to depress him—all that effortless and unattainable beauty. He knew he wasn't much to look at, nothing like Reed, who both men and women had fallen in love with on a whim. Even Reed didn't resemble the men in the ads. Magazine beauty was all illusion, Eddie knew this, but that didn't make it any less depressing. Maybe that was why it was depressing in the first place.

Some days Eddie resisted the compulsion, but other days he could not. On those days the compulsion grew so strong it propelled him up the stairs to his mother's bedroom. He'd open the closet door and face the closet's interior, a private voice urging him to touch one of the dresses; at least do that much; he was alone; would he stop shutting down? A battle between fear of discovery and the need to wear a dress would rage inside him, competing for control of his thoughts, his movements. When the compulsion would win out, his fear and guilt fell away, and there was only this *moment*, this fleeting, transitory moment in which he would try on a dress and complete that picture of himself.

Once he'd pulled a dress from its hanger, it would become the one he would step into, which was easier than slipping it over his head and trying to wrestle it first over his thick shoulders. He'd step out of his shoes, slip off his jeans, and remove his shirt. As he'd tug the dress up over his hips, his excitement would build to a heady crescendo, adding to the fever in his blood. He'd zip the dress as best he could and stand before the mirror, gazing at himself with the suspicion of a detective. He wouldn't know how to feel about this person in the mirror, for (s)he looked grotesque, malformed, incomplete. His ugliness would not be hidden nor his true self revealed. He'd simply created some monstrous sad sack in a dress. Sometimes, if he were feeling especially bold—or especially driven—he'd thrust his large feet deep into a pair of his mother's pumps until his feet hummed from the pain. He wouldn't walk around in the shoes and the dress, because that struck him as ornamental, too obvious and womanly. He'd merely stand in front of the mirror, staring at his absurd reflection, trying to grasp what he was feeling and how it related to him and who he was. When he'd stared at himself in the mirror long enough, the compulsive thrill gradually diminished to embarrassment and disgust. The clothes just hung on him, restricted him. A metallic taste rose in the back of his throat. What was he doing? This was all ridiculous, beyond what even Christian would do. If Danny or Bruce ever found out about this, or his brothers or his mother...but he would kill himself before any of that happened. Besides, no one would find out, because he was never doing this again. He had little desire to see that pathetic, slovenly creature he'd created in a dress. Now that he knew she existed, he could bury her and her slovenly softness in the deep soil at the back of his mind.

Only the next time would come, and he would find himself alone in the house with the compulsion again swelling to life inside him...

Iris didn't find out that Eddie was responsible for her over-stretched clothes entirely by accident. One afternoon she returned home for a quick lunch, mostly as an excuse to check on the boys and make sure they were okay. That ragged shadow of a killer still loomed, and she didn't want to let down her guard. Even to herself she had to admit this was just an excuse. What she really wanted was to walk into the house unannounced and catch her sons unaware. She supposed this was not an especially honorable impulse—in fact, it seemed deceitful—but she couldn't resist the temptation or fight it. Finding Christian in bed with a young man had opened a trapdoor of curiosity about the secret lives of her sons, and, like any sleuth, she wanted to know what mysteries lay beneath.

At first she was disappointed. Christian was not at home, and Eddie was merely posting vigil in front of the TV set, paying scant attention to the soap-opera woman with multiple personalities as she morphed from a crisp, judgmental woman into a bellicose boy with clenched fists. Iris fixed herself a sandwich and a tossed salad, but once she sat at the table to eat, she couldn't enjoy the meal, since Eddie was now staring at her from across the living room, as if waiting to see who she might turn into. A harridan, a depressed woman on a crying jag, a plate hurler? His stare wasn't bored or laconic or even exasperated so much as openly willful, anxious, even demanding—demanding and maybe pleading. Her swift exit, that was what he seemed to want; that was *all* he seemed to want.

Once Iris was driving back to work, she wondered if Eddie's defiant stare hadn't been laced also with anticipation. But why anticipation, and for what? With a spontaneity that thrilled her, Iris turned the car around and drove back to the house. She was prepared to discover something remarkable about her son, something lurking just beneath his silence and defiant, pleading, anticipatory glares.

She parked on the side street where Eddie could not possibly spot her car, and approached the house from the backyard. If Eddie questioned her return, she'd make up an excuse off the cuff. A prepared alibi would sound stilted and hollow. She walked through the back door, passing through the kitchen first and then into the living room. The TV was still on, but Eddie was no longer riveted to the sofa. Iris removed her shoes and climbed up the carpeted steps. When she saw a shadow in her bedroom through the half-open door, she paused, knowing with a sure intuition that the only way she could pass through the trapdoor was to remain still. And there stood Eddie, barefoot in front of her closet mirror, wearing the lemon-colored sundress she'd bought just last week, the price tag still dangling off the collar. At Eddie's feet his own clothes lay tossed in a resigned heap. Her breath boiled in her chest, but she didn't move. Fortunately Eddie's back was turned and he was unaware she'd stepped onto the scene. What immediately struck her was how Eddie didn't appear to be pretending anything, as she'd imagined Christian doing when she suspected he was the guilty party. Where was the inner life, the sense of drama and masquerade, the brief, daring parade before the mirror as he enacted a private fantasy she couldn't hope to know? She'd imagined that men who did this sort of thing were buoyed by some sort of exhilarating charge, but Eddie didn't look charged. He just stood motionless, his strong back stretching the material to its limits, a rugged schoolmarm cursed with a boy's troubled gaze, miserably mesmerized by his/her own reflection.

After a moment a small panic overtook Iris. She mustn't be here, she mustn't be seen. She hastened quietly back down the stairs, still holding her shoes, and stepped out the back door in the shade of the porch and the deeply rooted oak that the Jackmans' sprinkler was inadvertently watering. She was a little dizzy and her hands shook, although she was annoyed with herself for feeling so startled. When she'd imagined Christian was responsible, she hadn't felt nearly so stirred. This worried her, too, her own wrongful assumptions. She hurried across the backyard like a guilty child to the side street and her car. Of course she had no intention of letting on to Eddie that she knew what he was doing. That much was clear to her.

Since that day, she understood why Eddie avoided her and Christian, and seldom ate meals with them unless he was required to. She understood, and yet she couldn't quite look at Eddie in the same way, possessing as she did this secret knowledge. Now she understood what was eating away at him, digesting him, an emotional parasite he carried that was his burden alone. She noticed the furtive guilt in his eyes, a bitter confusion that hadn't existed before this summer, or at least, she hadn't noticed.

She thought about asking for Reed's advice on the situation, but decided against it, unable to explain what she knew without betraying Eddie's privacy, which she had already violated. Besides, she'd been relying on Reed for too much over the years, and sensed that his mind these days was on other things.

And his mind was on other things. Finding St. Justin's gay killer consumed most of Reed's thoughts now, although he was not a detective and had not been officially assigned to the case. He could no longer focus well on the routine of his job—the paperwork, street patrol, minor car accidents, petty domestic squabbles—when the killer, omniscient and unseen, had still not been found. Nearly a month had passed since the last victim, and the police had no fresh leads, which only increased Reed's conviction that the town was being lolled into a state of complacency, softened up for the next kill.

Some afternoons when he was rooted to his desk with paperwork, Reed daydreamed about what the killer might look like. Occasionally he carried the visualization one step further, attempting to sketch faces that loosely matched up with theories he or the police force had formed about the case. But what any of them knew about the man was vague and required conjecture, leaps of analysis. His method of killing—bashing the victim's head open with a stone—suggested that the killer was a man of at least moderate strength and a somewhat primitive mind, for why else the appeal of the stone? A rock, a brick, whatever was used, still conjured images of stoning, that historical method for killing the heretical and the perverted. Did the man lust for the violence of the act, long to stand beside his victims to experience their moments of death, or even to share in them? Shooting was too impersonal, after all, and bullets could be traced. Stabbing was more personal, but too messy. Strangling was possibly the most intimate murder of all, requiring sustained one-on-one contact, and it was clean, but suffocation required time, and a lithe or athletic victim might easily escape before the act was completed.

Reed suspected the man would be inward-drawn, someone who spent too much time in the swirling morass of his own interior, so his outward appearance would reflect this. He wouldn't be dirty, unwashed, or brazenly neglectful, which would violate his external need for order and cleanliness. Yet some smaller physical trait might point to his inner disorder. His hair would be grown out in some ridiculous way, for example, or both his eyes would be ringed with sleep crust he'd forgotten to wipe away, or his jaw would be lightly spliced from where he'd shaved with a dull razor and hadn't noticed he was cutting himself. His face might seem flushed, demonstrating how he was burning in his own hatred.

But how could Reed draw any of this and make it concrete? First he sketched a man's wide face, then added narrow eyes and a tight grimace for a mouth. How about a messy haircut that stuck out in random animal clumps? It was all conjecture, of course. Because the killer's victims were young, Reed imagined the man was young himself, no more than thirty, but what if he was actually in his forties? Who said the man was murdering his own shadow? Reed envisioned the culprit as a man who wore a uniform—was stuck in a life emblematic of a uniform—only this man could just as easily have been a teacher or an innocuous businessman, engaged in some other profession that required no uniform but nonetheless fit like a strait jacket. Instead of feverish eyes, what if the killer possessed cold, expressionless ones, which would suggest he was freezing in his own hatred rather than burning in it. The fires of hell were hot or they were cold; not even the ascetics had figured that one out. Reed couldn't rid himself of the maddening thought that this man was eluding him out of spite and thereby defeating him. He gave his sketch a Mephisto beard and menacing eyebrows for the hell of it, then took a marker and etched a large *X* across the mocking face.

"You realize what you're doing?" Alex asked Reed that night in bed. "You're creating a man inside your head." Alex tapped Reed's forehead, then used that finger to brush away a stray lock of hair that had dropped across Reed's brow. "Only instead of a demon lover, you've created the demon nemesis. The phantom menace."

"I've already got myself a demon lover." Reed kissed Alex, who only half-appreciated the joke.

"I guess it's almost like being in a threesome," Alex added. "It would nearly be sexy if it wasn't for the fact you're creating a man to *hate*."

They'd been drinking some J&B, so Reed suspected Alex was a little tipsy, but still...where was all this coming from? He turned over so he was lying on top of Alex. "He already exists. I'm trying to put a *face* on him. There's a difference."

"The Great Protector," Alex said. "At least you've stopped tailing your brother all over town."

Later they began to make love. After a couple minutes Alex turned overheated and insistent. Maybe he only wanted to battle against the shadow of the other man he insisted lingered inside Reed's head. His movements seemed too frenetic, too forceful and quick, as if their lovemaking were now under a time constraint. What Reed most appreciated about sex was the build-up—just lying beside each other, breathing, pressed together, kissing mouth and throat and chest, setting each other gradually on fire—so he tried to slow Alex down. They moved around in bed, gently insistent, one against the other, unable to find a rhythm, their former simpatico, with Alex's hand in Reed's hair, trying to urge his head lower, and Reed not willing to go there yet. In time they reached a compromise, and although the lovemaking was not precisely what either one had wanted, it was still good enough, welcome enough.

After Alex had fallen asleep, Reed watched the way a vein in the side of his lover's neck pulsed lightly with each breath. Alex, he supposed, was a distraction, too, although a pleasant one. *A necessary one*, or so he told himself. They were ex-lovers who had fallen back into the habit of sleeping together out of loneliness and need. Still, Alex could end up dead just as much as Christian, as any of them.

Reed fell into a light sleep with his face buried in Alex's neck. He dreamed he was lying on a bed of coals. A man holding a stick of firewood stalked over and stirred the coals, forcing those glowing to the surface so Reed's back would scorch.

In the morning Reed still felt unsettled. His back was actually hot. When Alex woke he leaned over Reed with one elbow, just gazing down at him with a sleepy, drugged smile on his face. "I don't think it's just gay men he hates," Reed blurted, trying to get at something.

"We're back to him, then? The Animus?"

"Suppose this guy hates all things gay. I mean, everything. Our life force, our life source, just everything. Hell, the society that allows us to exist, the mothers who gave us birth, the God that created us." Reed stopped before any more words condemned him. He believed in what he was saying, but then again, it seemed over-the-top in a groggy morning way. "At some point we're going to have to talk about what we're doing back together like this," he added gloomily. He hadn't meant to say this either. It was too early; he had to get hold of himself.

Alex frowned but didn't answer at first. He reached over to the bedside table, popped a couple of Tic-Tacs into his mouth, and kissed Reed slowly, the way Reed preferred. Then he stood up and slipped on his underwear. "Anyone ever mention you have a serious side, Officer Reed?" he said. Reed took a deep breath. He wished he'd chewed on a Tic-Tac before Alex had kissed him. "Work," Alex added. "I'd hate capitalism if it didn't pay the bills."

He leaned over the desk to open the window. "Don't," Reed said, and Alex turned to him with a slight confused smile. Reed didn't know how to explain that he couldn't bear the smell of rotting flowers and trailing vines mixed in with the vague chemical smell of the river, creating an overripe odor that was part of the anesthesia blanketing the town, part of what was distracting Reed from finding the killer.

But how do you battle a killer who is a wraith, an enemy whose face exists only in your head?

Late that afternoon Reed returned home from another fruitless day at work and found Eddie sitting outside the door of his apartment with a stubborn, mute expression on his face. His brother had a bruise beneath one eye, twin scratch marks along his neck and jaw, and a wad of coarse tissue plugged up one nostril. "Christ," Reed said, because Eddie was sweating so thickly it had turned his white T-shirt an unpleasant gray. It was clear he'd been in a fight of some kind, but Eddie refused to discuss what had happened. He said only that he'd walked a couple miles from the mall to Reed's apartment in the sinister heat—and it was sinister, this heat—which was why he looked like a janitor's mop and probably smelled like one, too. He just wanted to get cleaned up before he had to return home and face his mother.

Reed unlocked the door and let Eddie into the apartment. Seeing his brother beaten both physically and emotionally was numbing, a feeling similar to, but worse than, what he'd felt when he'd spotted Christian's name spray painted on that wall several weeks ago. Eddie stood shivering in the breeze of the air conditioner while Reed dampened a hand towel and rubbed at the dirt streaks along Eddie's jaw. Eddie seemed unfocused and his skin was clammy to the touch, the whites of his eyes suffused with pink. Reed noticed a lump across his brother's right temple, a swollen discoloration tender to the touch, although he didn't touch it. "How did this happen?" he asked. "Someone attack you?"

Eddie seemed to understand what passed briefly through Reed's mind. "It's not that," he scoffed, nearly holding his breath, his body rigid. "He's a fag killer, remember?"

There was so much that Reed could have said, and wanted to, but you couldn't say any of that to a self-lacerating brother who was both injured and most likely closeted. So he settled on, "It's okay to breathe, you know."

Misunderstanding, Eddie pulled the bloodstained tissue out of his nostril and tossed it on an end table. Then he snatched the hand towel from Reed. "Don't tell Mom," he said as he stumbled into the bathroom to help himself to a shower.

Reed stood in the doorway while Eddie removed his shirt and stared at himself in the mirror—his slick, damp self—his expression suggesting he barely recognized himself, or only reluctantly recognized himself, or even that he recognized himself too well. Then he turned, trying to catch a glimpse of the world at his back. "You can't hide this from Mom," Reed pointed out. "She's going to see the bruises."

Eddie shook his head at his reflection with a disgusted grimace, leaned over the bathtub, and turned on the shower. When Eddie looked toward Reed, he projected that same disgust toward his brother. "Why are you watching me undress?" he asked. "You that hard up these days?"

Reed opened a drawer, pulled out a fresh towel, and handed it to his Eddie. "That didn't hurt a bit," he said and closed the door.

In the living room Reed unbuttoned his shirt, popped an old Bob Seger CD into his machine, and drank half a beer, which did nothing to relax him. He picked up the bloody tissue Eddie had left behind. On the tissue his brother's blood was an explosion of violet; Reed stared down into it. The blood knew more than it seemed. He tossed the tissue into the wastebasket.

When a few more minutes had passed, Reed knocked on the closed bathroom door, but Eddie didn't answer. Reed tapped on the door again, and when Eddie still didn't respond, he opened it. Eddie was slouched on the floor, leaning against the bathtub, his chin rested listlessly on his chest, hair dropping away from his forehead and exposing the harsh bruise.

In a moment of prolonged fear, Reed saw his brother as dead, there on the bathroom floor, just dead, while the shower ran behind him to conceal that fact as long as possible. The image he'd carried around earlier in the summer, of Christian lying dead in a field of weeds with his skull broken open, now transposed itself onto Eddie. Reed's head and heart flushed of emotion, leaving behind a vast empty chamber. He kneeled beside his brother and shook him a couple of times. Reason returned in a headlong rush and he understood Eddie had merely fallen asleep. Was this some kind of concussion? Eddie was breathing out of his mouth in a slack, arrhythmic manner.

Reed didn't bother with calling for an ambulance since the hospital was only a mile away. He helped Eddie stand and walked him out to the car without stopping first for Eddie's shirt and shoes. "This pavement is *blistering*," Eddie marveled, staring at his feet as if expecting them to ignite into a magician's twin flames.

Reed turned on the car's air conditioner, but it still took a minute for the two of them to stop breathing as if pillows were pressed over their faces. Eddie glanced down at his bare chest, still moist with that unsettling sweat. "You can't take me anywhere *naked*," he said.

His voice sounded disoriented. Reed buttoned his own shirt as he drove, thinking that this killer had fooled him yet again, although he couldn't have said how he was being deceived and bested, other than made too aware of his own fallibility. His police training, his skill for detection and judgment, were apparently useless to him—unless he was useless to them. *You're creating a man to hate.* While he'd been absorbed in following Christian around town or trying to outguess a shadow, he hadn't thought much about how Eddie was doing, although Reed had been fifteen himself only ten years ago, suppressing his genuine sexual desire in favor of faking those emotions he imagined he was meant to feel. Reed could see the scar on his hand as he drove, but he couldn't pull Eddie out of his inner fire in the same way he'd kept Christian from toppling into a physical one so many years ago. There was a kind of calm in seeing so clearly his own limitations. He couldn't father Eddie or protect him; he could simply act the role of brother. Or no, not act the role; that was his problem. He was always acting the part, straining for perfection. He must simply *be* Eddie's brother, which of course was the greater challenge, almost an altogether different language. "We're nearly there, Ed," Reed muttered and squeezed Eddie's shoulder. The words didn't sound like much, which was exactly why, Reed supposed, he should trust them now.

As it turned out, the blow to Eddie's temple had caused only a mild concussion, exacerbated somewhat by a light case of heat exhaustion. The doctor suggested to Iris and Reed that Eddie remain overnight in the hospital for observation. If everything checked out in the morning—and there was no reason to believe it would not—then Eddie would be released.

Reed offered to stay with Iris, but she told him to go on home and meet up with Alex. Eddie's condition was not that serious, and Reed had done his part by shuttling his brother to the hospital before any real damage had been done. She didn't mention that she wanted to be alone with Eddie, without the distraction of her other sons, but Reed seemed to intuitively understand this. He brushed his lips against her forehead and said something encouraging, although his exact words remained indistinct to her.

After Reed had gone, Iris stepped into Eddie's room and found him lying in the raised bed, awake but expressionless, staring in a detached way at the TV that was not turned on. Eddie's eye possessed a sluggish look, as if pulled downward by gravity, which helped keep him from having to look at her head-on. Other than the scratches and the welt on his temple, he looked physically fine. Iris pulled up a chair and sat down beside him.

"What?" he said to the earnest look she gave him, his voice groggy but, for all of that, still a boy's wayward voice. Fifteen—he was only fifteen—why did she keep forgetting that? Now that she was with him, she was strangely inarticulate, as she often was with Eddie, her most rough-and-tumble son, her most challenging, contradictory, unhappy son, her baby.

"You know what your father would have said about all this?" she asked at last.

Eddie's voice sounded lifeless and shorn of personality: "I never knew him."

Iris's eyes welled with frustrated tears. She'd forgotten this, too. But Carl had been dead for too many years for either of them to turn sentimental about it now. Iris plunged ahead. "He would have said, 'You don't expect me to believe you got this messed up by accident.'"

The remark wasn't that funny, except for the way Carl had said it, but Eddie smiled in a flat, forced way, to please her. "I got in a fight," he said, and refused to elaborate, mostly because he didn't want to explain how he'd fought with Danny, and how the fight had been about everything and nothing. They had been at the mall, just killing time, staring through glass at a leather bomber jacket hanging from the torso of a male dummy positioned in the window for exactly that purpose of luring them away from their previous destination and into the store. Eddie was admiring the jacket, picturing himself wearing it, while standing quietly side by side with Danny who, he supposed, was imagining himself wearing the same jacket. For a moment they were so close together, linked by their trivial fantasy, that Eddie could smell traces of Danny's aftershave, a musky spice he breathed with caution, stealthily, a thief trying to inhale a scent to which he had no right.

Eddie glanced up from the jacket with a pleasant smile and, through the glass, caught a glimpse of a woman looking back at him. And for a dazed, surreal moment, Eddie thought that the woman on the other side of the glass was himself, his own reflection as he looked when wearing one of his mother's dresses. Had he forgotten to change back into his own clothes before he'd come to the mall? He sucked in a ragged breath; Danny turned toward him at the precise moment Eddie released that same breath. Danny rubbed his cheek in distaste and stepped back. "Christ, McGregor, you're *breathing* on me," he said. "You're that hard up?"

Eddie had struck Danny in the chin with his closed fist before he was aware of having done this. Once he'd swung and connected, his anger vanished, and he was left with a sick desolation anchored in the depths of his stomach. The surprise on Danny's face quickly turned to a scowl, and then full-throttle hatred as he lunged at Eddie. He grabbed Eddie's shirt with such violence Eddie thought he meant to rip it off his chest, and he swung a couple of times, too, striking Eddie in the face, the ribs. Then Danny grabbed hold of the back of Eddie's neck with both hands and pushed Eddie face-first against the wall, once, twice, disorienting him. Something loosened and wobbled around inside his head. Eddie just took the punishment. He had no more fight in him after that first swing. Maybe he'd meant to hit Danny, or maybe he'd been swinging at the woman in the glass.

The saleswoman that Eddie had mistaken for himself hurried out of the store and separated them, yelling something into Danny's face until he calmed down. A crowd had gathered and someone was gulping laughter. The woman spoke to Eddie as well, maybe asking if he was all right, but Eddie turned away from her frown and the cloying reek of her perfume. The exit—somewhere there was an exit out of this cold blast of a gladiator pit called a mall. As he pounded past the crowd an elderly woman handed him a tissue and indicated his nose; otherwise he might never have known he was bleeding.

Outside the heat had blasted him, dizzying him more, but he didn't care about that either. He walked the two miles to Reed's apartment, holding the tissue to his nose, then stuffing most of it up his injured nostril to staunch the bleeding. Cars passed by as he walked, honking their strident horns, puffing toxic clouds of exhaust that knifed at his lungs. The sidewalk ended and there was a brief stretch where he had to walk alongside the racing traffic, dimly aware that he should be careful, that everything felt so strangely apart from him, so strangely unreal. The sun beat down on his shoulders. Even the trees he passed looked as if they'd been dipped in oil. He didn't know why he was going to Reed's, except that it seemed the only place other than home, and he couldn't bring himself to go there. His mother would become undone and make a scene, and the last thing he wanted, in this endless summer of dead men and dead lambs, was any more drama.

"But you don't have to say a word until you're ready," Iris said, breaking into Eddie's memory. She sounded calm, but her eyes snapped with energy, an avid sharpness. There was something naked about his mother's face that both surprised and exhausted Eddie. "You don't have to say a word about anything until you want to."

She waited, but he didn't respond. Of course they both knew this wasn't a real conversation—they were dancing around what needed to be said, circling, at once approaching meaning and backing away again. "Are you feeling okay?" she asked. "Is there anything you want?"

He nodded, but in truth wasn't feeling much at all at the moment, or else was feeling so much he'd temporarily shut down, which was nearly the same as feeling nothing at all. As for what he wanted, some things were unsayable, and his mother should know that. He could have told her, if they were two different people, that his greatest torture was the feeling he was stuck with a life his brothers had already marked for him, that his identity had been mapped out and predetermined. For years Eddie had known his brothers were gay, and had felt early the undertow of expectation pulling at him. He hadn't wanted to be another gay McGregor brother, but his own person, distinctly individual, a lover of women. But over the years, against his will, almost, his own person had moved closer and closer to that of his brothers, until the fantasy images that leapt to his mind at night while he was drifting off to sleep increasingly involved men, often Danny. He was swimming at the city pool with Danny or grappling with him on the school's worn wrestling mat. His sexual needs, then, were not so different from his brothers' after all, only they wore who they were well, and Eddie couldn't find his comfort zone. All he knew was to hold down his feelings, pin them inside himself, wrestle them into submission.

But he couldn't tell his mother any of this. If he unleashed himself, what else would she hear? That he'd watched his friends murder a lamb and helped them bury it to apologize for the shame of not being able to participate in the killing? That he was driven by needs and hungers he couldn't control and still was not comfortable with, and the strongest of these hungers drove him to her closet? That whenever he saw Danny Fitzgerald without a shirt, he wouldn't have minded massaging Danny's shoulders and chest? He'd probably ruined any future friendship or alliance with Danny. The fight would exist between them, a barrier subverting whatever friendship they'd once had, and his existence without Danny's grudging comradeship seemed unendurable, a hell of his own making.

You couldn't say this kind of thing to your mother. You had to spare a mother what you could, even now, when she was flushed with a commitment to make things right. But sometimes things could not be made right. Eddie sensed his mother's determination battling with her helplessness, the two forces struggling against each other for supremacy. A battle, a fight, warring factions—he couldn't seem to grasp the world outside of wrestling terms. Domination or submission, strong or weak, top or bottom, pin or be pinned. He knew the world was more than he was seeing, but now he could only see in black and white. He was too tired for anything other than black and white. The only color left in the room was the dazzling heated blue of his mother's eyes, which he couldn't help staring at, although he'd tried to keep away from eye contact.

"I'm tired, Mom," was all he could bring himself to say.

She nodded, but the look of expectation did not leave her face. "Go to sleep then," she said. "You won't mind, will you, if I stay for a while anyway?"

He shook his head, feeling drugged up, weary, the words alone ushering him toward sleep. "Go ahead. Stay," he said, and meant it.

Iris sat for some time beside the bed, and the soothing sound of Eddie's breathing must have drawn her into her own dreamless sleep, because the next thing she knew a plump nurse with a silver tooth was shaking her awake. "Mrs. McGregor, visiting hours are long over," she scolded.

Iris was astonished to see it was nearly eleven o'clock. "Yes, of course, I'm sorry," she said, yet it was difficult to leave Eddie behind in this impersonal hospital for even one night. Eddie's mouth always dropped open when he slept, often giving him the look of a dead man, but tonight his parted mouth seemed oddly hopeful, frozen in a half-formed whisper. He had no idea, her son, how much she knew about him, or how much this knowledge only deepened her love if not her understanding. She considered spending the night down in the business office where she worked, sleeping in the small private lounge area on the battered sofa next to the dicey vending machine that always spat out a snack you hadn't ordered. But Christian would have returned home from work at the copy center long ago and would be waiting for an update on Eddie. And so she must return home.

Eddie, Christian, Reed—her sons' names swirled in her head as she rode the lurching elevator to the lobby, entwining together like a helix molecule. She was restless for them, restless for herself. Iris started walking toward employee parking, then remembered she'd parked in the visitor's section behind the hospital, so she veered off and went in that direction. A scant rain had begun to fall, hardly noticeable, yet it suggested the weather was shifting and the unspeakable heat, at last, was breaking. A few lightning bugs darted in and out of view around the lampposts. She recalled how Christian and Eddie used to chase the bugs at night, snatching at the bursts of light, and how she had to wash the yellow smears off their hands before putting them to bed.

Iris was digging around in her purse for her keys, although she hadn't reached the car yet, when an orderly wearing green hospital scrubs shuffled out of the shadows and stood before her. He was simply not there and then he was. "Mrs. McGregor?" he said. "Iris McGregor?"

His voice sounded so dim and reserved she could only make out what he was saying by straining to hear. She had the odd sense she knew him, yet was sure she'd never met him before. "Yes?" Iris said, and offered him a half-smile of greeting, as was her custom.

The man did not return her smile. He was in his middle to late twenties, wearing a crumpled jacket over the scrubs, although the heat made the jacket impractical and even a little foolish. He was neither tall nor short, but seemed well built, although the jacket was baggy and she couldn't know for sure. There was something bastardized about his face, or that was the word that came to her, bastardized, sunken as his expression was into a look of forlorn emptiness and frustrated rage—unless it was frustrated pain. His hair was too short, as if he'd navigated the cut himself with a pair of stiff scissors while staring in the mirror, and there was a cold, agitated sheen to his eyes. Something was weighing him down—his face, posture, the heavy downward curl of his mouth—she could sense that weight, feel it. Her first instinct was that he might be injured.

When he spoke again, his voice sounded clogged, a little echoing, as if it were coming up at her from a kitchen drain. "I know who you are," he whispered in that way words sound when they're spoken to someone but not meant for that person. "Don't you see, I know. Fag mother."

He took a stumbling, pleading step toward her. In the moment before he withdrew the plaster arm cast he was carrying under his jacket—a cast, not a stone!—Iris understood who he was. And like a blurred movie image abruptly brought into sharp focus, she saw how all along she had been his target, too, a woman he passed anonymously dozens of times in the hospital halls, a woman whose body in its youth had given birth more than once to those he hated.

How could this be anything other than fate, the strings of some unknowable moral pattern pulled tightly together, to dump this man into her path with such paralyzing suddenness?

Weeks later, after it was all over and Iris thought back on that night, she supposed what had startled the man most was how she hadn't shrunk away or screamed or tried to run when he was slipping his right arm into the perfectly formed cast. Instead she had attacked. "You!" she screamed in a whisper as clogged as his own, her car key gripped in her hand like a tiny dagger. She charged him with her dagger, grabbing hold of what listless hair she could, jabbing her key at one of his eyes, that cold, uneasy eye, wanting to blind him, temporarily or permanently, it didn't matter, she knew no distinction between the two. He grunted and tried to pull away, but Iris held firm, raking the key down his face. She meant to scar him, yes; and in this way he would be marked, he would stand out in a crowd, unable to blend into the stagnant human wall of normalcy. The man regained his balance, raised his arm—now fitted in the cast—and drove it hard down across her right temple, causing an explosion of white light inside her head. She collapsed to her knees, but still clutched his arm in a tight grip, her fingers digging so deeply into his flesh she might have meant to break through to his very bones, to his basic physical essence. He raised his heavy arm a second time, panting in pain, and in that last fleeting second remaining for her, Iris managed her final act of rebellion by memorizing his face.

And though she would lie in a hospital bed in a coma for three days, she clung as tenaciously to life as she'd clung to the killer's arm in the parking lot. Once she emerged from the coma, following the voices of her sons out of the void and back into the concrete world, she spoke with a slur out of one side of her mouth, an affliction that would remain with her thereafter. Yet still she was able to describe the man's face. His image hung in the forefront of her mind more sharply defined than the police sketch they'd assembled from her description—the self-mutilating haircut, snarling mouth, dead eyes. Iris described her attacker with such dogged detail that, only hours later, the police (and Reed among them) stormed the house of one Emma Mooney. They found her son Jack hiding in a closet, crouched low among his shirts and jeans and several pair of stolen sneakers, his left eye swollen and face scratched from the marks of Iris's key, clutching to his chest the arm cast scratched with several signatures, and spotted here and there with threads of dried blood. In the background his mother called out in a tragic voice—*Jack, Jack honey, don't run, what have you done, don't be afraid, don't hurt him, my baby...*

Iris knew none of this the night she faced down Jack Mooney. She knew him only for who he was, the killer of sons, an embodiment of every danger she couldn't place, now made flesh and weak as anyone. What fear she'd felt gave way to relief and a stunned, dark thankfulness, that a fleeting moment of opportunity had been presented her, and she might end, at least, this much. So she rushed toward him with a muffled cry, this burning, ragged figure of a man with his plaster arm, while he stood in front of her still, while she could see what it was they were fighting.

SILENCED VOICES: SHI TAO

by Siobhan Dowd

Shi Tao

As China's economy grows exponentially, Western multi-national corporations are chasing each other to take advantage of the burgeoning markets which the billion-strong population affords. Up-to-the-minute technology, high fashion, and international tourism have all come within reach of many Chinese for the first time ever; these are exciting times in terms of access to material goods for the richer portion of the nation. Unfortunately, however, the new climate is not accompanied by a political thaw. As the case of imprisoned poet Shi Tao demonstrates, the government remains unwilling to embrace a softer approach

Glimmer Train Stories, Issue 59, Summer 2006

to civil liberties and, in particular, freedom of expression is still in short supply. Even more unfortunately, Shi's case also indicates that at least one Western corporation is quite willing to aid and abet the Chinese government in its suppression of dissent, in order to keep its business in China safeguarded.

Shi Tao was born in July 1968 in Yanchi County in Ningxia Hui Autonomous Region. He is of Han ethnicity and a university graduate, who, at the time of his arrest in November 2004, was married and living in Taiyuan, Shanxi Province. The official court verdict against him states that he was then "unemployed," but prior to that he had been working with Hunan's *Contemporary Business News* as head of the editorial department. It was in this role that trouble befell him.

The year 2004 marked the fifteenth anniversary of the Tiananmen Square Democracy Movement. Many Chinese citizens sympathetic to the aims of the students of that time were planning to commemorate the Movement in some way. The authorities, however, wanted to forestall any reawakening of the old revolutionary ardor. They therefore imposed a set of media restrictions designed to keep all discussion of the Movement out of the public arena.

Shi Tao, like other journalists across China, found himself summoned to a meeting in the spring of 2004 by his bureau's editors. He and his colleagues were read an official document entitled "A Notice Regarding Current Stabilizing Work" (Party-speak for "press censorship of a sensitive topic we'd rather not refer to directly"). Shi took notes of the meeting and soon afterwards emailed a summary of the restrictions to the Asia Democracy Foundation. In doing so, he used a Yahoo! account and the pen name 198964. (The numbers comprise the date the Chinese army tanks famously crushed the Tiananmen Square Democracy Movement before the shocked gaze of the world.) Shi's memorandum was then posted on the on-line Democracy Forum under this pen name.

It is not clear precisely how the authorities traced the memorandum to Shi Tao. However, it has been documented by the French human-rights group Reporters Without Borders that at least part of the process involved the American-based corporation Yahoo itself. Yahoo Holdings (Hong Kong), Ltd. provided the state security authority with account details that helped to establish Shi Tao as the sender, according to the court's official verdict. As Reporters Without Borders claims: "Yahoo obviously complied with requests from the Chinese authorities to furnish information regarding an IP address that linked Shi Tao to materials posted online, and the company will yet again simply state that they just conform to the laws of the countries in which they operate. But does the fact that this corporation operates under Chinese law free it from all ethical considerations? Information supplied by Yahoo led to the conviction of a good journalist who has paid dearly for trying to get the news out. It is one thing to turn a blind eye to the Chinese government's abuses, and it is quite another thing to collaborate."

Soon after having been thus identified, Shi Tao was taken into custody near his home by members of Changsha security on November 24, 2004. His computer was confiscated, along with other documents, and his family was told to keep quiet about the matter. Three weeks later he was issued with a formal arrest order. Then, on April 27, 2005, the Changsha Intermediate People's Court found him guilty of "illegally providing state secrets to foreign entities." His lawyer's plea that his action had not engendered "especially serious circumstances" fell on deaf ears. The court concluded that "Shi Tao leaked this information to an overseas hostile element, taking advantage of the fact that he was working overtime alone in his office to connect to the internet." He was sentenced to ten years' imprisonment plus two years' subsequent deprivation of political rights. He is not due for release until November 23, 2014.

Shi Tao is known to the world outside China through his various postings on overseas Chinese-language media, such as Democracy Forum. He is also a published poet and a member of the Independent Chinese PEN Center. He would have been twenty years old at the time of the May/June 1989 Tiananmen Square Democracy Movement and presumably still a student. Exactly what his role was in the demonstrations of that time is unclear. However, the following poem indicates that he *was* involved in some way, and perhaps lost a loved one to the fray:

My whole life
Will never get past "June."
June, when my heart stopped,
When my poetry froze.
June, when my lover died,
Left behind in a pool of blood.
June. The sun scorches open my skin,
To show the wound that lies beneath.
June. Little fish swim from the blood-red sea
Looking for another place to hibernate.
June. The earth changes shape. The rivers fall silent.
Letters pile up, undeliverable to the dead.

Polite letters appealing for Shi Tao's release can be sent to:

His Excellency Hu Jintao
President of the People's Republic of China
State Council
Beijing 100032
People's Republic of China

Some readers may also like to write to Yahoo by snail mail (which, ironically, may have more impact than email) expressing grave concern at Yahoo's involvement in Shi Tao's case to:

Terry Semel
Yahoo Inc.
701 First Avenue
Sunnyvale, California 94089
USA

Siobhan Dowd, an author and journalist living in Oxford, writes this column regularly, alerting readers to the plight of writers around the world who deserve our awareness and our writing action.

On the back of this photo it says "Samantha and her old man, to my old man. Happy old man's day." I was six weeks old.

Samantha Schoech spent portions of her childhood in a fishing village in Mexico, at a Buddhist meditation center in Vermont, and in a leafy suburb north of the Golden Gate Bridge. She now lives and writes within salt-spray distance of the Pacific in San Francisco. Her stories have appeared in *ZYZZYVA*, the *Gettysburg Review*, the *Sun*, *Seventeen*, and other journals and magazines. Her husband and her dog often keep her company on the beach.

ASCENSION

Samantha Schoech

I've just stopped by to change my clothes when I first see her wings. She's sitting there at our kitchen table with her hands wrapped around the #1 Mom mug I gave her for Mother's Day in seventh grade. At first I run past her, but then I stop and walk backward to the open kitchen door and stare at her. Her eyes are sort of half-closed in this beatific way, and there are two smooth, white humps behind her shoulders. I know she's heard me come in, but she doesn't look up; she just stays in that pose until I say, "What's up with the wings?"

She opens her eyes slowly and it takes her a moment to focus on me. When she does, her lips bend into a coy little smile.

"They're angel wings."

I roll my eyes, but I'm intrigued. My mother is not a great kidder. She is the type to light incense and candles and consult tarot cards and rune stones, but she is not the type to joke about angels. She takes spiritual beings very seriously.

I walk around behind her and check out the wings. She doesn't turn around or stand up. From the two arches above her shoulders, the folded wings descend to about her knees. They are pleated neatly and hang down over the back of her chair, folded and tucked, and huge. I touch one, and it quivers like the hide of a horse. I snap my hand back in horror.

"They're sensitive, like breasts," my mother says. She is always saying stuff like this. She loves words like *breasts* and *vulva* and sometimes even *yonni.*

"Look," she says. There is a rustling, like someone snapping a sheet before folding it, and then her wings spread out from her horizontally. She's got over a six-foot span; it's an impressive thing to witness.

They are not exactly how I've imagined angel wings to be. They have no feathers, just a thin, pearlescent membrane connecting the fine, finger-like bones. They look like white silk bat wings, and I wonder again if she's joking, if she has rigged these elaborate wings out of fabric and pulleys, which she is manipulating beneath her poncho. But of course she is not. These are her wings, attached with the certainty of limbs to her shoulder blades.

I walk around the table and sit down across from her. She looks at me with that same calm smile, the one she has been working on since my dad left and she turned to goddess worship and transcendental meditation. It's an over-compensation thing, that smile, and usually it doesn't fool me. But now, I have to admit, she looks convincingly calm. The line between her eyebrows has relaxed and her eyes are heavy lidded.

"So, how'd it happen?" I know that Claudette is waiting for me at her house. We are going to her parents' club to go swimming later, and I only just rode my bike home to get my bathing suit and a clean pair of shorts. I should be hurrying; we are trying to time our arrival with Steve Menendez's lunch break, and, by stopping to talk to my mom, I am messing up our schedule. But my mom has grown angel wings, so I make the decision to skip the club.

"I woke up with them," she says, sipping from the #1 Mom mug. "My back felt a little itchy last night before I went to sleep and I was rubbing it against the door jamb, like a cow." She laughs lightly at herself. "Then, this morning..." She shrugs. The rest is history.

"Did anyone talk to you about them? Like, did they come with a message?" My mom shakes her head and shrugs again. She hasn't a care in the world. "Well, how do you know they're angel wings if nobody has, like, given you any instructions or anything?"

She looks at me with kind pity in her eyes and I know she's right. They are so obviously angel wings. They couldn't be anything else.

"So you're an angel?" It bugs me to ask this. If there is anyone on the planet who thinks she is an angel, it is my mother. It annoys me that this image of herself seems to have been realized. She nods with confidence and slowly folds her wings back down and stands up.

"Are you hungry?" she asks. "It's lunchtime. I could make tomato soup and grilled cheese."

I have barely eaten at home all summer. I spend most of my time with Claudette. At her house there are seldom parents, and the pantries are stocked with chips and sodas and cookies that the maid bakes every other day. At my house the kitchen smells of yeast and tea leaves and mildewing fruit. My mother bakes her own bread, and so any attempt at making a sandwich is thwarted by odd, uneven slices that fall apart too easily. Tomato soup is the one prepared food my mother still buys. She loves Campbell's, and although she has to make a special trip to the regular grocery store to buy it, she always has a few cans ready.

I say okay and watch as my mom goes about the business of making lunch while her wings bounce and shimmy slightly with her movements. The wind chimes outside tinkle and sing.

I look down at my arm, the fine hairs bleached white by the summer sun. "I thought angels had to be dead first."

"I guess not," my mother tells me without turning around. "Unless I died in my sleep." She laughs, but a wave of nausea passes through me when I think of the possibility that she has died. Then I look at her, turning the can opener against the soup can, and realize that even if she did die, it doesn't seem to matter. I mean, here she is. I am looking right at her.

I stare at the place on her back where the wings are coming from. Her clothes must have slits cut in them or something, because they seem to fit all right; nothing's bunching up or anything. "Did you cut your poncho?" I ask.

"No. It just sort of works when I get dressed. I put on my regular clothes and they just fit, and my wings are on the outside, and I don't have to struggle at all." She shakes the soup out into the pot and it lands with a splat, holding its cylindrical shape for a moment before dissolving. "Take a look," she says, coming toward me. "Tell me what's going on back there."

I stand up and sort of peer around the edge of her wings, trying to see where they connect, but it just seems like they disappear into the nubby wool of her poncho. I don't really want to touch them, but I'm curious. I pull the edge of the fabric away and hold open the hole so that I can see the skin of her back where the wings are attached.

"It looks like a chicken," I tell her, and it does.

"Does it look irritated?"

"No." I let go of her poncho and lean against the counter.

She goes back to the stove to stir the soup and I butter the bread for the grilled cheese.

When the phone rings my mother and I look at each other. It is as if we realize simultaneously that other people are going to have to be told. Word of my mother's ascension is going to get out sooner or later. I pick up. It's Claudette. "Where are you?" she pleads into the phone. "We're already totally late."

"Go without me," I tell her. "I'm gonna stay home." She exhales dramatically into the phone. She has been my best friend since freshman year, but she can really be a brat. My mother says she has an over-developed sense of entitlement.

"Claudette?" my mom asks when I hang up the phone. I nod. "You didn't tell her."

I shrug and continue preparing the bread. "Do you have any, like, powers or anything?" I ask her after a moment, when I'm done with the butter.

My mom shrugs and her wings bounce slightly. "I don't know. I feel great, though."

This shrugging, easy-going person is not the version of my mother I am used to. The mother I am used to is tense and likes a lot of quiet and soft lighting. The mother I am used to shrieks into the phone when my father calls to talk to me, and then practices her breathing exercises on the living-room couch until she feels centered.

"Maybe after lunch we could try some stuff."

"Like what?" my mother says.

"Like, to see if you have special powers."

"What kind of powers do you think I might have?" She has turned to face me again and she looks excited, a little flushed.

I don't know very much about angels. I try to think of what her special powers might be, but I keep coming up with the kinds of things superheroes have, like x-ray vision and extra-strong hearing. Then it hits me, and I am suddenly excited.

"Do you think you can fly?"

My mother grimaces and shakes her head. "I sort of tried," she says, pointing to a bruise on her forehead that I hadn't noticed. "I jumped off the landing, but I just fell and hit the bookshelf."

"Oh," I say. "That's too bad." We are silent for a moment, then I say, "Okay, what am I thinking?" I look straight into my mother's eyes, and she looks straight back into mine, frowning and unblinking. We are both concentrating very hard. This is a trick I have tried with my friends at various times over the years. Once, in sixth grade, I kept telling Rachel Grimes she was right every time she guessed what I was thinking even though what I was really thinking the whole time was how dumb I thought she was for believing me. She still brings it up sometimes, even though we haven't been friends since junior high. She thinks we share a secret about her psychic abilities.

"Umm," my mother says, "are you thinking about Taffy?"

I wrinkle my nose at her. Taffy was our neighbor's pony when we lived in the country when I was a little girl. I think for a minute about telling her that she's right, but I shake my head instead. I haven't thought about Taffy in about five years.

"So I guess mental telepathy isn't one of them," I say.

"I guess not," my mother says, turning off the flame under the soup and then starting in on the sandwiches. She always does this, leaves the soup in the pot too long before serving it. It grows a skin, which I refuse to eat.

I accidentally knock over the salt shaker and then trace designs in the spilled grains with my finger. "What about good deeds? I think angels are supposed to do good deeds. I mean, you're put on earth for a reason, right?"

My mother nods solemnly. I can tell she likes this. She's into all that higher purpose stuff, giving of oneself. Last summer she started volunteering at the juvenile hall, but she didn't last long. Nobody signed up for her self-esteem through beading workshop, and she was totally offended.

She puts the first grilled cheese onto a small plate and cuts it diagonally. She won't serve me until everything is ready and we can eat together. Ritual is very important to her.

"Well, like, do you feel any special calling?" I ask. I am making a series of wavy lines in the spilled salt. She looks up and drums her nails against the counter top. They are perfect, as always. Even after my dad left and my mother started dressing only in the colors of the sunset and decorating our house with batik prints of gods we can't name, she kept her weekly nail appointments. She has always been extremely well groomed.

"Umm," she says again, rolling her eyes back into her skull to think. "I definitely want to do something with women." She reminds me of the way me and my friends talk when we talk about the future, except a lot of them want to be models or do something in fashion.

"Like what?" I ask.

"I don't know exactly." She looks at me with her head cocked. She is waiting for me to come up with something, but I'm not into all her vagina goddess stuff. I shrug at her and pour myself a glass of milk.

"I wonder if there are certain individuals I am supposed to look after, you know, like a guardian angel, or if I'm just here for a sense of general well being," she says dreamily, to no one in particular.

She finally serves lunch and we sit back down at the table facing one another. Except for the humps of her wings, she looks exactly like she always looks: smooth blondish gray hair, blow dried with a slight flip at the end, dangly moonstone earrings, expensive peach-colored T-shirt under her Ecuadorian poncho with the llamas along the border, a skim of pink frost on her lips.

I study her for a minute while she calmly spoons tomato soup into her mouth, blowing on each bite beforehand, even though it's barely hot anymore. There is something different about her, but I can't place it. Occasionally, she looks up at me and smiles, and then turns back to her soup. It's not just the wings; it's something else.

My dad has been gone for sixteen months. He lives in Dana Point now and tells me he's bought a sail boat. I have never been to visit him, although he has invited me, saying he will pay for my plane ticket. When he calls and I answer the phone I sometimes lie to my mom and tell her it was someone else. I can't stand how she gets when the subject of him comes up, and I can't help feeling, when I watch her face harden and her lips pinch up, that I can sort of understand why my dad didn't love her anymore. But then I feel bad because, as she is always reminding me, she gave up twenty years of her life for that man.

My mother has been pissed off since the day my father left. Big time. But now, as I look at her, and as she looks back at me with her watery navy blue eyes, she doesn't seem quite as mad as she usually does.

"Why do you think they picked you?"

"Who?" she says, as if she's lost the thread of the conversation, as if there could be anything to talk about except her new angel status.

"I don't know. God or St. Peter or whoever. I mean, I guess we have to believe in God and everything now."

She looks up from her soup and puts down her spoon. "I have always believed in God, just not necessarily the Christian version of it." This is not technically true. My grandparents are Episcopalians, and I happen to know that my mom spent much of her life believing in the Christian version of things. This is typical of her though; she revises freely and unselfconsciously.

"Okay," I say, letting it slide, "but why do you think God picked you?"

She looks back into her skull again, the little line of a smile appearing on her lips like she's remembering something extremely pleasant. "Well, I've been a good person."

I think of the way my mother violently sliced my father out of every single photograph in the home, the way she screamed as she tore apart their wedding album and threw its pages into the fireplace, of the way she once hissed at me, "You will have nothing to do with that bastard. He hates us and we hate him back." It is difficult for me to see my mother as an angel, but obviously she rose to the top in somebody's estimation.

We finish our lunch and I clean up the kitchen, and then we sit around as if we are waiting for something, only we don't exactly know what we are waiting for.

I have not spent a single afternoon in our house all summer. There is nothing to do, really. I take a basket of my dirty laundry down to the basement and do a load. I get out the as-of-yet-unopened SAT study books I demanded my mother buy me at the beginning of summer and flip lazily through the practice tests.

My mother sits at the kitchen table with another cup of tea and works on the beaded earrings she makes and sells at the farmer's market. I hate them; they are totally hippie and eighties, but she doesn't know this. She gives me a pair for every occasion. Sometimes I wear them around the house on Christmas morning to make her happy, but that's all. After Christmas they lie in my jewelry box like sparkling, out-of-style reminders of how little my mother knows about me.

At four, Claudette calls. She's back from the club.

"I rode by your house on my way home, but I didn't stop. There was this totally weird guy standing in your front yard." I lean over and look out the living-room window at the front yard, and, sure enough, there is a man standing there on our flagstone path looking back and forth from our house to a little notebook he's writing in. It looks like he's sketching, or somehow recording the details of our house, but our house looks pretty much like every other house in the neighborhood—fake Tudor, sloping front yard, little black lamppost sticking out of the lawn—so I don't know why he would do this.

"Gross," I say. "He's still there."

"Who is he? I didn't want to have to talk to him, so I just rode by." This is so Claudette. She is interested in very few people.

"I'll call you back," I say, and hang up before she has a chance to respond. I watch the man some more. He is old, about fifty, and he's dressed in a pale yellow golf shirt and very neatly pressed khakis. He has white hair combed over to the side and dark blue boat shoes. He reminds me a little bit of my father. He continues to scribble in his book.

"Mom," I stage whisper, going into the kitchen where my mother's hands are struggling with the tiny beading loom she uses. "There's a man in the front yard."

She looks up at me slowly and her wings rise and fall like a shrug. "What do you mean?"

"Look out the window," I tell her. "Do you know that guy?"

My mother sighs and disentangles herself from the loom. Little beads skitter across the hardwood when she stands. She looks out the window for a minute, and then something occurs to her, and she charges toward the front door, leaning forward and stomping. Her wings rustle as she passes me and I turn and follow her.

She rips open the front door so hard it bangs against the wall and leaves a mark, then she charges down the flagstone path toward the man in the golf shirt. He looks up and sees her, and starts to back away down the path, staring like he's seen a ghost.

"He will *not* get this motherfucking house!" she screams. She is still walking toward him, but the man is frozen in place. "It's mine, motherfucker, and he will never get it. Never."

Her performance is so dramatic I almost start giggling. But I don't, because it is obvious she is dead serious. Instead I stand back, on the lawn, and watch her. A car drives by and slows, and I see the driver crane his head and stare. It's about six o'clock, and people with regular jobs are starting to repopulate the neighborhood.

My mother has stopped her advance, but she stands her ground, her chest heaving, and challenges the man.

He gapes like he's the first person on earth ever to see a middle-aged angel in an Ecuadorian poncho, and then he makes a little sound, like a grunt, and runs back to his tan Buick parked against the sidewalk. He does not peel out. Instead he pulls slowly away from the curb, watching my mother until it is unsafe to do so.

When he is gone she heads back inside. When she passes me she stops and turns around so that I almost bang into her back, into her wings, and says, "Your father is a horrible person, but I will be damned if I am going to let him ruin my life." She goes back into the house but I stand outside for a while watching a dragonfly flit around the hydrangea. I want to yell back at her, to tell her that nobody likes her when she's like this, but at the moment I am a little afraid.

When I go back into the house my mother is on the phone with her lawyer. I listen to the conversation while I make dinner: organic pasta with olive oil and parmesan and little cherry tomatoes from my mother's garden. At one point I hear her say, "Okay, I'm breathing, I'm breathing." And I know Christof, her lawyer, is calming her down.

When she gets off the phone I ask her if she wants dinner, but she shakes her head and goes into the living room where she puts on her CD of Tibetan chants and lights some incense. I eat alone at the kitchen table listening to the guttural intonations of the Tibetans.

By nine o'clock my mother is fully recovered and we watch a rerun of *ER*. She has to sit in the straight-back chair so her wings can drape over and hang down the back. We pass a bowl of popcorn back and forth and drink herbal iced tea. At one point she lets out a little cough and says, "I can't believe how they treat the women on this show." I don't say anything because it seems to me they treat women fine. The whole head of the ER is a woman, for Christ's sake.

When the show is over we go upstairs to bed. I have not been to bed this early in a long time. I wonder what Claudette is doing, and only then remember that I was supposed to call her back. I fall asleep imagining her reaction when I tell her that my mom is an angel.

The next morning I run into my mom in the hall outside our bedrooms. She is fresh from the shower, wrapped in a thick white towel, and she looks beautiful. Her wings are still there, hanging down her back and sparkling with little droplets of water.

"Beautiful day," she says, grinning. I squint at her and then head into the bathroom to pee.

My mother has made us oatmeal for breakfast and she has cooked the raisins in, which is the way my dad and I like it.

"Is it uncomfortable to sleep?" I ask as I pour syrup into my oatmeal.

"I don't think I've slept so well in years." She takes a deep laundry-detergent-commercial breath, stretches her arms, and says, "I feel absolutely glorious."

I get up for the milk, and that's when I notice the guy from the day before parked outside our house. He is in the same yellow golf shirt. I decide not to say anything. Even though her new angel mood is a little annoying, it's way better than her shrieking.

After breakfast I leave for Claudette's. Her parents are skiing in Chile, where it's winter, and it's the maid's day off, so we will have the place all to ourselves. Claudette's dad is a chemist and he invented some sort of sealant, and now they are the richest family I know. I like to be around her parents, who never yell at her about the price of clothes or cancel cable because it's too expensive. Ever since my dad left, my mom has been on what she calls her "belt-tightening campaign." She earns a little money from her beading, but mostly we live off child support.

I decide to see what the guy in the golf shirt is up to. As I approach his car, he starts to fumble with the keys as if he's afraid of me, but when I tap on the window he rolls it down and smiles a tight, nervous smile.

"Why are you in front of our house?"

"Are you Patricia?" he asks, raising his eyebrows expectantly, as if it would be a great relief if I were.

"No. That's my mom. And everyone calls her Patty."

"Is she home?"

"Yeah. Why?"

He glances at a clipboard lying next to him on the seat, and then shrugs and rolls up the window again without answering me.

"Whatever," I say, hopping on my bike. My mom is going to kill him if he tries to fuck with her about the house. She fought my dad in court to keep it.

At Claudette's we watch movies in their entertainment room and give ourselves pedicures. I paint my toes red, white, and blue for the Fourth of July. Claudette does hers in Pussycat Pink. Later, when our toes are dry, we will walk to the club to swim. I don't mention my mom's wings. She is already considered a little strange.

• • •

It's late when I get home from Claudette's and the house is dark from the outside. I put my bike in the garage and go in through the kitchen.

I am on my way upstairs when I notice a lump on our couch covered in a purple chenille throw blanket. I tiptoe back across the living room and peer down at it. It's the man in the golf shirt, and he is sleeping soundly, emitting a little whistle as he breathes. He is dressed in a white T-shirt and a pair of my sweat pants. They say "Central Wildcats" in a little circle near the hip. In his sleep he looks older than he did before. He is on his side and his belly hangs and strains against the T-shirt, and sits solidly beside him on the couch. The sides of his eyes are crinkled like the fans we used to make out of construction paper in grade school. "La-ti-da," we would say, fluttering them in front of our faces.

I watch him for a few minutes, listening to the tick of our kitchen clock and noticing the way his mouth twitches into a smile and then relaxes, as if he is laughing in his dream.

In my bedroom the clock glows 1:00 a.m., casting a circle of green light near my pillow. I undress and slide right into bed, without even brushing my teeth. I can smell chlorine in my hair and Banana Boat suntan lotion on my skin. I stare through the darkness at the pimply texture of my ceiling until my eyes sting. Then I close them and fall asleep.

I awaken to a hum, some sort of low, continuous vibration. It's still dark outside when I open my eyes, but there is a sort of weird, silvery glow in my room. I blink and prop myself up on my elbow, and only then do I notice my mother standing at the foot of my bed in her white cotton nightgown. The glow is coming from her, like a halo.

"What?" I say, sitting up.

"I found out," she whispers at me, her voice husky.

"What?" I ask again.

"They sent a messenger, like you said." When she says "messenger" she jerks her head toward the staircase and I assume she means the golf-shirt guy.

I sit up and squint at her through my heavy eyes. "So?" I want her to get on with it so I can go back to sleep.

She smiles and clears her throat like she is about to audition, and then she unfurls her wings, all six feet of them, and says in a clear, loud voice, "I am the Angel of Bitterness."

I frown. "Meaning what?"

My mother rolls her eyes. She can't believe I am not more impressed. "Meaning that's my calling," she says, her shoulders slumping slightly.

"You go around making people bitter?"

"No!" she says, folding her wings back down against her back.

"Well, what then?"

"I'm not exactly sure yet. He was tired." She does the head jerk toward the golf-shirt messenger again.

"But he said you were the Angel of Bitterness?"

She nods. "I'm like a patron saint. I'm in charge of the bitter ones."

Now it's my turn to nod. I can picture this.

"So?" she says. She wants my reaction.

"So, it sounds good. I'm sure you'll be great at it." I yawn.

She sighs and her shoulders relax. "I think so, too," she says, smiling. "I really think I've found my calling." She stands there nodding like she's waiting for something. When I don't say anything she says, "So?" again, but slowly, like there is something obvious I should be doing.

"What?"

"Well, is there anything you want to get off your chest? You know, try me out."

"You want me to confess or something?" I ask.

"Not confess, just share. Only if there is something bothering you."

I roll my eyes back to think about what I might tell her. I think about my father and his new boat and about Claudette and her rich parents. I think about the way my mother is always home bent over her beading or sitting silently, looking at nothing. I look up at her. Her wings are quivering and her face is flushed and lovelier than I've ever seen it. But there is nothing I want to tell her. Her powers, it appears, do not work on me.

They taught me to play ball wearing mittens?

Jean Colgan Gould is the author of *Divorcing Your Grandmother*, a novel, and *Forty Years Since My Last Confession*, a memoir, as well as the editor of two anthologies: *Dutiful Daughters* and *Season of Adventure*. Her short stories and poetry have been published in *Cosmopolitan*, *Sojourner*, *Fiction Monthly*, *Nimrod*, the *Carolina Review*, *Clare*, *Passager*, and others. Several have been anthologized. She has been Writer-in-Residence at Hollins University, Fellow-in-the-Novel at Wesleyan University, and Resident Scholar at Northeastern University.

A FINE FATHER

Jean Colgan Gould

The hawk drifts across the blueness like an unattached kite. Once, a long time ago, Paul Maxwell saw a hawk swallow a field mouse so quickly there was no blood. He lifts the sunglasses from his eyes. One arm is loose and wobbles off its hinge. Squinting, he focuses on the delicate triangles of the hawk's wings and their dusty pink undersides. A cramp the size of a bullet takes shape in his hamstring. Later he will remember the hawk that circled the clear Colorado sky the day he kidnapped his daughter.

Leaves shimmer their silver in an easy wind, as small tufts of pollen travel through the air in slow motion. Maxwell jams a stick of gum into his cheek with one hand and with the other brushes the unruly auburn hair from his eyes. Emily has grown. That's what kids do. They grow. They learn to skip and swim, and if you're not careful you miss the whole thing. Nearly four, Emily can blow her own nose.

"Let's go," she says, pulling him toward the rental car in front of the house. Is it the green eyes with those barely visible lashes, or just the way she tilts her head when she speaks that is so like Laura? Her knees are scabbed from a recent fall. She has picked at them so that the new skin shows beneath the hardened brown like bull's eyes.

They decided not to marry. Mostly, they agreed, they just wanted a child. He was forty-six; she was thirty-nine. How many more chances would they have? He tries his sunglasses again but they no longer fit. Emily hop-skips on one side.

He talks with her and with Laura every night on the phone, but because of the demands of his new sales territory in the East, it's been months since he's seen her. Removing the foil from a second stick of gum, he rolls it up like a sleeping bag.

"Mummy says chewing gum is bad for your teeth."

Laura Briggs, DDS. She had worked too hard to establish her practice to leave, she told him, after he found out about his transfer to Boston. *He* should quit *his* job, she said, find another. She had no intention of relocating. Besides, the East was too unfriendly, she said, too crowded. People triple-locked their doors and never made eye contact.

"Daa-dee." His daughter's hair is thick like his and gleams not quite popsicle-orange. In the tangle of his fingers, her hand flutters.

"Yes, baby," he says, leaning against the car. The cramp disperses. This is the first time he hasn't stayed at Laura's since the transfer. Raising his leg, he shakes the knot out of it. Just now, just ten minutes ago, Laura told him she plans to marry someone else, a periodontist. The wad of gum is huge in his mouth now.

"Come on," he says. "Let's get out of here." As he lifts his daughter into the car seat, her arms fit around his neck in their old way. This new guy wants to adopt Emily. The child will be confused for a while, Laura told him, but she will get over it. He hates it when she calls their daughter "the child."

"I'm hungry," Emily says.

"Me, too," he says, buckling her into the car seat, nibbling at her cheek.

He and Laura met when she backed her car into his, although she claimed it was the other way around. Right away, she told him it was odd that he had never married. Neither car was much damaged. He didn't think it odd, he said. What was strange was that there he was in mid-winter right on Market Street in rush-hour traffic having a discussion about his marital status with someone he'd known for thirty seconds. Laura's blond eyebrows twitched and she stumbled into a snowbank. She'd been married once, she said. Maxwell had already noticed her dazzling, even teeth before he knew her profession. His own parents had been married for fifty-three years, he told her. That should count for something. He was glib, she said. She had never met anyone so glib. What if you wanted to be a dentist and had terrible teeth, he asked her.

He had wanted to keep his options open. Over the years, something always stopped him from a legal commitment. His mother matched his father's socks with such devotion before putting them away. She set the table for breakfast after she finished the dinner dishes. The two of them sat on the sofa every night holding hands while they watched TV. He had never been ready to surrender to that kind of predictability.

After the accident, Laura called him. He should have said no. She didn't ski. She thought the Broncos were a basketball team. Later, he discovered she used an electric blanket and was a teetotaler. She thought steady breathing solved all the world's problems. Still, there was something about her. Once or twice, he attempted to identify exactly why, despite their differences, he was so drawn to Laura. Sure, her body curved in ways that matched his, and he loved how she locked her limbs around him until he could hardly breathe. But it was something else. She could see through him, into him, in a way that made him more complete. He moved in with her, but he didn't give up his own apartment until Emily was born.

Now, he drums his fingers on the steering wheel while his daughter squirms behind him. From the moment the baby's crown emerged between Laura's legs everything changed. Laura claimed that once you were the parent you could no longer be the child, but that was too pat an explanation for him.

"I was there when you were born," he says.

"Grr," she says. "A tiger, Daddy. I'm a tiger."

Baring his teeth, he growls back at her, nearly losing his wad of chewing gum. He has been driving slowly through their neighborhood, past the movie house, the vegetarian restaurant Laura favors, past the store where they bought Emily's crib.

"Silly. So silly, Daddy. All you want to do is play."

"No sir," he says. Laura has never quite approved of him. Sometimes she accuses him of having too much fun at his job.

"The tiger is hungry, Daddy."

Yes. The tilt of the head. That's what it is. Approval. Loving has nothing to do with approval. Laura teased him about his job—his demonstrations with new basketballs and track shoes and lacrosse sticks. A life promoting games was not sufficiently serious, she told him. It was not professional. There were more important things than winning and losing or making a sales quota. Athletic supporters. Hockey sticks. Baseball helmets. Couldn't he see he was contributing to a violent world?

Jock straps, he'd say. Why don't you call them jock straps? Once he chased her around the house, with one, waving it in her face, until they collapsed on the floor, and she admitted that a dentist's drill was, in fact, more violent than a jock strap or a tennis ball.

When he learned Laura was pregnant, he was the one who urged her to keep the baby despite her doubts. He was even willing to consider marriage, he said. Eventually, she said that she planned all along to have the baby, but she did not want to marry him. He would be a fine father, she told him, but a dreadful husband. He knew nothing about intimacy, she said. But when she agreed to name their baby after his mother, he was certain that some day she would change her mind about him.

"French fries, Daddy. Do I get french fries?"

A fine father. A dreadful husband. Those were Laura's exact words.

"How about gum?" says Emily, licking her lips. When he gives her a piece, she shoves it into her mouth in an attempt to mimic him.

Perhaps it is this moment of his daughter's small treason against her mother that makes his fingers shake, the pulse in his neck throb. Some animals mate for life. Wolves, for example. Mourning doves. In the rearview mirror, the huge brown eyes of a stranger with no plan startle him. At the next traffic light, he knows that he will not take Emily back to her mother.

He does not drive to the airport. He heads south. In mid-afternoon on Route 25 there is no heavy traffic. Without marriage, he probably has no legal right to his own daughter, who after her last whimper for french fries is now sleeping. Though the sun continues to blaze, a light rain falls. He rotates his shoulders in their sockets. Laura must have thought it had been easy for him to start over in a new city. He puts the car on cruise control, reaches for his sunglasses on the dashboard, remembers they have only one arm, but tries them anyway. Emily stirs. The sunglasses are impossible.

As he crosses the border into New Mexico, a jogger in blue shorts glides over the blacktop. A lawyer friend in Boston told him he's lucky. Because there was no marriage, he can avoid child support. The blue shorts fade in the rearview mirror.

While the car, no longer on cruise control, winds up, around, and through the mountains toward Taos, the roads become more menacing than scenic. Most fathers don't want to avoid child support, he told his friend. Dark trees and shadows angle toward him in a constricting tunnel. Emily yawns in her sleep. Her voice warms him and forces his mouth into its widest grin. He has never totally absorbed the facts of her birth, her growth, her new words. He was the one who got up in the night when she was an infant, to feed and soothe her, and sometimes just to look at her. A few houses appear now in the woods. Another car goes by in the opposite direction, and the driver waves. As Maxwell waves back, the road becomes straighter, wider, and he knows he has done the right thing.

Without the snowbanks that make Taos a ski resort, the main street with its one-story buildings is more like a stage set than a real place. He has never been here in warm weather. The one time Laura agreed to try skiing, he brought her here. She was a good sport, putting on layers of warm clothing each morning, enrolling in ski school, smiling over dinner each night as he raved about this mogul or that, drinking red wine. But after the third day of their vacation week, Laura stayed behind while he went to the slopes. He had no idea what she did with herself those days, and she was vague about it when he asked. An intermission, she said. Only an intermission. No more. No less. But she never returned to ski with him. On their way home, she told him she'd explored the Indian pueblo. The settlement was nine hundred years old, she said. When he pressed her for more details, she said the place had spoken to her. He had no sense of her meaning, and when he asked if she had spoken back, she got angry. He was trying to make her invisible, she told him. After that trip, he tried to be less flippant, more serious, but an awkwardness developed between them. A month later she announced the pregnancy.

At the inn where he now registers with Emily, there are hand-tiled fireplaces. A waiter with a drooping moustache brings Emily a peanut-butter sandwich with jelly, and, miraculously, someone else produces french fries. When passersby, wearing the bright-colored clothing of a brilliant sunset, remark that Emily is *maravillosa*, he feels that he is, by extension, also *maravillosa*. They buy him whiskey and are patient when he tries his high-school Spanish.

"Paul Maxwell," says Laura when he phones her, "I'm putting out a warrant for your arrest."

"Drop dead," he says, astonished by his own angry words.

"Where are you?"

Stunned into silence by the panic in her voice, he does not answer.

"Are you all right? Is Emily all right?"

He places the receiver in its cradle and touches the buttons that are her number. Her feelings. He hadn't considered her feelings.

That night, still clacking away at his chewing gum, he is unable to let go. When he closes his eyes, something like sandpaper rubs across them. On the other bed, Emily sleeps the way she did as a newborn, with her arms framing her delicate features. He envisions the two of them on the run. They will change their names, find a new place to live. Melting ice cubes settle in the glass on his night table. He never expected Laura to marry anyone but him.

"It's four in the morning," she says this time when he calls. "When are you bringing Emily home?"

"Don't do it," he says, working his jaw with considerable effort to speak.

"Paul, I'm asleep. Goodbye. I expect to see you and Emily in the morning."

"Don't marry him," he says. But she has hung up. Probably she's not alone. Once, when he was living with her, on a warm night like this one, her electric blanket smoldered and almost caught fire. She used it without regard to season. Sometimes, in the night, she would reach for his hand and suck on his fingers. He empties a bottle of soda into his watery glass. Probably she is lying there right now with another man's fingers in her mouth.

In the morning, he does not call Denver. On the short drive from the inn to Taos Pueblo, a sense of inevitability takes over. Emily is already restive and misses her routine. She has begun to talk about her "other" daddy. As they enter the pueblo, he sees at once there will be no clues here about Laura. Dwarfed by mountains and smaller than he expects, the five-storied adobe structure might as well be a fortress for all it is going to reveal about her. Whatever Laura's secrets, she did not leave them here for him to find.

"See those ladders," he hears himself speak in Laura's intonation. "In the old days, an Indian would climb a ladder and go inside through an opening in the roof."

"Oh," says Emily.

"They did it to keep safe," he says. But Emily runs away from him toward a group of children playing with a litter of puppies. "Now they have doors," he says anyway. "Now they are safe." Sweat gathers at his temples, and his mouth is dry. The light is almost blinding. With others, he is drawn to the mission chapel and the rich voices of choral singing. Inside the ancient structure, a priest and children, teenagers in jeans, conduct a service in several languages. A boy with shoulder-length hair strums a guitar for the congregation, while Maxwell takes a seat in a back pew. Next to him, a woman offers to share her hymnal. A drop of sweat falls from his forehead. In his purple robes and deep-set eyes, the priest passes out brown bread, which Maxwell does not refuse. Weightless on his tongue, the grain has form but no flavor. Presently, a collection basket passes from hand to hand, pew to pew. From his pocket he gathers all his change except for pennies and deposits it into the basket. Clapping her hands to the music, Emily sits at the foot of the guitarist. And now they all kneel for a final blessing.

Before bowing his head, his eyes meet those of the priest, whose chant is soothing and whose hands take the shape of doves.

The service ends. Voices silence guitar strings. Feet shuffle. Everyone speaks but the priest whose lips are still. And Maxwell remembers that outside these comforting walls the day is scorching and that in his whole life his throat has never been so dry. The young men, the teenage boys with their long sixties hair, tattered blue jeans, and bare feet, lead the procession from the church. One carries a golden crucifix. Others follow, holding satin banners with undecipherable messages. The priest walks, his arms lifted in parentheses. Old men and women, with faces too cracked to be called wrinkled, trail behind. Maxwell smiles at the men, some of whom wear blankets, and at the women with their lively, black eyes. Emily marches with the children.

Outside, the midday sun wrings perspiration from his pores, and he sits on a bench in the courtyard, while the procession breaks up into small groups. "I've lost her," he whispers. His torso rises and falls, heaves as if some wild creature were trapped inside. "Lost," he repeats, again and again until it seems that the word itself whips at him instead of his own misery. As he stands, heat rises from the dust through his soles and he shifts from one foot to the other. His nose runs over his upper lip. He leans back, sliding low onto the bench.

And that's where they find him—his daughter, her playmates, and their families. A woman, the one who shared her church hymnal, presses a handkerchief the color of buttercups to his lips. She wears Reeboks and bifocals. And an old man in a gray blanket gives him a lighted cigarette which Maxwell accepts, although it burns his mouth. Someone else—he sees it is the priest in khakis and a sports shirt—offers water. Under protection of the few scrub pines in the square of the pueblo, the Indians feed him and his child red beans and rice followed by cornbread and plums. With a cloth smelling of cloves, they wipe the sandpaper from his eyelids, and the water they give him, so cold, so pure, quenches his long thirst. And despite the cigarette, the texture of the communion bread remains imprinted on the roof of his mouth. Though he senses the futility of his action, he removes

Laura's photograph from his wallet and asks if any of them remember her. As if it were an important document, the picture is passed from one set of hands to another. Heads shake no.

The priest drives off in a pickup truck. One of Emily's playmates offers her a puppy and his daughter selects a black one with gigantic paws. Maxwell draws geometric figures in the red earth with a twig and considers how many plums he has eaten, how many cups of sparkling water have cooled his throat.

On the gravel road out of the pueblo, a bird flies into his windshield. Emily lies in the backseat with her puppy whom she calls Mary Lou after her best friend. The small brown bird, a sparrow, appears stunned for only a moment before flapping its wings and taking off. The past twenty-four hours have been full of omens he is unable, or perhaps afraid, to acknowledge.

"I expected you this morning, Paul," Laura says when he arrives.

"We saw Indians, Mummy. I ate a plum. Look at my dog. You make cornbread in an outdoor oven. It's called a beehive."

But Laura, after a distracted hug for Emily, grips Maxwell's forearm and drags him into the house. "You idiot." Spit oozes from the corners of her mouth. "What did you think you were doing?" Her hair is arranged in two flopping pony tails which make her older rather than younger. The dog has already peed on the carpet. Emily jumps up and down as the puppy runs in circles. "I thought I knew you," she continues. Two red circles form over her cheekbones, as her eyebrows do that same blond flutter.

Maxwell stands in the living room watching the stain spread on the rug. "You do know me," he says.

As if he were elderly or sick, she takes his elbow and seats him on the sofa, recovered since his last visit. "Sit," she says.

"We went to the pueblo," he says, "in Taos."

She takes his hand. "I should have told you sooner about Dan," she says.

"I was looking for you," he says. Maxwell tightens his grip on Laura's hand. Her bangs are perfectly squared above her brows.

"When you went East, I thought you didn't care," she says. In a pair of worn jeans, her hip grazes his thigh.

"Let's just hold each other," he says.

She wraps her arms around him. "Mister Cool," she says over his shoulder. "You just roll with the punches. Right? That's what you said."

"Not care?" he says. "Cool?" He buries his head in the curve of her neck.

"And what am I supposed to do with a puppy?" she says as Mary Lou whines from the kitchen.

The doorbell rings. The dog barks a baby bark. At least the fiance, Dan, doesn't have his own key. Maxwell stands as they are introduced, and then tumbles back into the cushions next to Laura.

Bearded, the other man is taller than he, with crisp creases in his trousers, brown hair that stays in place, the requisite teeth. "Sorry," he says. "I forgot my key."

"I'm going to have two daddies now," says Emily standing halfway between them. "Two. One and one are two."

No one speaks. Laura's thigh still touches Maxwell's. "I don't think so," he says, rising. "Not two fathers. I don't think so." Thrusting his hands in his pockets, he jingles his pennies. Maybe he had been wrong to bring Emily back.

"I had chewing gum," says Emily.

"Sorry," he says.

"It's okay," says Laura.

"Remember when your blanket caught fire?" he says.

"Stop jiggling your dimes," she says.

"Jingling," he says. "Jingling."

The other man, Dan, says nothing. He removes his suit jacket, loosens his tie, and unbuttons his collar, as if that were the most forceful way to mark his territory. Emily follows her puppy to the kitchen. The living room has darkened, but no one moves to turn on a light.

"Besides," says Maxwell, "they're pennies, not dimes."

And for no reason, they grin at each other. His dime-jiggling-jingling is an old bone of contention between them.

"I didn't call the police," Laura says.

"You should have, sweetheart," says Dan. "If you were smart you'd let the authorities handle this."

"It was my fault," says Laura, ignoring Dan. "But I knew you'd come back."

"Are you saying she's not smart?" Maxwell says.

"What?" says Dan.

"Look," he says. "Let's forget about fault. How about if I move back to Denver?" The change is moist in his hands. "Will you marry me then?"

"I don't believe this," says Dan.

"No," says Laura. "No." She reaches over to an end table and flicks on a light. "I was wrong in not telling you about Dan. But no."

The beams bounce off the spokes of Emily's trike in the corner and attack Maxwell's eyes like a flame. "Do you have any beer?" he says. "Is it okay if I get a beer?"

"Yes," says Laura.

He turns to face Dan, but fixes his eyes over the man's head. "You want a beer?" he says.

"Yeah," says Dan. "Thanks."

"No," says Laura before she is asked. "Nothing for me."

In the kitchen he makes Emily some chocolate milk and pops open two green bottles with a wolf on each label. Not his brand. Does he mean to move back to Denver, or was he sure, before asking, what Laura's answer would be? Only crazies kidnap their children. He peels the labels off the bottles. Emily blows bubbles in her milk with a straw. With his disheveled hair and two-day beard, he must look like a maniac.

"If we could all just try to be civilized about this," he says, handing Dan his beer. The words are pompous, wooden. They are polite. Maxwell needs to be polite. He needs to be calm.

Laura removes a piece of lint from the cuff of her jeans. She could be picky about things of no consequence. He reminds himself that she and his daughter are not the same person. She coughs, clears her throat. "Centered," she says. "We'll all stay centered."

Maxwell starts again. "About Emily, I mean. We all want what's best for Emily. Right?"

Laura nods. Dan nods. "Of course," they say in unison.

"I'm sorry about...," he says, taking a swig from the wolf bottle, knowing the apology is crucial, "about taking her."

"You mean the kidnapping," says Dan. "Let's call it what it is, shall we?"

Maxwell closes his eyes. What about betrayal? Laura's betrayal? Shouldn't he call that what it is? He rolls the bottle across his forehead, opens his eyes, and keeps his cool. She couldn't possibly want to marry this jackass.

Laura speaks very slowly, very clearly. "The reasonable thing to do," she says, "is for us"—her eyes and hands search the air—"to share custody."

Dan goes to her on the couch and puts his hands on her shoulders. "He has no legal rights, you know," he says.

"Didn't you hear her?" Maxwell says, he hopes not too triumphantly. "Joint custody."

"Paul was with me when Emily was born," she says. The sound of his name in her mouth is still exquisite. "Paul did every single night feeding and sometimes held her for hours when she was teething. He arranged daycare and interviewed her teachers. Paul"—she pauses—"has every right."

"Well," says Dan, "I guess there's no reason we can't be civilized. None at all." He has gotten a glass for his beer and gives some to Laura.

"You hate beer," Maxwell says. He sits in a straight-back chair at the edge of the carpet.

"What's civilized?" says Emily from her trike in the corner. Not waiting for an answer, she rings the bell on her handlebars. The puppy barks.

"We'll want to document our agreement legally," Maxwell says. Is he pushing his luck? "No marriage until then. Right?"

"Of course," says Dan. "Having a stepchild is quite a bit different from adopting Laura's child as my own daughter."

"Wait a minute," says Laura. "What's that supposed to mean?"

Emily climbs into Dan's lap.

"It's not the same thing. Right?" Maxwell says, pressing for additional advantage.

"Hold it," says Laura. "A daughter is okay and a stepdaughter isn't? Is that what you're saying?"

"We'll talk about it," Dan says, bouncing Emily on his knee.

"More," says Emily when Dan stops. "More, Daddy Dan."

Daddy Dan takes off his shoes and socks, showing ridges of hair resembling emaciated centipedes atop his feet. "What a day," he says.

Maxwell piggybacks his daughter to her room, gets her ready for bed in monster pajamas, and tucks her in. Smoothing the quilt, he kisses his fingertips and touches them to her forehead, to each cheek, and to her mouth. In the dim light from the hallway, the blue and red train he painted over one white wall before she was born still sparkles.

At the front door, they begin their goodbyes. "I would never have really kidnapped her, you know," he says.

"Look," says Dan, shaking Maxwell's hand. "Look, Max. It's all going to work out just fine."

"How do you know?" he says, pulling away. He swallows. Had Dan and Laura settled their differences while he was upstairs with Emily? "You. You know nothing about what's fine."

"Civilized," says Laura. Her ponytails bob like distorted slinkies over her ears. "And Dan? Don't call him Max."

Dan rolls his hands into fists. The guy hadn't counted on being a stepfather, or on having another man, the real father, in his little family. "Get out," he says now, shoving Maxwell hard against the door.

"Civilized," says Laura again as if the word were a mantra. "Stop. Breathe. Think about what you're doing here."

Maxwell rubs the back of his head. He folds his arms across his chest to keep from breaking the guy's face.

"My God," says Laura, "you pushed him, Dan." She makes his name into two syllables. *Daaah-annnn.* Her mouth forms a grimace.

Dan backs away as if he were the one assaulted. "Sorry," he says, just missing the puppy's accident on the carpet. "Look. I'm sorry."

And Maxwell laughs. Though the muscles in his arms and hands have turned to steel and are ready to kill, he laughs. He laughs so hard that the sound thunders in his ears and threatens his rib cage. Has he won? His eyes tear, and he stops only to catch his breath.

"Are you all right, Paul?" says Laura.

For a moment then, the three of them stay in frozen positions as if they are afraid of what will happen next. A collective sigh beats the silence to the room's corners.

"You'd better go, Dan," says Laura.

In the split second before Dan hangs his head and pads upstairs, Maxwell imagines the guy putting on his shoes and jacket and walking out the front door. He even hears the clink of the house key on Laura's coffee table. Instead, Dan gathers his things and makes no noise on the stairs.

Laura opens the front door. "I'm so sorry, Paul," she says.

Maxwell looks up the stairs. "But why don't you want me?" he hears his mouth say to Laura, to the green eyes, to the blond lashes, to the ponytails, to the perfect, even teeth, to the frayed blue jeans, to the mother of his perfect little girl.

She looks away. When she turns back, he sees her lip trembling.

"Marry *me*," he says.

"Dan and I are alike," she says. "Mirror images."

Maxwell's head feels heavy enough to drop off. His body has lost whatever power it possessed only minutes ago.

"More in common," says Laura. "With a life partner, you need to have more in common."

"You want me to be a dentist?" he says. "You want me to be a guy who spends his life looking into people's mouths?"

"See what I mean?" she says. "You just don't get it. You just don't."

"Of course I get it," he says. Fingering his two-day beard, he regards his rumpled clothing. Loving can make you crazy with longing and regret. It can make you glib when you mean to be serious, or make you violent enough to imagine annihilating a total stranger. It had made him desperate enough to think he could live on the lam with his daughter. Laura is right, of course. Except for Emily, they have little in common. A person might make you feel more complete, might complement your weaknesses, but in the end, you resent them for their differences. He closes his eyes and recalls the soft triangle of vulnerability beneath the hawk's wings he spotted only yesterday. Stepping through the doorway into the night, he finds the North Star in its usual place. A crescent moon climbs silver.

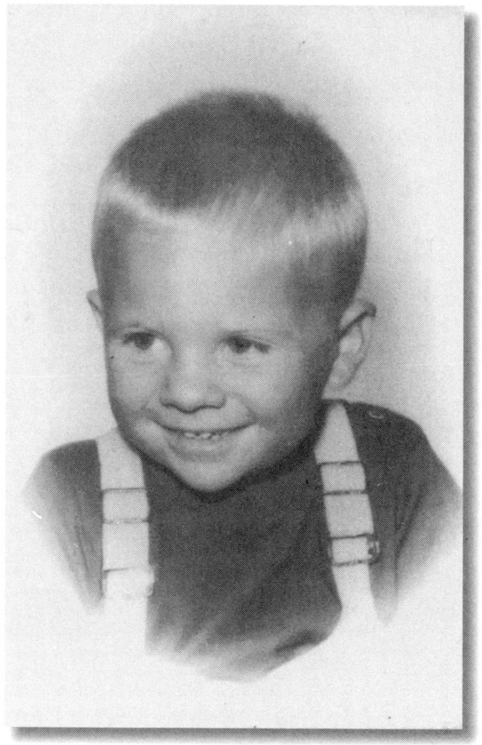

The well-dressed and happy two year old.
I am envious of the overalls and the smile.

David Borofka teaches composition, literature, and creative writing at Reedley College in Reedley, California. His stories have earned such awards as the *Missouri Review*'s Editors' Prize and *Carolina Quarterly*'s Charles B. Wood Award for Distinguished Writing, and his collection, *Hints of His Mortality*, won the 1996 Iowa Short Fiction Award. His novel, *The Island*, was published by MacMurray & Beck, portions of which appeared in *Gettysburg Review* and *Shenandoah*. New work has appeared in *Image*, *Southern Review*, and *Manoa*.

FIRE

David Borofka

The fire starts in the back bedroom upstairs. The bedroom no one ever uses because it is stacked floor to ceiling with forty years of her grandmother's hair magazines. Not to mention the boxes of her grandmother's wigs and falls and extensions. Ancient synthetics, ripe for an explosion. So, while Cheryl Kendell stands on the sidewalk across the street with a blanket around her shoulders in the cool night air, she watches the firemen at their work and thinks of beehive hairdos fighting for their lives. Synthetics contracting in the heat. Slick pages with their fading colors curling at the edges.

Flames lick against the upstairs windows, and Tina, Cheryl's mother, sobs furiously. "Goddamn it, Mom. All your fucking junk." She snuffles into the blanket she dragged from her bed. "Here I swore I'd never swear again, and now look. Jesus, forgive me."

Nana has been dead for two years, but Tina still talks to her on a daily basis, usually in argument. Old grudges, old scores. The undeclared war of family life. Not even salvation can touch the anger she feels, not on this Friday after Thanksgiving when she is already sensitive to irony.

When the fire breaks through the roof, sparks shoot upward into the black early morning sky like the birth of new stars, like the intimation of danger, and, despite themselves, they *ooh* and *ah* with the rest of the onlookers.

Glimmer Train Stories, Issue 59, Spring 2006

"Our life is going to be different now, Cherry-Pooh." Tina sniffs. "No doubt about it."

Her mother has used the nickname she was awarded as a toddler, not long after Cheryl's father departed for Canada and the judicial refuge from which he never returned. To be called Cherry-Pooh was to be aware of her mother's bravery, her spunk in the face of long odds. Tina has no idea where they are going or what they might do, but she has made up her mind that they will survive.

Cheryl snugs her blanket more tightly around her shoulders. Fog is forming around the street lights, but their house is still a beacon, a warning in the night. "Now what?"

"We'll find a motel somewhere, I guess." She looks brightly into the black sky made blacker by the bonfire of their home. "Whatever the good Lord decides!"

If her mother begins singing "How Firm a Foundation," Cheryl will not be surprised.

Firemen come streaming out of the house, then watch like the rest of the spectators as the roof caves in. They turn their attention and the hoses to the houses on either side. Streams of water arc gaily through the searchlights. They might be standing at the entrance to an amusement park. It might look that cheerful to someone passing by.

"About time," Cheryl hears Mr. Glendenning say. "Who'd want to save that rat trap, anyhow?"

Maggie Anderson, who is a Catholic and therefore not a pure follower of Jesus, what with the Pope and Mary and all that, puts her arm around Tina's shoulder. "You're welcome to stay with me."

Cheryl's mother sniffs again, a prelude to the gush of tears sure to follow. "That is so kind," she says. "So kind. I guess there's goodness in the world after all. And in the most unexpected places."

I do not invite confidences from students. Not anymore. In this case it was inevitable, however, since Cherry-Pooh was explaining to me why she had missed the last week of class and why she couldn't submit her last paper on time. All of her notes had burned in the fire. Her rough draft. Her books. *Library* books. Goodness gracious, she was in trouble. She didn't even have the luxury of deciding what waterlogged, charred thing could be saved. It was all gone—*poof*—up in smoke, as the saying goes. She had been writing a paper about *Mariette in Ecstasy*, and she would have to start over. Her notes, her mother's out-of-date computer, her backup floppy disks, the book itself—all gone. She should have saved the paper to her webmail, but she hadn't thought of it, and she should have hidden the book from her mother, but she hadn't thought it would be necessary. She should have known. The young woman, a nun practically having an orgasm on the cover—all of that blood and Catholicism. The confusion of sex and spirituality. A book like that could have made the house explode. Her mother had called me twice that semester as it was. They'd read Greene, they'd read Buechner. Now this. Wasn't the stigmata a sign of Satan? All the students were troubled, she said. They'd signed up for the class thinking it would feature real Christian writers such as C.S. Lewis and Tolkien. Peretti, of course, and the *Left Behind* series. Instead they were getting Catholics and other perversions of the gospel. Buechner was a Presbyterian, I murmured. Peretti was a hack, *Left Behind* was a comic book with suspect theology, and Tolkien was a Catholic—did she know that? I wanted the students to read writers who respected the mysteries of life and possibilities of transcendence. But she was no longer listening. Instead, she said that no daughter of hers should be required to read filth, not at a good Christian school, not when good, decent people such as herself were paying my salary.

Had she read the book? I asked. What precisely was she referring to?

She hadn't read it; she didn't need to read it to know trouble when she saw it. Wasn't I the college chaplain as well as a teacher? Didn't I have some responsibility to protect the souls of my students? What did I think about that?

I didn't think much about much.

Not anymore.

I didn't tell her that, but I probably should have. I wouldn't miss such exchanges with the parents of students, that much was true. And

I wouldn't miss knowing what my students and their parents had to tell me.

How much of Cheryl's story about the fire was true, I couldn't tell. Her complexion was fair and dusted with freckles, and when she was nervous or anxious, which was often, blood rushed to her throat and along her jaw as though she were bruised, and she was bruised now. She twisted her fingers as though an illustration of the phrase *wringing one's hands*.

"Look, Cheryl, I'll give you an Incomplete for the semester. It's no big deal on my end. You take your time, you finish off this last paper before the end of the spring, I'll read it, and then you'll get your grade. I'll still be here. For one more semester, anyway."

She was shaking her head. "Thanks, Taylor," she said, "but I really can't do that."

A creature of the sixties, I had encouraged students to call me by my first name. The propriety of which was just one more thing for me to question.

"There's nothing on your transcript," I said. And then I couldn't help myself: "There's no stigma attached." She looked at me, a blank look on her already troubled face. "Stigma, stigmata. Po-tay-to, po-tah-to," I finished. Lame.

"I'm graduating this month."

"Same difference," I said. "You graduate, you just don't get all the official seals until the paper is done."

"Isn't there something else I can do?" The mottling along her throat had grown like lace, like the filigree of a chain. I thought she was going to start pulling her hair. "I don't want an *A* or even a *B*; I don't care about the grade, only the units. I just want it to be done. I don't want it hanging over my head. I try and I try and no matter what I do, there's always something hanging over my head. My mother is crazy. You know that. I can't deal with anything else."

On and on she went. Those who have taught will recognize the signs: the student who just wants class to be over: the bell has rung, vacation beckons, life is waiting to begin.

If this were a piece of fiction, we would end up together, Cheryl and I, two poor sad sacks with our various problems. We would suddenly discover each other, and our physical union would embody the emotional complicity we imagined in each other. But this is not that kind of story.

At least I don't think that it is.

No. Not exactly.

Help me, Jesus.

Since Tina's ancient Volkswagen burned along with everything else, Cheryl and her mother take the bus when they return to their house. Maggie Anderson watches from her porch as they stand in the middle of what was once their living room. Two days have passed so the ground has cooled. With the toes of their shoes, they poke at the lumps of char, their life reduced to its essence. There are no more offers of free neighborly shelter. They are now just a mother and daughter without a home of their own. The night of the fire, a woman from the city's social-service liaison gave them a coupon for one night at a decent hotel. Still, by the time the fire crews were gone and they had filled out all the paperwork, it was four in the morning. Cheryl and Tina fell into bed by five, and by eight o'clock there were vacuum cleaners roaring outside their door. The next night they rented a room for the month at the Lazy Eight on Motel Drive in the sleaziest part of our town, two double beds and a bathroom, a dysfunctional television, and a Gideon's Bible, cheek by jowl with the railroad tracks, and at six every morning they hear the Southern Pacific rumble through the twilight of their dreams. Her mother keeps talking about graduation, what they will do once Cheryl has her credential and her degree. Look for jobs, both of them. A first real job for Cheryl, substitute teaching at least during the spring. A better job for Tina. She can get out of the hair business for good, leave behind her mother's legacy, maybe train at a travel agency. All these years while Cheryl has been in school—nothing but scrimping and saving and getting by. They've filled out God's own number of scholarship applications. But now, they'll finally have some options. They'll see the value of higher education. They'll get some *return* for all that sacrifice. His will be done. Amen. So, despite the fire and their loss of the house her mother was born in, Tina is as happy as Cheryl has ever seen her. She sees good times around every corner, and she wakes up singing "Amazing Grace." Even that first night when the police kicked in the door of the drug dealer's place on the second floor.

So how is she to tell her mother that there is still this one last paper to write?

For the burned-out apostate, no less. The chaplain with the murky reputation.

Me.

Confirmation of what I suspected came a month before the beginning of the fall semester. My family was gone. Molly and Clark and Hannah left at Easter—*how ironic was that?*—and except for a few desultory phone calls with the children, we had little contact. Molly already had taken up with her yoga instructor. Nothing could be worse, and I took some comfort in that. I was working in my office, filling in blanks for the schedule of services—themes, guest speakers, and so on for the fall and spring semesters—when Gloria Albright opened the door and brought the furnace of August inside. As Dean of Students, Dr. Albright had hired me seven years earlier. In rosier times. Now, the upwardly mobile Dr. Albright was the College President in charge of a sizable deficit, and according to the campus scuttlebutt, the Board of Trustees, all of whom were conservative, reactionary men, had appointed her unwillingly. She had only one mandate: bring the college to fiscal respectability or lose her job in the bargain. If she was successful she made the board look like progressive, forward-thinking men; if she failed, they fired her, and it was just one more proof about the inadequacy of the female. So she had no reason to visit me unless she was making the rounds in search of allies or firing people in person, and somehow I didn't think that a cabal was on her mind.

She didn't waste time on the niceties.

"Pink slips are going out tomorrow," she said. "The Board approved the list. I thought you should know."

I felt sorry for her. I have felt sorry enough for myself between then and now, but at the time I felt sorry for Gloria Albright, as she touched and retouched her helmet of hair and delivered the bad news as though she were a judge announcing a sentence.

"You'll have," she said, "until the end of the spring. You'll have a chance to find other employment."

"A Baptist college without a minister," I said. "Isn't that some kind of error? Something on the order of a college run by a woman?"

She ignored the taunt.

"You can't turn around in this place without running into ministers." She folded her arms across her breasts, picked a piece of lint off the lapel of her blue suit jacket. "Even the biologists have ministers in their midst. You know that. We'll make do for a time."

"Ah. Spiritual life on a rotating basis."

"Something like that. You made the decision easier for them."

"The divorce wasn't my idea," I said, "and let's face it, I'm not the only one who's had marital difficulties."

Her face darkened; Gloria Albright had experienced her own problems in this regard. She and her husband had nearly come to a parting of the ways. Who knows why? Time passes, passions cool, desires change. Her husband was no academic; he was a plumber, or a pipe fitter, I believe, so they were an interesting match right from the start, and it was no wonder that there was some tension. There were rumors of one of those almost-affairs between herself and a younger temporary instructor in foreign languages. That Gloria Albright and her husband had patched things up at the same time as the end of the instructor's appointment was purely coincidental, I'm sure. There was a time, just after Molly's departure, when I thought she might be casting her eye in my direction. That's probably just male ego talking, however, of the wounded variety, no less.

"It wasn't just the divorce."

"No?"

"No." She looked at me as though she were a coroner, and I was a corpse on the slab. "I never wanted to mention this."

Just before the end of the spring semester, I had taken a week of vacation time. Big mistake. Molly and Clark and Hannah were long gone, I was holed up in my little rathole apartment, and I was bored and restless, but the idea of leaving town never entered my mind. I suppose I thought that if I left, I might miss my family's return. They might come to their senses only to find me gone. I felt so sorry for myself that I drank a pint of bourbon and six airline bottles of gin, and then spent the better part of four hours in the bathroom losing my miseries. *This is fun*, I told myself while leaning over the toilet, *we're on vacation now!* Two hours later, spent and exhausted, while lying curled around the cool stem of the commode, I had my vision: Jesus loved me! The whole cliché in technicolor with the white of the bathroom porcelain as a bonus. You might be surprised to learn that Jesus wasn't wearing the traditional white robe and beard. No, in my vision he was clean-shaven and his head was closely cropped, and for clothes he sported jeans and a T-shirt. Instead of thunder and lightning, we talked about everything and nothing: his preferences in movies, pitchers of the National League, and the dating scene. His particular favorites were *The Princess Bride*, Sandy Koufax, and dinner followed by a walk around the duck pond. I was impressed. So down to earth! Why hadn't we heard this before? Oh, He said, you can tell people and tell people until you're blue in the face, but who listens? That is so right, I said. Just try it sometime, He said. So I did. I hoisted my carcass from the tiled floor, rinsed my face, brushed my teeth, and then stood on the corner of Blackstone and Shaw in front of that group of right-wing fanatics who every Friday night shout their support for war against the rest of the world. Iraq! Syria! North Korea! Iran! Bomb the axis of evil to smithereens. Make the world safe by destroying a third of it. *Father forgive them, for they know not.* Damn fascists. Even in a whisper my voice was as damaged as Louis Armstrong's, and my sermon on love and the consequences of its opposite was seriously compromised, I'm sure. I wanted to tell them that Jesus and his T-shirt asked for better behavior. Respect what you don't know for sure. My eyes were burning with my own convictions while tongues of fire danced above my head. Pentecost had nothing on me! But then a long black car slid to a stop against the curb and Dr. Albright and her French instructor boyfriend got out. What in God's name are you doing? she asked. Her hands were on her hips. Have you completely lost your mind? She held out her cell phone. I'm already receiving calls. I think I said, The price of telling the truth is ever so high, *n'est-ce pas?* And then I winked at the boyfriend, and I may have waggled my finger in front of his nose. *Bad boy*, I might have said. I may have used some other phrases appropriate to the two of them as well. Get in, she said, and together she and Pierre bundled me into the backseat of her Town Car. You can't keep a minister of the gospel from preaching the one true faith, I said. You can, she said, speaking over her shoulder, if said minister wants to keep his job. This is tyranny, I said, and religious persecution. I have First Amendment rights. I have academic freedom. Shut up, she said. *Shutupshutupshutup*. They took me home, pulled me up the creaking stairs, and poured me into bed. And when I woke the next morning, my headache told me that the drinking and the bathroom of the night before were real enough, but I hoped that subsequent events were merely the chaos of dream and alcoholic nightmare. And when Gloria Albright said nothing in the days and weeks afterward, I consoled myself with the thought that it was only that, a dream, nothing more, and for dreams, of course, we are not held responsible.

However, when Dr. Albright faced me in my office that August morning, I knew that such hope was nothing more than an illusion. "Oh," I said, holding my head, for it had begun to ache, much as it had two months earlier. "Good Lord, I'm mortified. Did I really call you the whore of Babylon? I seem to recall that happening."

"I hate to do this, Taylor. I like you, but you were out of control for a while. Preaching to the multitudes. It's understandable, the way you were acting, but you can't say you didn't see it coming."

It was a freight train, and I'd been lying on the tracks, waiting and waiting for the blow yet to come.

"No, you're right," I said. "The writing was on the wall, even if I couldn't make out the words exactly. A Baptist minister giving a sermon on the street corner—what was I thinking? I mean Baptist ministers preach on street corners all the time, but they usually don't do so with Jack Daniels on their breath."

"I think you'll be happier doing something else," she said. "Don't you?"

As though there was something else for a failed minister-slash-teacher. "I managed to screw up two jobs in one," I said. "What's left?"

"You could always try your hand at insurance," she said, "or real estate. It's a boom market. Look at the interest rates. You're not so old you couldn't switch gears. Maybe you should go back to school."

So now here I was, at the end of the fall semester with my one class filled with bitter students and sour, suspicious parents, and an administration only too willing to see me go. Was it any wonder that when I opened my newspaper, I turned first to the classifieds to read about my future?

Two weeks after the fire, Cheryl wakes late. Her mother is gone. Amid the falls and permanents and gossip, Tina is about her mother's business. Unwilling though she may be. There are customers whose grooming needs must be met; there are bills that must be paid. Fire or no fire. Cheryl rolls over and looks at the arthritic alarm clock on the end table. Eight fifteen. By the time she showers and dresses, and then catches the bus to campus, it will be nine thirty, at least. Just enough time to reach her ten o'clock seminar. But why? She has no paper to turn in, in all likelihood she never will have a paper to turn in, and Reverend Tyler—Taylor—is a pain in the ass. The Reverend Taylor Tyler. "A pain in the ass." She shouldn't say it, but there it is. The words make her giggle. To hear them from her own mouth. She lies back against her pillow, listening for those noises on the other side of the door. The *glug-glug, cough!* of a motorcycle trying but unable to turn over. The hoarse expletive of its rider, and the too-bright, too-brassy laughter of a woman too many years past her prime. Why are they up so early? Or are they just now leaving a party that has lasted all night? Their voices are a doorway to a life not recognized by her mother. What must it be like to straddle the seat of a motorcycle, to ride with her face pressed against someone's back, her arms around his waist? To wear leather, to taste the wind and her own mortality? She hates her own timidity. What else has she never known, protected as she has been by her fearful, unhappy mother? What else has she yet to discover?

Her father, unlike the draft resisters of a decade earlier, left her mother and her two-year-old self for criminal rather than ideological reasons. He used the wilds of Canada as a fresh start against drug charges and his own demons, and he found salvation among a community of New Agers and the language of addiction therapy. He has written Cheryl and her mother on numerous occasions, urging them to join him in the new world of British Columbia, but they never have, not even in the context of a vacation. And this is what she thinks: ever since her father's departure, her mother has retreated farther and farther into her own brand of fundamental Christianity as a charm against fresh misfortune. Her vicarious brush with the illegal has left her shaken, fearful of risk, and afraid of the body with its appetites and cravings, its ability to overwhelm reason and good sense. This is her legacy for Cheryl. And from Tina's standpoint, it has worked, hasn't it? Until the night of the fire, they have known a relatively peaceful life, although that peace has been somewhat hand-to-mouth in the financial sense. But even in that regard, their poverty, there is an affirmation of God's plan and His blessing of the poor. She clings to her beliefs with the tenacity of a Huguenot.

So, when Cheryl can hear the sounds of a shower and a man singing "I Could Have Danced All Night" in a voice so off-key as to defy song, she listens as though she's hearing another language. She knows that the man next door is a divorced liquor salesman in his sixties. Why should he be singing one of Audrey Hepburn's songs from *My Fair Lady*? And the drug dealer in the room upstairs, out on bail and no more chastened than the day before his latest bust, must have a guest, because the two of them have just commenced a vigorous session of morning lovemaking, and the rhythm of their exertions, the vibration of windows and walls and ceiling, is as fascinating as it is repulsive. In another hour she will no doubt smell the smoke of burning cannabis as it drifts through the opened windows.

Is there anyone more mystified by the ways of the world—and of her own body—than she?

"Mom," she says to the air above her head, "you are a pain in the ass."

Let me tell you about the place where I used to live. It was nothing fancy, a tract house, one of five repeating models. If you drove down the street where I used to live, you'd swear it was Stepford. I could have told you where every bathroom was located, and in the winter when the trees were bare, every roof ridge was identical. But I loved it there. We had a patio, and on summer nights, when the heat lingered past sunset, I barbecued, sending up my own column of smoke to join with the rest of my fire-loving tribe. My children had their own rooms, and my wife had her way with the house as a whole, but the room above the garage was mine. The windows looked east, toward the purple razor of the Sierra, and before the houses were built on the other side of the street, before the trees grew up and obstructed the remainder of the view, I could watch the sun free itself from the mountains every morning. Then the neighborhood changed, and our family changed, and none of us lived there anymore.

In the divorce, Molly took the house, thinking to keep it, but then out of the blue, she sold it, and she and Hannah and Clark moved to New Mexico, and I suppose they're happy enough in the land of enchantment with Molly's pottery classes and Sufi dancing and her displaced yoga trainer from the Bronx. And although the schools are nothing special, the kids are happy, and soon enough they'll be on their own.

And this is where I landed: a one-bedroom efficiency on the third floor of an older building. My room was jammed under the eaves and the ceiling was filled with the odd corners and cutouts of its dormer windows. Duct work had been wedged between the ceiling and the walls, late efforts at air conditioning. At least once a week, I stood up or turned around only to whack myself in the head. I'm not tall, but the ceiling, with its many impediments, was that short, and although I am hardly old, I was beginning to walk with a permanent stoop.

But the college was across the street, and while I drank my morning coffee, I could watch the parking lot as it swelled with more cars than slots, one of the many frustrations of a sheltered, private education on a budget.

I wasn't going to be there much longer, and I suppose I was savoring that sense of belonging while I still had it. Seven years—hard to believe that I had lasted that long. Molly had seen the writing on the wall even if I couldn't, and she and the kids had taken off before the end had come. Lucky them. Ten years ago I was doing church work and listening for the voice of God in those dreamy moments before sleep. I was happy enough even though the collection plate was never full, and Sunday after Sunday I listened to complaints about whose husband was cheating with whose wife, why Mr. X didn't appreciate the music the previous Sunday and why Mrs. Y didn't approve of Molly's dress or the way we were raising our children. The money in the collection plate was never enough in those days when Clark needed braces or when Hannah wanted clarinet lessons. The money in the collection plate was never enough when our twelve-year-old Toyota needed to be replaced. Did I mention that the money in the collection plate was never enough? So when the chaplain's position became available at the college, and when Dr. Albright offered me the job, I grabbed it as I would have a life preserver, and we settled into the academic life and our tract house. I taught one class each semester and listened to the children of the middle class complain about their parents. I conducted services every Sunday for an entire campus of believers, but the chairs in the chapel were rarely filled. The paychecks were better and more regular than those offered by a small congregation, and I thought our troubles were over, that Jesus had heard our prayers. Maybe He had. And maybe I just didn't like the answers. And maybe I needed to be prepared to listen—to Jesus with His buzz cut and T-shirt and His talk of inconsequential things.

I know what you're thinking: as epiphanies go, mine was pretty weak, the product of mid-life and alcohol poisoning, and you'd be right.

Still, we cling to what we have.

• • •

She has only the vaguest notion of what she might do, what she might say, but if she thinks too specifically about what she's planning, she will know her stupidity for what it is. There's every rational reason why it's the wrong thing. But if she doesn't think, if she lets nature take its course, then what is meant to happen will happen. Stay loose, she thinks. Be in the moment. Don't become your mother, don't worry everything to death. She selects the sheer cranberry blouse that her mother won't let her wear, and her tightest jeans, so often washed they are more white than blue. Bone white. In all of the turmoil of the past weeks, she has lost five pounds, and her clothes feel *good*, as though they have been made specifically for her, so there is something to be said for the positive effects of catastrophe. Her blouse with its spark of color gladdens her, even as the gauzy, see-through material annoys her mother. Her hair…well, her hair is another story; it's a mess, it needs to be trimmed and layered, some highlights wouldn't hurt, but there's nothing to be done at this very moment except pin it back and hope for the best. Her mother may be a hair stylist, but her mother's daughter's hair is a disaster, her worst feature. Isn't that just the way life is?

She closes the door to their motel room with the sense that something big, something momentous, is on the verge of happening, but at the bus stop she only regrets not wearing her coat. The December sky is clear, the morning fog has burned off, but the sun is all light and no heat. And even after she steps aboard the bus, she continues shivering. This is what vanity will do, she thinks, and the words echo her mother's voice. Vanity and superstition. She is hardly vain; she has never had money enough for clothes to be truly vain; she has always had to make do with discount-store discoveries: last year's tops and skirts, second-hand jeans, resoled and serviceable shoes. In her mother's mind, their poverty is a guard against the larger sins. Still, her coat *is* terrible: a threadbare canvas thing with cuffs that are frayed and dark from use. Wearing it would give away her disguise; the sophisticated college student would be revealed for what she truly is: a penniless drab just this side of welfare.

Across the aisle in the seat opposite hers is a man fallen asleep with his head against the window. His mouth is open, but for some reason she has the uncomfortable sensation that he is only pretending to be asleep, and that as soon as she turns away, his eyes will open to slits, so he might watch her every move. Such self-induced panic nearly threatens to dislodge that sense of imminence that rests near her stomach, and she lurches off the bus one stop earlier than she intended. Why does she do this to herself?

A cold wind has begun to blow, and so accustomed is she to hauling twenty or thirty pounds of books in a backpack, she tries to duck under it, but since the fire, she has neither books nor backpack, and bending over makes her feel as though she's someone's bad idea of Marcel Marceau. Look who's pretending to be a student! Whatever good feeling she had located below her heart has burned away and has left only a knot inside her stomach, queasy and yet not quite entirely sick.

She's ten minutes late for class, but when she arrives there's no one in the room, and when she looks again at the door, she finds, in the middle of other announcements, a note that Reverend Tyler is not holding class today. The last class of the semester, and he's gone fishing. Another note is likewise tacked to his office door in the chapel. Now what? She can slide a message under his door, or she can call or e-mail. But that's not the reason why she came. Earlier in the morning she thought that if she could just face him, make him understand the singularity of her predicament, her unique problem, if he would just *look* at her in her best set of clothes, he might make an exception in her case, let her pass the class without that final paper. But now it seems as though her confrontation is not to take place after all.

Shit.

In the chapel office, Victoria, a student aide that Cheryl knows, is typing the program for this Sunday's service. Hymns, readings. The sermon topic. She's wearing a headset and typing from habit and the chaplain's dictation.

"So what's up with Taylor?"

Victoria looks up, her eyes a blank from listening to the voice in her ears. She stops the cassette player and pulls the headset away.

"What?"

"Have you seen Taylor? I need to talk to him."

"He's probably at home."

She inclines her head toward the other side of the road facing campus, then writes down an address.

"His apartment?"

"He won't care. He's lonely. Just knock on the door."

Cheryl thanks the girl, then walks past the administration building and across the street. All this walking. She's still cold, and now there's a heaviness deep in her guts as well. A hint that she might be getting sick. A cup of tomato soup sounds heavenly.

Taylor's building is one of those grand old houses that has been diced up into cubbyholes, terrible little apartments, and, of course, with her luck, his apartment is on the top floor, and with every step she takes, she can feel a pull in her lower abdomen as though extra weight has been attached to her abdominal wall with thumb tacks.

At the top of the third-floor landing, she knocks on the chaplain's door. No answer. She knocks again, but now the pain in her abdomen is announcing itself much more insistently: *this is the body*. The thumb tacks have become nails and knives, and whatever pleasure she took in herself earlier this morning is most definitely gone.

"Taylor," she calls. "Taylor. Are you in there?" She knocks one last time. "I need to talk to you about my paper. Are you at home?"

The only sound on the other side of the door is the silence of a held breath, she is no longer able to stand upright, and even her body has begun to form a question mark.

She imagines the chaplain sitting in his apartment, waiting for her to leave. Why is he hiding from her? she wonders. What does he have against her? Is this what Jesus does to those who take too much pleasure from their own bodies? And why is a school chaplain named for two dead and mediocre Presidents?

And that's when she passes out.

I canceled the last class of the semester. I hadn't planned on it, but when I arrived on campus, there was an envelope in my mailbox with the briefest of notes. From Molly. She was getting remarried in January. I shouldn't have been surprised. Our divorce had gone through without a hitch, as though even bureaucracy agreed that we were no longer meant to be a match. But opening her letter knocked me to my knees, and I said, "Oh, shit. Oh, God," loud enough to alert the angels, and it was my good fortune that none of my self-righteous colleagues were in the mail room just then to witness my discomfort.

So, without a word of warning or explanation, I posted an announcement on my classroom door ("No class today; turn in your final papers to my office by Monday at 9:00 a.m.") and then a companion note on my office door before I lurched off-campus to the coffeehouse two doors from my building.

"Molly," I kept muttering. "Molly, Molly, Molly. You have done me wrong, and someday you'll realize the depth of your mistakes." Our marriage was over, and I was stunned, but I wonder if I was as tormented as I might have appeared.

So why did Molly leave? No marriage is without complication, and ours was no exception. The easy answer is that we just ran out of gas. We woke up one morning, looked at each other in the full light of day, and realized that enough was enough. You know how you can look at something—a picture, a word, your lover's eyes—and if you look too hard it no longer makes sense. After sixteen years, two children, and four debt reconsolidations we knew each other so well that we didn't know each other at all.

The more complicated answer is that we both lost our faith, but we lost it in different ways. Molly lost her faith in Jesus and she lost her faith in me. She was jaded, all right, and she knew too much. *I am so goddamned tired*, she said. *I am sick to death of all these pious, goody-two-shoe Baptists whose eyes are like knives and their hearts are like flint.* She was sick of it, and on Sunday mornings when I stepped down from the pulpit fresh from the delivery of my sermon, I could tell that she was sick of me. *Superstition and make-believe*, she said, *fairy tales for fearful adults. And I suppose all the Buddhists and Moslems, Hindus and Jews are dead wrong?*

Who was I to argue? *Pay no attention to that man behind the curtain.* For by that time, I had traded my spot at the church house door for my office on the sunny side of the college chapel. I felt fraudulent either way, but what was I supposed to do—become a travel agent in the middle of my life? *Use whatever name you want,* I said to Molly, *we're all just trying to make our way through the complexities of life.*

No, she said, *no more phoney baloney. I'm burning my bridges, buddy boy. It's time to be honest with ourselves.*

She could no longer tolerate the rigor of our conventional life and faith while I couldn't conceive of any alternatives.

So I left the house, and then she sold it so she and the kids could discover the Land of Enchantment. Life is what it is, but I had followed all the rules! I can't say I thought very highly of the divine at that moment. Which made it all the more surprising when Jesus paid me a visit while I languished in the bathroom that night of my binge. Did I mention that I called Molly before I took my position on the street corner? Although the hour was late and an hour later for her, she answered the phone on one ring.

Molly, I said, we're two lost souls, you and I. Why should we be so unhappy?

There was a pause on the other end of the line. Oh, Taylor, she said, speak for yourself, and then she hung up, so quietly I didn't know right away that she was gone. So I spoke for myself and Jesus in his T-shirt; is it any wonder I spoke with such passion that night? She had a life, while I only had a headache, and now she had her yoga instructor besides.

Since that night, I had spoken with Molly only once, and that was over something innocuous: the new owners of our house had called with some question about the manufacturer of the living-room carpet, a question I couldn't hope to answer. And then her letter came. *Dear Taylor,* it read. *I just thought you should know before you hear it from the kids...*

In the coffeehouse, I ordered two large cups to go, thinking that caffeine might be the spark I needed to get myself back on track. No more Mr. Booze for the minister, I decided. The last thing I needed was an additional headache.

I walked home, a cup in each hand with steam rising from the lids, like twin smokestacks of grief. So this was the end. Of so many things. The end of my marriage, which until that moment I hadn't believed would finally occur. And then there was my job: although I had one more semester left, I had to take stock of what I might do once the month of June arrived, but at the moment I couldn't think of a thing.

And yet...

And yet...

Our sky, which during the summer is brown with dust and the heat of trapped exhaust, was deeply blue, scoured by the cold wind gusting from the ocean one hundred miles away. It may have been the first time in months that I had looked at that brilliant blue dome, seen it for what it was, and appreciated it as the threshold of the divine.

I was such an ass.

So Molly had found a new life, a new love. A new way of looking at the mysteries of our life. The tone of her letter was happy and optimistic, and if there were any darker moments they only came when she worried about how I would take the news.

I was such an ass.

I would have to quit running in place, hoping that the axe would not fall. It had already fallen, and I would have to make some decisions, take some steps. *The first day of the rest of my*...etc., etc. What was the worst that could happen?

I walked upstairs with my coffees, and that's when I saw her. In a heap on the landing in front of my door, with her jeans and the inside and backs of her legs streaked red.

"Cheryl?" I said. I set my coffees down on the floor and shook her by the shoulder. "Can you hear me?"

She blinked her eyes and groaned.

"Come on," I said, "I'll make you some tea. Or coffee. I bought extra. I thought I needed two, but I guess I was buying it for you and just didn't know it."

"You weren't in class," she said finally. "I looked for you."

"I'm playing hooky today," I said. "Call it an early vacation."

"You teachers. My mother thinks you're all lazy as sin."

"It's a wonderful life," I said, "if you can get it." And I was reminded all over again that it wouldn't be mine much longer.

"Oh, god," she said, sitting up. "I feel awful." She looked down at herself, and her face and throat began their familiar flush. "And totally stupid."

"I have some sweat pants you can borrow," I said. "They're too big, of course, but you're welcome to them. I thought I was going to start working out, but you know how it goes. They've never left the drawer. So much for good intentions."

"Oh, god." She grimaced and rolled into a ball on the floor. And then she began to laugh and hiccough and cry. One right after the other. "Can you believe it?" she said. "My mother believes the stigmata is the mark of Satan. What would she think of me?"

This is not the story I had intended to write. I thought I would tell you about how I left the ministry—parish as well as educational—about how I tried my hand at several things in the aftermath. Real estate for a time, until it became clear that I was completely unsuited for the work, even if it was a boom market—every house seemed perfect to me, and I couldn't help feeling hurt when buyers didn't see the same potential as I did. I made more money than I was used to, but it seemed like a bitter way to live. And then landscaping, but I couldn't stand to cut things as short as most customers wanted. Grass must be sculpted into putting greens, bushes must be tidy, and hedges must be boxed. What's the point of Nature in your front yard if you're only going to chop it down, trim it into unnatural shapes, clip it so it's near death? That seems like an unnecessary need for control, if you ask me. I sold my equipment the day that Dr. Albright called me. It was the end of that next academic year. Finances at the college had been restored—an alum had died, and he had been most generous in his will; who says the *deus ex machina* ending is dead?—and Dr. Albright was generally hailed as the school's savior since her powers of persuasion were responsible for such beneficence. She was calling, she said, to offer me a job.

"It's nothing great," she said, "but I need a coordinator for Student Activities. You'll have to put up with ping-pong tournaments and movie nights, car shows and fashion shows and software exhibits. Not to mention the annual Mission Boards Fair."

"When do I start?" I said, for the past year had been like a year of waiting in the desert. "Normally I don't take charity, but this time I'll make an exception."

There was a moment of silence between us, before she said: "I don't know what you did for the Kendell girl, but her mother has been calling all year, demanding you be rehired. This after wanting you fired. What are the odds?"

"Go figure," I said. "I don't have a clue."

"Well, whatever it is, can I tell her you're back in the fold?"

"Be my guest."

The morning that I found Cheryl in a heap on my floor, I tried to help her to her feet, but the moment I let go, she slumped back down.

"Whoa," she said. "A little too soon."

"Maybe you should sit here."

"Yes, maybe I should sit here."

"And maybe I should call a doctor."

"Don't be ridiculous." She shook her head. "Look, I think if I could just lie down for a while. I'll be fine."

"I don't know about that," I said, but I put her arm across my shoulders and picked her up; Cheryl wasn't very heavy, but I wasn't too steady either, I have to admit, and I nearly dropped her when I opened the door.

"You can lie down for a little while," I said, "but after you wake up, I'm driving you home."

"Fine," she mumbled against my shoulder, and then I spread her across my unmade bed because I'd left my place in something of a shambles that morning. Newspapers on the floor, dishes in the sink, sheets and blankets in a jumble. I picked up as best I could while she snored. I found my sweat pants and laid them next to her feet. She was a mess. Molly was getting married, and my kids were a thousand miles away. And I was soon to be unemployed. But then I have mentioned all of that previously, haven't I? I didn't know then that Cheryl wouldn't wake up until three hours later—a little groggy, but feeling some better, only a little light-headed—and she would change into my sweat pants and a sweat shirt while my back was turned. I didn't know then the reception her mother would give me when I delivered her daughter back to the parking lot in front of their motel room, for she was at least semi-crazy if not a full-blown lunatic.

"Oh, my god," Tina cried. She had been looking out their window when we pulled up, and she came charging out, looking back and forth from me to her daughter as though we were a mystery that needed to be solved. "My baby, where have you been?"

"Oh, Mom," Cheryl said, "don't go ballistic. You knew I'd be at school."

"But—"

Cheryl stopped her mother before she could get going again: "I had the worst cramps of my life, and Pastor Tyler brought me home. Look at me," she said, "I'm a wreck." And she held out her jeans which looked like evidence in a criminal proceeding. Which was when I tried to excuse myself, but her mother grabbed my arm and wouldn't let me go, this woman my own age, who was only trying to keep her world in some kind of order.

"I've been so awful," her mother said, beginning to weep. "I've been so awful."

I didn't know then that her mother would believe (and no argument to the contrary would convince her otherwise) that my pink slip was somehow related to her earlier complaints about my class, and that she would see my situation as one particular mission in her life. Getting me rehired might not get her to heaven, but in her mind at least, it would keep the divine scales of justice evenly balanced.

I didn't know all of that then, but this is what I did know while I washed my cereal bowl and watched the blanket covering Cheryl rise and fall: I knew that I'd give Cheryl her *C* and exchange academic integrity for compassion. I mean, what does it really matter in the long run, one paper more or less? We all wanted to be through. Done and done.

Through the dormer window above the sink, I could see the sun beginning its early December descent, a smooth flat disk, a lens into the future. Throughout the morning while the wind whipped dry leaves along the sidewalks and gutters, it had shined weakly in the pure blue sky without offering much in the way of heat. But, soon enough, summer would come, and with it the one-hundred-degree temperatures our community is known for. We would dash from air-conditioned home to air-conditioned car to air-conditioned office, and still we would sweat. We would bank our blinds against its rays. We would think of reasons to stay indoors. We would curse the fire of its zealous and jealous life.

May 1950

Chicago Sunday Tribune

UTH ON THE CAMPUS

A camera tour of the Midway suggests how the University of Chicago might nurture its sons and daughters from cradle to grave . . . Story in Grafic Magazine.

URSERY SCHOOL, Miss Peggy Jenk
teacher, reads to Kenny Kaye.

I was brought up believing that the Laboratory Schools had identified me as a literary genius by the age of four. This was the (only) evidence. Miss Peggy Jenkins, where are you?

Ken Kaye was a closet fiction writer for nearly forty years, while making a living as an academic and then a family therapist. He helps families throughout North America resolve conflicts in passing businesses or wealth to the next generation (www.kaye.com). His books as a psychologist include *The Mental and Social Life of Babies* and *Family Rules*. After providing for the education of two sons and two daughters, he entered the MFA program at Bennington College, where he finds each semester's ten-day residency "the best vacation money can buy."

SEE BEN'S FAMILY

Ken Kaye

See Ben now, browsing *The Family of Man*, nestled on his mother's couch under an afghan (his sister's got the AC on full blast). What a hopeful title: *The Family of Man*. Did many households like theirs own the book? If not, what possessed them—his parents—to buy the catalog of a photography exhibition and keep it on their coffee table, permanently? In Ben's memory it's as prominent as the Bibles were in his Christian friends' houses. His family must have had one of those, too, an Old Testament, maybe even a New for reference, somewhere in the house, but it wasn't on the coffee table, nor under it where a shelf held other books that were too big, and, Ben the boy perhaps thought, too canonical to be consigned to an ordinary bookshelf. Of those coffee-table books, only the collection of *New Yorker* drawings occupied as many hours of a contemplative boyhood as this one did. The two books together, he supposes, constitute his intellectual parentage. He's the product of Edward Steichen's photographic choices and the cynical commentary of an elite coterie of cartoonists.

The corners of the room are in darkness, his face in shadow as the lamp above his head illuminates little more than those black and white pages and the blanket's knit pattern of blue and gray waves. He recollects most of those pages as he turns to them; many he could have described without opening the book. Before asking what he's doing here, awake in Mom's apartment at 3:49 in the morning, two thousand miles from home, take a moment, if you will. See Ben at the age of nine or eleven or thirteen, in the fortress-like cubic armchair or sprawled on the floor of the four-bedroom house in Rogers Park, the northeast corner of the city of Chicago, half a mile from Lake Michigan, continent of North America, turning the same pages and contemplating these same pictures. What's going on here? Could the several images of Ben span time, in some way akin to that in which the photographs were/are linked across six continents? Where is the wool that knits those images into the patterned fabric of a man? It might be true that the *family* of Ben, which is to say the *person* of Ben, the man himself, consists of snapshots from different ages, each equally a moment in the making of him. One could even say that the middle-aged sociologist whom we "now" see reading the Prologue by Steichen's brother-in-law Carl Sandburg, reviewing this textbook of human connections, rediscovering the old young men women children like long lost friends, one could say that this adult shaped the boy Ben's experience with the either widely or distinctively owned treasured book as much as did the hours of boyhood exposure, maybe alone in that living room, or while one of his sisters practiced the piano, or when relatives visited and he had to sit there because it would be rude to go upstairs and watch TV. Yes, the man-to-be could have shaped the boy. The photojournalists' images (and the cartoons, too, and the television of course) told what growing up would entail, signposts for the kid's journey to manhood. The photographer for the high-school paper. The college student who switched from pre-med into sociology. First job: a teacher of all grade levels in a boys' detention center. Graduate school at Berkeley. Junior faculty appointment at San Jose State. Marriage. Tenure. One child, Eliza, now twenty. Family encounters with sisters and their boyfriends, husbands, children. Illness and deaths of in-laws, then father. Now, mother. All prefigured in this book that's lived in his parents' living room for nearly fifty years.

Ben's going to sleep on the couch because his sister Sharon is in the guest room. She offered to help him change the rumpled sheets on Mom's bed, but it didn't seem right to sleep there while their mother's cooling her heels in the hospital morgue. So he tucked a sheet around the cushions, and he'll try to get a few hours' sleep here before Rebecca (winging her way on the red-eye from Portland) shows up to complete what his wife calls the four-ring circus.

His other sisters' tears—Ann's and Sharon's—seemed excessive. Mom would have been eighty-seven next month; it's not as if she were in the prime of life, or as if they were children. He wanted to tell them, Be realistic. Ben's wife, Carolyn, lost her mother thirty years ago, to breast cancer at fifty-three. And they've all been through their father's slower, painful death. Sure, Mom's death was a surprise; but she'd had a full life. Ann and Sharon acted like it was a tragedy.

Ann, who lives nearby, in Wilmette, was the one who ten days ago took Mom to the doctor, complaining of shortness of breath. Sharon came in from Minneapolis a few days later. After a week in the hospital, efforts to stabilize her heart having failed, Mom contracted pneumonia. When Ben flew in yesterday, his appearance at the bedside elicited her last words: "Oh, for God's sake." Then she closed her eyes. For hours Ann and Sharon kept saying, "Open your eyes, Mom," and, "Can you hear us, Mom?" as her breathing slowed and the cardio monitor above their heads took its determined course from erratic, to weak and slow, to the unambiguous flat line. At the end, it was Ben who removed the plastic mask from over her nose and mouth, releasing her face from the strain of living.

His eyes won't close.

The Family of Man tells a story, scenes flowing from sex to pregnancy to birth to childhood, work, play, religion, aging, death. A full page shows a boy in an ill-fitting suit standing on a fallen tombstone in an old cemetery. On the next page, among funerals in Mexico, New Guinea, Korea, a younger boy looks up at the weeping faces of three Austrian women in black.

Ann and Sharon seemed okay with each other tonight. He imagines the craziness once Rebecca hits town and the three of them start pushing one another's buttons. There's danger that these next few days could become more of an unearthing than a burial. After Dad's funeral, he can't remember what it was Sharon said that made Rebecca start screaming at her, "You've been killing him for twenty years! You're the cancer in this family!"—until Ben pushed her out of the room and Ann went in the bathroom with Sharon and didn't reappear until Rebecca was gone. Rebecca and Sharon didn't communicate for a few years, but eventually, for Mom's sake, they resumed their former relationship—adolescent sniping.

Rebecca's fifty-six, three years older than Ben. Ann, next in line, refers to Rebecca as "the law" (she's a labor lawyer). Sharon calls her "the control freak." Rebecca does tend to be the self-appointed circuit judge of the family, riding into town. Ben doesn't think she's all that bad. The time Rebecca visited his family in San Jose, she busted them for improper recycling. He said, "I think we'd know better than you what our town's requirements are." Later she made a point of lecturing Carolyn, his wife, why they should have a separate category for plastic bags and if the city doesn't require it, you should call someone and get it looked into. Alone with Ben later, Carolyn laughed it off; one needn't take it personally. But it's not so easy for Ann. When their mother had the heart attack a year and a half ago, Rebecca didn't fly in until after Mom got home from the hospital. Then she was full of ideas how they should have handled it differently, what Mom should tell (not ask) her doctor, how much help she needed in the apartment. Last night, by the bedside, Ann was already planning what she'd say when Becca starts issuing orders. Ann takes it personally, because she's the one who does the most for Mom. Did the most.

Ann quit teaching high school in her first pregnancy and never resumed, even after her kids grew up and her husband left. She's the insecure one, whose life hasn't reinvented itself after divorce. She lacks both their older sister's imperious rigidity and Sharon's provocative flakiness. Not long ago, Ben's wife remarked, "Ann's investing too much of herself in your mother. Mom's not going to be around forever."

Both of them, Rebecca and Ann, have been divorced for years. Mom's death has spared Ben from having to break the news that he and Carolyn separated. Then there's the youngest, Sharon, with a string of men in her wake, two of whom she briefly married. She calls herself "your crazy sister," waggling her hands above her head (or, to her nieces and nephews, "your Auntie Mame," a reference lost on them). She thinks she's crazy in a fun way. She left for New Mexico twenty years ago on the back seat of a Harley. Somewhere between Santa Fe and St. Paul she lost the biker and found the Lord. Ben had no problem with her professed Christianity, nor with the Buddhism she claims now; he understands the need for community, wherever it's found. But she wears it as an element of her quirkiness. She's not crazy funny, she's crazy annoying. When she called from Puerto Rico last year "on a retreat" to ask him for an emergency payment on her credit card—only a loan, she'd pay him back—he refused. It sounded fishy; she may or may not have been in Puerto Rico, but if she was, he doubted that the word *retreat* properly applied. Later Ann told him she responded to the plea and loaned Sharon five hundred dollars. She'll never see it.

The other problem with Sharon is she's paranoid; Ben is more or less professionally qualified to use that term, though the rest of the family does too. She's convinced they conspire to avoid her. This is true. She's told them, "I'm not paranoid, you do leave me out of things." "That doesn't mean you're not paranoid." "If I am, that doesn't make it okay to be mean to me." Then she laughs, as if she weren't serious. Sharon can get the rest of them fighting with each other when they don't even know why. A harsh reaction to her shenanigans by either of her sisters, or Mom, would lead one of the others to counterattack on Sharon's behalf. She's impossible, but they tend to make allowances, thinking she really is crazy. Which, as she says, "is more than I can say for the rest of you."

Ben has invested many an hour with therapists discussing the psychodynamic history of his family. How did they turn out so different? The *Family of Man* book, hymnal to universality and diversity, offers no clues tonight. The bossy one, the insecure one, the sensible one (how he sees himself), and the crazy one, all from the same parents. Parents who were solid citizens, married over fifty years. All but Sharon got college and higher degrees: a lawyer, a teacher, a college professor. Why, then, the lingering feeling that Mom, Dad, or the family itself held them all back in some inchoate way?

Thoughts about tomorrow intrude into his nostalgic book-browsing: *Should I tell the family we're separated, before Carolyn gets here? Now I'm like her in having both my parents gone. Should I change my return flight from Friday to Sunday?*

How she looked: toothless, irritated, wired to a computer, tubes dripping from the clear plastic bag above her bed and out between her legs into the dark amber bag below. Her hair, always clean and brushed in elegant white waves, was matted in gray curls against her scalp. He has barely admitted this once-in-a-lifetime snapshot into his mental album.

This is the place for a portrait of his mother: Not to speak ill of the dead, let's say she was difficult to communicate with. She didn't listen. Conversation with her consisted of you starting to say something and being interrupted by whatever association your first words triggered. If Ben reported that he just sent his new book off to the publisher, she'd start talking about a lady in her building who used to work at Barnes & Noble. This conversational trumping had nothing to do with being old—she'd done it all their lives. Consequently, she was oblivious to what concerned them, but that was no bar to her giving advice. On his last visit, he witnessed this exchange about Ann's ex-husband, Howard.

Mom: "How are the boys?"

Ann: "I just had a letter from Danny, he…"

Mom: "Howard wrote me a lovely letter."

"You told me. A birthday card, three weeks ago."

"Well, all I have to say…"

"You don't have to say anything. I've asked you—repeatedly—to stop bringing him up."

"Maybe he realizes he made a mistake. Do you ever think he might want another chance?"

"Goddamn it! Don't you ever think about how you make me feel when you…"

"It should make you feel I care about you."

"You don't! It shows me that I don't matter to you at all, if you…"

"Why do you bother to come visit me when you're in a bad mood? If you're going to yell at me in front of your brother, you'd better leave." Turning to Ben: "She's sick of me still hanging around, with the rest of you too far away to help."

He believes that he, unlike his sisters, immunized himself with a healthy sense of humor about Jewish mothers. Long ago he gave up hoping for any validation from her. He learned not to agitate for what she'd never deliver; nothing expected, nothing lost.

In hopes that the book will settle him for sleep, he's thumbing through it as he did decades ago, transfixed by its paean to the life cycle. The boy pored over the photographs until he could tell each person's story. He made up what they'd been saying just before the camera caught them, and how the people in each frame felt about each other. Where the couples in the courtships and weddings first met. What circumstances weighed on the lives of the poor or lonely; how the well-off made their money. Here is the section on childhood. A two-page spread of boys playing is captioned by a Kwakiutl chant:

When I am a man, then I shall be a hunter,
When I am a man, then I shall be a harpooner,
When I am a man, then I shall be a canoe-builder,
When I am a man, then I shall be a carpenter,
When I am a man, then I shall be an artisan,
O Father! Ya ha ha ha.

So what did he grow up to be? A college professor. When he was a boy, did he think he'd be a salesman like his father? He told Dad once, at ten or twelve, that he was going to be a congressman like Jimmy Stewart. He had barely heard of sociology before he found himself majoring in it. O Father! Ya ha ha ha.

Ben asleep: He's back in Mom's hospital room with his sisters. It was like a logistics command center, with the calls to Rebecca, to various children and friends and cousins, to his wife. Talking about Mom as if she weren't there.

When he hears Rebecca let herself in, he starts to open his eyes, but they rebel against the first light of dawn. His sister goes to survey the bedrooms, then returns for her bags. She says, "Thanks for leaving the bed for me—would it have killed you to change the sheets?" He hears her luggage roll over the carpeting into Mom's room.

Later, the sun still low in the sky, beams of gold fill the high-rise apartment and shimmer off the case of a clock that presided over the mantelpiece of their old house; a brass wall fixture; the glass on a framed print Ben doesn't recognize. Near his head, studio pictures of himself and his sisters stand on the end table. He reaches for the one they're all in, nested one-two-three-four like bobsled racers, Rebecca's hands gripping little Sharon's shoulders. Was it like that? Were they a team, barreling through life? At ten, did they rely on Becca? Pamper Sharon? Or was he the pampered one, the boy? Did he wear that merry gleam every day? And was Ann's brow once wrinkle free, or did the airbrush lie?

Sitting up, he stands the portrait back in its place, retrieves the book from the floor, and slides it into his suitcase, under his clothing.

The little bottles on Mom's bathtub shelf—hotel souvenir shampoos, conditioners, body lotions—appear unused. It seems she made do with an economy-sized bottle of shampoo and a jar of bubble bath, on the floor beside the tub. Think of Mom luxuriating in a bubble bath, like Eliza, his child, when she was little. Ann had sent her handyman to install grab bars on the walls. Mom's only other accommodation to age was an emergency call button she wore around her neck, when she remembered to. She didn't use a walker, or a cane. As he showers, he pictures her as if through frosted glass—stepping into the tub with one hand on the grab bar, lowering herself into the bubbles. Afterward she'd have to stand and rinse under the shower head, climb out of the tub and dry herself.

Shaved, he comes out dressed in blue jeans and a T-shirt: *San Jose Girls Softball 1999*. Sharon's door is still closed but Rebecca is up, in Mom's room, looking older than he remembers her. She's going through the drawers of Dad's old desk. She stands up perfunctorily to accept his hug. He asks what she's doing.

"Starting to get organized. I'm the executor, you know."

"Mom's not even…"

"I've got to go home in two days, Ben. I have a job. Not that you don't, but I know you can take off whenever you want. I'm just saying. We've got the funeral tomorrow." Her white jeans don't flatter her. She's put on weight around her belly and butt—as has he. Her hair is pulled back in a scrunchy like his daughter used to wear in middle school. "I'll probably have to come back at least once, but I want to take Mom's will with me, and a list of her assets so I can get started with…"

"I think it can wait, Rebecca."

"I don't." Her tone recognizes his objection and overrules it. "If you want to be helpful, figure out which of these is her current policy." She hands him the folder marked Health Insurance in Dad's rounded block letters. "Throw out everything that doesn't pertain to her current HMO and major medical. There's old dental bills and all kinds of irrelevant stuff in there." She pulls out another thick folder: Taurus. They sold Mom's car two years ago. "Just make sure nothing important got stuck in here. Then toss it." She's already filling a second waste basket, setting some kind of record for efficient executorship.

Ben and Rebecca at the kitchen table. He's made coffee; she has tea. His sister says she's too jet-lagged to eat anything. He pours himself a bowl of Cheerios. She says, "I would have been here two days ago, you know."

"If…what?"

"If they'd have told me the truth."

"Come on, Rebecca. Don't start blaming…"

"It's interesting, isn't it, that Sharon gets here, you get here, but Ann doesn't manage to tell me how serious it is until it's too late for me to get a flight out."

"Believe me. There was no conspiracy. I didn't know, Ann didn't know Mom was going to die. It's just I was able to get away, so I wanted to come and help."

"And see Mom before she died."

"I told you... no one expected her to die. This wasn't..."

"All I know is she had everybody there except me. Did she ask where I was, even?"

"You sound like Sharon. Mom didn't ask where anybody was. You know what she said when I walked in? 'Oh, for God's sake.'"

"That's great," she laughs, the outburst of a jumble of emotions. "I can just hear her saying that."

He thinks, the whole day was bizarre. He was awake for twenty-four hours: rose before dawn in his not-yet-furnished studio apartment, flew across the country, watched his mother die, and curled up on her couch amid the furnishings and books of his childhood.

Rebecca is looking past him, out of the kitchen, at the dining table eight feet away. "That's odd."

He turns to follow her gaze. "What's odd?" Something has changed, though he wouldn't be able to say what.

"Where's the fruit bowl?" Mom kept a large ceramic bowl full of ceramic fruit; ugly semblances of fruit, in dull shades that clashed with the deep blue glazed bowl she bought at the art fair. (She used to say, "I bought it at the Old Town Art Fair," as one might say, "I bought it in Paris.") Almost fifty years ago, Ann and Rebecca laughed at Ben's thinking it must be terribly old because of the crackles in the glaze. He doesn't remember Mom ever using the big bowl for anything but decoration. He does remember her getting mad one time when she found it on the floor in front of the TV, with potato-chip crumbs.

The bowl's gone, but the fruit isn't. A few pieces—a banana, a peach, and a bunch of grapes—form a centerpiece on a straw placemat. Beyond the table, the rest of the ersatz fruit is arranged along the sideboard.

Rebecca says, "Ann took it, I bet."

"Naw, it must be around somewhere."

"I wonder what else she's helped herself to." She opens the doors of the sideboard. It's empty except for a folded tablecloth and set of napkins. "The Passover dishes," she says. Not being kosher, Mom used them for all holiday meals, but they always called them the Passover dishes. Gone. Now Rebecca's fuming. In the corner cabinet, only a pair of silver candle holders stand, one framed in each glass door. Even Ben knows those two top shelves held matched sets of rose-colored champagne glasses, wine glasses, and water goblets. Eight or ten of each, delicate, with twisted stems. More special than the Passover dishes, they must have been a hundred years old, because they belonged to grandparents—Dad's mother gave them to Mom as a wedding present. He doesn't recall the glasses being used, ever.

"Fuck," his sister hisses.

That shot of Ben and Rebecca in the recessed dining area is snapped from the perspective of the living room, where Sharon comments, "Nice language for a lawyer." She appears in a tank top and a pair of men's boxer shorts; whose, he wonders. She comes around the dining table to hug Rebecca—holding her long enough for Ben to see, over Sharon's shoulder, the storm brewing in their older sister's face.

From Sharon's face, the puffiness and smeared eye shadow are gone. That was yesterday; this is today. She says, "You missed all the drama yesterday. Just came for the fun part, eh?"

"I came when I got through to the doctor and *he* told me what was going on. Did you take my Passover dishes?"

"Whose Passover dishes?"

"The Passover dishes Mom was giving me. Did you take them?"

"Noo-o."

Although the tone sounds so much like an offended teen that Ben thinks Sharon's probably guilty, Rebecca says, "I didn't think so. It's obvious who did. What about the stemware?" She nods toward the corner cabinet.

"No-o," says Sharon, catching Ben's eye.

"And the bowl?"

"What bowl? The fruit bowl? Mom gave it to me. Hey, I noticed the bedroom, Becca. What's going on with Mom's desk? Are you ransacking the place?"

Rebecca retreats to the bedroom, ignoring the question. Sharon shakes her head. "We're looking at some serious obsessive-compulsive behavior there. You think she'll make it through the next few days?"

"I don't know," Ben says, as if agreeing that it's touch and go.

"I need thirty minutes of quiet time out here, okay?" She has to perform her twice-a-day yoga/meditation ritual.

The picture in the living room, when Ben goes in to get his cell phone, is of tranquility itself: his sister, cross-legged in front of the window. It faces the lake, across which the morning sun shimmers, backlighting Sharon's loose, golden hair.

Last night, as Ann drove them here from the hospital, Sharon reminded them that she's Buddhist. "Couple years ago, I'd have said Mom was going to burn for all eternity. She wasn't saved. Now I know we only change forms. I don't believe in hell."

When neither Ann nor Ben responded, she added, "Aren't you glad I saved your parents from the fires of everlasting hell by converting to Buddhism?"

Back at the kitchen table, he calls his colleague about a research meeting he forgot to cancel. "How's your mother?" the man asks.

"She died last night." He's impressed with how dispassionately he can say that, and accept condolences.

Next he dials Carolyn to find out when she and their daughter are coming. Their flights will arrive at around the same time, Carolyn's from San Francisco and Eliza's from Newark. "Don't worry about it," she says, "we'll get a cab. How are you doing?"

"I'm fine," he says, with a defensive edge for no reason. "How are you doing?"

"I'm sad about Mom. I'm thinking you are, too."

"Of course." It was easier with the colleague.

She asks, "How are your sisters?"

"Rebecca got in this morning and went right to work in Mom's files. Sharon's meditating in an unspecified man's boxers. I'm expecting sparks when Ann gets here." In a low voice, he tells how Rebecca found the bowl and dishes missing, suspecting Ann, but then Sharon owned up to taking the bowl.

"Look," she says, "make it easy on yourself. Keep your mouth shut."

"I am." He wonders whether she means he shouldn't let them draw him in to their sparring, or shouldn't say anything about himself and Carolyn. Or both.

She adds, "I'm glad I'm not there. I could skip it, couldn't I?" He knows she wouldn't; his family is part of her, too, notwithstanding what's dying between them. "Did you tell them about us?"

"No."

"It doesn't actually have to come up at all, if you want to hold off..."

"Yeah, let's."

"Rebecca's taken her share of stuff, too, you know. She took all those old framed pictures of your mom's and dad's families."

He didn't step all the way into the bedroom before, or he'd have noticed them missing. They're half a dozen formal family photographs, some from nineteenth-century Russia, which he hung for Mom when they moved her here from the house, after Dad died. Those, too, were formative images in his childhood: the men's trim beards and stiff collars distinguishing them (perhaps falsely) as men of business rather than peasants; the toddler standing in the ankle-length white dress, identified as his grandfather. "Wait a minute," he says. "How do you know they're not there?"

"Your mom must have let her have them, sometime last winter. I saw them when I was in Portland in April."

"You didn't mention it."

"I forgot. Or maybe I thought you'd be better off not getting involved."

The picture of Eliza in his wallet is of the two of them, father and daughter, in her prom dress, in a playful tango dip. Eliza, his last, best hope, chose to stay in Princeton as a professor's summer nanny instead of coming home. Although she didn't say so, her parents' marriage breakup news must have prompted that decision. Ben hasn't spoken with her since he moved, earlier this week, but he and Eliza have talked by phone more these past few months than during the five years before that. She told him she felt bad for his having stayed with her mother so long, unhappily, for her sake. He should have assured her it wasn't like that, she shouldn't feel responsible. Yet her saying it meant so much to him that he let it stand.

Who might his other daughters have been, the ones he didn't have? By the time Carolyn accepted the fact that she couldn't get pregnant again, Eliza had started school and Carolyn was more interested in the challenges of a new career than those of adoption. Luckily, as they used to tell Eliza, they hit the jackpot the first time.

Ann arriving, not the oldest but the largest, filling the narrow hallway to the living room. Sharon has disappeared into her room, maybe to put on some pants, maybe to go back to sleep. Ann is dressed for a hot day in a cotton skirt, lime-colored Polo shirt, and sandals. Despite the cool attire she looks haggard. She's had a long ten days; or is she always haggard? Except for her reddish blond hair like Sharon's, she is the sister who most resembles Ben, round eyed and round faced. Before she can plop herself in an armchair, Rebecca charges in like a prizefighter from her corner.

"You took the Passover dishes, didn't you? And the antique glasses."

"Hello, Becca." But Rebecca shows no sign of submitting to a normal greeting. Ben feels he's seen this picture before. Finally Ann responds, "I didn't take anything. I was given them."

"I *told* you Mom said I could have those. I'm the only one who has a seder."

"You're not the only one who has Thanksgiving, are you. She didn't say anything about promising them to you, when she gave them to me. But if you want them that much…"

"I do. And the matching glasses."

"They're not matching glasses." He can tell Ann's determined not to raise her voice. "It's a whole different pattern. I'd really like to have those. And they may be antiques, but they're not worth a fraction of that china. Plus you've already taken the old family pictures…"

"It sure as hell is worth as much, or more than the china. If it's not, why do you want it?"

"Because I like it. Shall we get everything appraised, including the jewelry? I knew you'd nickel and dime me, Becca, so I already took the glasses in to find out what they're worth—about two hundred bucks, total."

"No way." They're in high school, Ben in eighth or ninth grade, Mom pleading, *Don't you three ever have anything nice to say to each other?* Rebecca says, "I've seen wine glasses like those, going for thirty or forty bucks apiece. There's how many—the wine, champagne, and water glasses—five or six dozen pieces?"

"You better come over and count them, if you think so. They didn't all survive the last fifty years."

"All right, why don't we just split them between us?"

"Between you?" Ben hears himself speak up, though he doesn't even care about the glasses.

"Four ways, then, if you want."

"You going to do that with the Passover dishes?" Ann challenges her.

"No. Of course not. They're a set."

"And the glasses aren't?"

"We'll talk about it later. We have a lot to do now."

Good, he thinks. Let's just do it.

Ann and Rebecca in Mom's room, choosing what she'll wear to her funeral. In sisterly accord, they're pulling a plastic garbage bag down over a hanger holding a blue dress. In Rebecca's hand are a bra, underpants, and panty hose.

"Does she need underwear where she's going?" Ben asks. "Not to mention panty hose?"

"Of course," Ann says. She sounds giddy. "You think Mom would go out without underwear?"

"Is it like the Egyptian kings needed to take their thrones and beds and stuff?" They ignore this. He remembers Carolyn's advice: keep his mouth shut. When Ann takes the dress bag, Rebecca hands her the underwear and then a pair of navy-blue pumps and a red and white silk scarf. Mom was famous for her scarves. He wonders how many her daughters filched over the years.

"Make sure you get at least ten copies of the death certificate," Rebecca says. "They're supposed to give you as many as you need. They can copy them right there."

Ann says, "I think I can handle it," throwing him a look that says their eldest sister is impossible. "Quit bossing us around."

"I'm not bossing anybody. Ben, go with her."

Outside, it's scorching—and humid, with barely a breeze. She drives with all the windows open until the AC gets cool. Ben says, "I hope they have her in the icebox."

She whacks him playfully on the leg, laughing, "That's awful."

"I'm surprised Becca didn't put that on the list of things for you to remind them."

"She probably told them herself when she called them this morning."

He shakes his head, bonding with this sister over what a piece of work the other is.

"Like I told you yesterday, I'm not taking any of her crap this time."

"Okay," he says. "So you'll ignore her when she says you deliberately didn't tell her Mom was going to die."

"No, I'll tell her, 'Fuck you.'"

"Oo-kay…"

"Sharon, too. She's driven me up the wall this past week. Like she's the patient. She insisted on staying here instead of my house, so I'd have to come out of my way to pick her up and bring her back every day. So she can sit there and hold Mom's hand. What a good daughter. Meanwhile I'm chasing after the doctors…"

"I should have come back sooner. I'm sorry."

"Do you have any idea how much of Mom's jewelry she's taken in the last couple of years?"

"Sharon? No idea."

"Most of it. You know the antique stuff Mom inherited from Grandma? Every time Sharon left after a visit, Mom went right to her jewelry case to see what left with her."

"Is it valuable?"

"I don't think so, not in dollars. She just wanted to make sure she'd get more of it than me or Becca. Or Carolyn, or Eliza. It's not enough that Dad supported her for thirty years."

"He did?"

"Where have *you* been? How do you suppose she lives? Alimony, like me?"

Neither of Sharon's husbands was ever in a position to support anyone. "I thought maybe from you lending her money."

"Very funny. Anyway, how are you?"

"You mean other than being an orphan?"

"Yeah, other than this..."—has she sensed something about his marriage?—"How's life? Do you still like lecturing?"

"Yeah." He hardly ever lectures—he teaches seminars, directs research, writes and edits—but no one in his family has the remotest idea of his work. "How are you?"

"Mixed. I got too caught up with her needs, the last few years. It should be a relief, in some ways, but it doesn't feel like that right now." She shakes her head.

"You were doing a lot for her, weren't you?"

"Is there such a thing as a love-hate-*guilt* relationship? Where you hate your mother only because you're knocking yourself out for her, so then you feel so guilty about that, you knock yourself out even more? I told my therapist she was a loyal, good person, and I loved her, but if she didn't kick the bucket this week I just might strangle her myself." After a moment she adds, "He gave me permission."

It's his turn to laugh. "Your therapist gave you permission to strangle her."

"Yeah, he said when you've had a reciprocal kind of adult relationship, you don't resent having to be their parents at the end of their lives. But if you never..." She trailed off.

Ben says, "I know what you mean." But what he thinks is, We know Mom was a pain, there's no point dwelling on that. As he learned when Dad died: Try to hold onto the affectionate memories, let the frustrations go. He was a good man who did his best. Mom was a good woman who did her best. She loved us. We loved her. That should be it, period.

In Pizer's parking lot, he waits—his Grateful Dead T-shirt deemed by Ann inappropriate for a funeral parlor—while she delivers the final outfit. She's taking longer than expected. Rebecca wrote out the vital newspaper facts for them to give the funeral director, as if he and Ann wouldn't have known them: date and place of birth, maiden name, deceased spouse, children, number of grandchildren. But Rebecca omitted Mom's one distinction, which he added: she studied at Hunter in New York City, the only one of her brothers and sisters to go to college. He's not sure she graduated, so he wrote "attended."

Apparently Ann has more to do inside than just dropping off the stuff. Insulated by the Toyota's purring engine and air conditioning, he watches two men arrive for a funeral. Tomorrow, that will be him, in the suit Carolyn reminded him to bring. He needs to polish his shoes, or get them polished this afternoon. The men are carrying their jackets, too hot to wear outside. The bereaved, of course, must be inside already. These tricklers in are the bereaved's friends or co-workers, attending as a courtesy. Last to come is a couple in a Lexus. Striding quickly through the parking lot, as they pass Ben, the woman—the wife—says something that makes the man turn on her angrily. His lips form the words "Stop it! I'm not—"...telling you again, or something.

Ann back at the wheel, they're five minutes from the apartment when she asks, "Everything okay with you and Carolyn?"

"What makes you ask that, out of the clear blue sky?"

"When we talked on the phone yesterday, she didn't sound...I don't know."

So he tells her—"just between us"—about the separation.

"That's terrible." She's at a loss for words, obviously. "Is it a bad one?"

"Not really. We're very civilized."

"Were you seeing someone else?"

"What?" The question astonishes him, until he realizes it's just what his sisters would think. Not that he's the type, but that's how they explain their own husbands leaving. He has become involved with a graduate student who has a four-year-old child, but Carolyn doesn't know about her, and it's not why he moved out. He doesn't share this detail, saying only, "We came to the decision mutually, as a result of counseling. Our therapist gave us permission."

From the apartment door, the view he sees is Sharon in a black kimono, with her foot in the bathroom sink. He and Ann stopped at Subway for sandwiches, after phoning home to ascertain each sister's requirements. (Vegetarian for Sharon, turkey for Rebecca.) His first thought: Sharon's limber for a forty-nine year old. His second thought: she's posing. Ann takes the Subway bag to the kitchen because Sharon has a request for Ben: "Will you run out to White Hen and get me a razor? I think Mom's been using this one for twenty years. Ouch." She has nicked herself in a couple of places. Notwithstanding the request for a new razor, she presses a Kleenex on the blood and goes on nicking. He won't respond. See, he's keeping his mouth shut.

Actually, Sharon's got something more urgent to discuss with him. She pulls him into the bathroom and closes the door. Her breasts sag under the kimono—his wife's don't, though she's older. Is it Sharon's genetic bad luck, or is she paying a price for all those years not wearing a bra? "Listen," she says. "This is confidential, okay?"

He should say no before letting her go on, but he's rattled by this tête-à-tête in the bathroom. For all she ostensibly distanced herself from the family, Sharon's never been one for boundaries. He has no idea what secret she's about to lay on him.

Outside the door, his older sisters' voices are raised—he's half listening for the promised *fuck you*. Sharon confides, "Mom had a few necklaces and bracelets, and a couple of pins, that are really old but still fashionable? She gave them to me for safekeeping because she didn't trust Maria or Ann." Maria's the lady who comes—came—for half a day on Tuesdays and Fridays. Ben is sure Mom would have trusted her or Ann before Sharon any day of the week. Mom was no fool. Catching himself and his sister in profile in one of the mirrored medicine-cabinet doors, he can't believe she doesn't see the skepticism on his face, but she hasn't paused. "I know she'd want Carolyn and Eliza to have some things. So I'm going to take them aside when I get a chance tomorrow or whenever, and find out what pieces they want, okay? I just don't think it would be smart to leave it up to certain other members of the family, right? Enough said?"

"I'm not going there, Sharon. I didn't hear that, and I'm not getting involved between you and Ann and Becca, in any way."

"You always take their side," she says, turning back to work on her legs.

Rebecca looks somber. "Come here, I need to ask you something." Is this about Sharon, the missing jewelry? Or what she and Ann were shouting about? She leads him into the bedroom and closes the door. "You're getting divorced?"

"Jesus! She told you?" He makes a face toward the absent Ann. "Carolyn and I wanted to wait until...with everything else..."

"Just tell me this. Did you cheat on her?"

"Rebecca..."

"Did you?"

"How would that be your business?"

Now, on her face he does see something like genuine concern. As though it's crossed her mind that she shouldn't sit in judgment, she manages to express the appropriate feeling. "Sorry to hear about it," she says.

"Thank you, Rebecca. Let's not tell anybody else, okay?"

As he says this, Ann is opening the door. Sharon's in the hall behind her. Ann says, "Come and have lunch."

Sharon says, "What aren't you telling anybody else?"

"He's getting divorced," Rebecca says.

"Omigod! You're kidding! What happened?"

He looks from one sister to another, shaking his head. "Thank you, Rebecca. Thank you, Ann. And thank you, Sharon, for not asking me if I was cheating on Carolyn."

"You're welcome," Sharon says. "Were you?"

He groans. "Wouldn't that be a simple explanation?"

In the kitchen, unwrapping the sandwiches. Rebecca cross-examining Ann about her trip to Pizer's. "Did you tell them we might be as many as fifty? Did you show them how she'd wear the scarf?"

"I told them tie it like a babushka."

"What?" Rebecca jumps out of her skin.

Ann giggles delightedly. "What do you think, I'm an idiot?"

"I won't answer that."

"They asked me where to announce we're sitting shiva. I told them only the one night, tomorrow night, at my house."

"No," Rebecca says. "Too hard to give everyone directions. I get lost every time, the way those streets curve around." That's not it, of course. She just doesn't want Ann to look like the lead daughter. As if having the cousins and Mom's few surviving friends come by your house to pay condolences is a status thing. "We'll do it here. The turkey's mine." Ben's stomach is too tight to eat anything; he feels like it's tied in a knot. He thinks Ann deserves to have them sit shiva at her house if that's what she wants. But she doesn't press it.

In Mom's room, the wall that held their ancestors' portraits is, as Carolyn reported, bare. He can visualize where each picture hung: there, the great-great-grandparents in Russia; here, Mom's mother's large family; to the left, Dad's young grandparents with their three daughters in matching ruffled dresses. The newest photograph, taken eighty or ninety years ago, was of a big family reunion at the side of a lake somewhere in New Jersey. Their father appeared in the front row, in knee pants.

Ben peers at the ghosts of those ghosts and sees what the photographs never showed. It was missing from the *Family of Man* pictures, too: the domestic struggles that are the real stuff of human development. A posed family group is a lie—a good lie, full of hope. Steichen chose lies for his postwar exhibition of global hope, showing brothers and sisters and parents and spouses making common cause against nature, weather, economics, racial and ethnic subjugation, foreign wars. As though they didn't aggravate the hell out of each other, on a daily basis. Literature tells us of family feuds, but in photographs couples and families appear as solid bulwarks against the world. As the cameras flatten the noses and distort the perspectives, they crop conflict out of the frame.

"Where's *The Family of Man*?" Sharon calls from the living room. "Did one of you take it?" His sisters ignore her, so Ben does, too.

Ann's sitting on the edge of Mom's bed, picking through the wastebasket to sample the papers Rebecca discarded. "What are you doing? Throwing away every record of Mom's existence?"

"Bickering as usual," Sharon observes, joining the crowd in the bedroom. To herself or an invisible companion, she mutters, "What else is new?" Then, to Rebecca, "Did you take my *Family of Man*? To go with our grandparents' portraits and our Passover dishes?"

"'Your' *Family of Man*," Rebecca says. "Excuse me, but we had it before you were born."

"So what? I loved that book. It's why I took up photography in high school. As a little kid I used to read that book for hours. I made up stories for every picture."

"It's a book, for God's sake," Ben says. "I'll buy you a copy."

"It must be out of print," Ann says.

Sharon says, "That's not the point. The one I want is the dog-eared, soft-covered copy that used to be on the underneath shelf of the coffee table when we were little. Last time I was here it was in the living room, middle of the second shelf, next to the..."

"I have it," he confesses, like an idiot. "You got the fruit bowl, dishes, jewelry, whatever. I got *The Family of Man*."

Suddenly all three of them want the book. "It has special meaning for me," Rebecca claims. "I was with Dad when he bought it."

"Bullshit," Ann remarks.

Sharon insists, "Mom always said I could have it."

"No, actually, Mom promised it to Danny, who's feeling bad enough because he can't make the funeral."

"Actually," he says, "it's the only thing you guys haven't already cleaned her out of that I would really like to have."

"Shut up, Ben," Rebecca says. "You got Dad's Army medals and his watch."

"Only because you all said I..."

Sharon says, "Ann, you take the *Atlas*. You like to travel. Becca can have Dad's joke books. Ben, take any other books you want, but I want that one."

"Bloody hell." He should have kept his mouth shut. He goes out to the living room to get the book out of his suitcase. This cramp in his abdomen is grief. The more he fights it, the more it's there, screaming to be heard. There's a lump in his throat, too. Not that he's about to cry if he can't have the book, but it just seems like the last straw. When he comes back, though, they're already arguing about something else. Rebecca is saying, "You can't not tell him. At least make sure the boys tell him."

Sharon reaches toward the book in his hand. Rebecca appeals to Ben, "Ann isn't planning to tell Howard. I'm sure he'd want to come tomorrow."

"He might, that's why I'm not telling him," Ann says. "He's not a member of this family, hasn't been for six years."

"Eddie's flying in all the way from Los Angeles," Rebecca retorts. "Carolyn's on her way."

"Well, that's your business," Ann says. "In my case, if the boys happen to tell Howard, that's between them. It's not my responsibility to call him. And it certainly isn't yours."

This is it—one squabble too many. So suddenly that he surprises himself as much as them, Ben erupts. He hasn't relinquished *The Family of Man* to Sharon's outstretched hand. "Look at this!" his voice breaks as he brandishes it in his sisters' faces, open at the middle of the book. "Satisfied?" He tears it apart through what happens to be a two-page procession of African women with baskets on their heads. He throws the second half on the floor and rips the first half into two quarters, throws them down and picks up the other half and rips that apart. The book lies in four pieces at their feet. "Take your share," he says.

His sisters look at him, speechless. Ben returns their stares, torn between laughing and crying. Both his parents are dead. Gone. In their place, out of the past, a hundred episodes come swirling around him and the girls, like a covey of dead ancestors. Do his sisters feel their presence, too? Fiercely trying to exact from their mother's treasury what they never got from her mouth, don't they see how the room is filled with holographic snapshots of themselves at eight, ten, twelve, fourteen, twenty, thirty, forty—the family they were, and are, and are doomed to be, into eternity?

INTERVIEW WITH DAVID MALOUF

by Kevin Rabalais

David Malouf

Nearly a decade after Patrick White became the first Australian writer to receive the Nobel Prize in Literature, he nominated a fellow countryman, David Malouf, to share that honor. By that time, 1982, Malouf had already established himself as a poet and novelist of international importance. Since then, he has published some of his finest work, including The Great World *(winner of the Prix Femina Etranger and Commonwealth Writers' Prize),* Remembering Babylon *(winner of the International IMPAC Dublin Literary Award and short-listed for the Booker Prize) and* The Conversations at Curlow Creek. *In 2000, Malouf received the International Neustadt Prize in Literature for his body of work. Born in Brisbane in 1934 of a Lebanese father and English mother, Malouf's first books were the poetry collections* Bicycle and Other Poems *and* Neighbours in a Thicket. *His debut novel,* Johnno, *met huge critical and public success and is now an Australian classic. After the publication of* **An Imaginary Life** *in 1978, Malouf moved to Italy, where, until recently, he lived for part of each year.*

Malouf is also author of the novels **Fly Away Peter, Child's Play,** *and* **Harland's Half Acre,** *the story collections* **Antipodes** *and* **Dream Stuff,** *the memoir* **12 Edmonstone Street,** *and three opera libretti, including* **Jane Eyre.**

The themes you explored in your earliest novels continue to appear in your later work. Did you have a vision of what type of body of work you wanted to write, even before you completed your first novel?

Johnno is the book I always knew I would write. I didn't have any thoughts beyond that. It took me ten years to write *Johnno* because I kept trying to be too clever. I was being indirect, trying to write in the third person and from an elaborate narrative point of view. I made many false approaches. These, I discovered, were attempts to escape the actual material. I don't think I wanted to face up to the relationship between the main characters.I had planned *Johnno* for some time. Even when a book begins as an attempt to come to terms with fact, then fiction—all that emerges from the material—becomes more interesting than actual fact.

How much do you know about the structure of a book when you begin writing?

I certainly have a sense of the book's dimensions when I begin. I know if it's long or short. That may mean only that I already know how the subject will unfold and that it will reveal further facets and depths of itself. When I start, I sometimes have nothing but the end. I'll begin somewhere inside the story and work to discover where the book should start. The book is something you walk around inside. As you go, you discover bits and pieces of it. Then you try to find a structure which works in terms of what the book reveals itself to be. In *An Imaginary Life*, for instance, I began with the "poppy" section, which is about 4,000 words into the finished novel, and it was quite late that I went back and wrote the section that leads up to that point.

Frequently, I'll begin with a scene, sometimes involving one or two characters and their surroundings. I will then say to myself, "Who are these people? What's this all about?" Or I will say, "What kind of world are these characters in? What's going to happen to them?" I often have a feeling about something and will write the first paragraph in order to get it going. The first task is to strike the right tone. I often don't have much idea about what's going to happen as far as plot goes. I may have a strong sense of a life or of a person. Often, that comes from something I've heard. This could be as simple as somebody telling you a story and you think, "Oh, what an interesting idea that is." And then you make up characters. But often I begin and don't have a clear idea of the character at all. Somebody, then, will suddenly pop into a paragraph, and she may even turn out to be the main character.

Your first two novels are first-person narratives, but they are extremely different in voice and tone. How do you find the voice and tone of a novel? Do they, like the story as you've just described it, grow out of the landscape of the story?

I wrote the scene with Ovid and the poppy without knowing if it was a scene in a novel or a short dramatic monologue. The voice established itself strongly from the start, and it was enormously easy to let that voice develop over the rest of the material. In the first paragraph of *Johnno*, for instance, the kind of irony we get, or comic view, is part of the novel's tone and of the narrator's character. His voice tends to be innocent and transparent, but it also throws up all sorts of contradictions and comic reversals. *Johnno* begins, "My father was one of the fittest men I have ever known." In the first paragraph, we are told how he is examined for a new insurance policy, and the letter that declares him A-1 in health turns up two days after his death. That's very much the tone of the book, and so much like the kind of reversals on which the book is based because it plays with one of the problems of first-person narratives. What he knows then is everything that comes after and that went before. The narrator is often aware that what he told us earlier was wrong, because he didn't know enough then or didn't see things in their proper light.

At almost every point in *Johnno*, what the narrator thinks is happening and what is actually happening are completely different. The novel is about the way people change, and what changes they are capable of. It's not only what happens that changes, but the difference between what they see now and were able to see then, and what they once felt and feel now. The two main characters in the book, who are certainly real and separate people, are in some ways playing that game we all play. We become different people for whoever it is we're talking to. In a way, both characters are more themselves, and at the same time too much themselves to be real, when they're with one another. Johnno always plays up to the idea that Dante has of him; Dante feels forced to be the kind of person Johnno sees him as.

You could be talking about An Imaginary Life *there, as well. In that case, though, language becomes one of the main characters in the book.*

The equivalent of that is another character in *Johnno*, which is the town itself, Brisbane. It's always in the background. In some ways, the real antagonist of each of the characters is not the other character but the place.

You grew up in Brisbane but left Australia in your mid-twenties and didn't move back until ten years later. Did you feel a certain responsibility to write about Brisbane?

That is a first book. But it's a first book of somebody who was thirty-seven when he wrote it, and who had read a lot of books and had time to grow. It's the book of an experienced reader. Its claims to innocence, which are present in the writing, are entirely false.

I was aware that almost all the cities in literature—Balzac's Paris, Dickens's London, or Dostoevsky's St. Petersburg, for example—are not real places. They're literary places that have displaced the real ones. In putting a place on the map in literature, you don't just record it. You create it. If you can do that well enough, it becomes such a magical place, even to the people who live there, that it replaces the real one for them. I knew perfectly well that this was possible. Until I wrote *Johnno*, I didn't know that I could do it.

You've described this as "mythologizing" a place.

Places are established in our memories by *feeling*. That's why the atmosphere of a place becomes so strong for a reader.

Speaking of fact, how do you know when your research has started to take over the feeling of the book? When do the facts become too present?

That's something I've always been interested in, and I don't know the answer, but I think it's a matter of tact on the writer's part. Look, for example, at a poet like Alexander Pope, who knows exactly how many facts to present in, say, ten lines, so that every one makes its point. There's never too much detail. In Pope, you never feel that the argument is crowded or dense. Instead, every idea comes at the right time and in the proper order to supplement or deny whatever came before.

Another thing puzzles me about writing. Anyone writing a novel, particularly a long novel, is taking the material forward just a thousand words or a few pages each day. So where in all of that does the long arc of the book come from? You can't simply have in your mind the whole arc of the book, but what impresses us enormously about novels is the perfect arc they make. Where does it come from? How does that arc establish itself in the mind of a person who is working piecemeal day after day? It's not as if you have this mess of a thing and then, by taking this or that out, you manage to make the arc.

How much did your background as a poet affect the writing of your early fiction? Was moving from poetry to novel writing a logical step?

As most poets will tell you, about eighty-five percent of any poem exists in the first draft, which you might have jotted down in ten minutes. It may take a long time to get the poem into its final shape, but you know that all the clues are in the first draft. Even the unexpected thing that might happen later, when you conclude the poem, somehow comes out of what you first wrote.

In poetry, you get used to trusting a quick first draft and being willing to spend as much time as it needs to finish. Novels, of course, work differently. You write in small patches, and somehow you have to trust that the arc that I previously spoke about is taking shape. You have to trust that its shape is leading you somewhere. In the poem, you only have to hang on to that trust for ten minutes. Novel writing asks us to maintain it for much longer.

If the work is truly organic, then the second part of the book inevitably prepares itself in whatever happens in the first. When I reached the middle of *An Imaginary Life* and didn't know what should happen next, I reread an early part of the novel. Then I realized what must happen in the second half. I hadn't planned for it. Something inside the *work* was preparing itself.

Does one book grow organically out of the one before it? While working on one book, are you already thinking about the next?

I'll often have what seems to me like a good idea and write a few scenes or sketch some dialogue, but somewhere along the way, interesting as the idea may be, I will see that there's not enough there to take me through a book. It's not going to be a novel. Or, it may start developing a kind of tightness of plot that I recognize as being a good idea for a book, and even a good book, but for someone else. It's not one of *my* books. I wait then until an idea comes along that does seem to have enough blank spaces, enough complexity, to keep me curious.

You seem to be as interested in the arc of your body of work as in the arc of an individual book.

It's really about knowing what it is that you do. You must be able to recognize that there are other things that you could do but basically they're not *you*. You could write those books, but it would be like producing imitations rather than real creations.

If we are to look back over the early work now, it seems that you were already beginning your mythology of Australia and its inhabitants.

There are a lot of preoccupations in *Johnno* that I recognize as themes I continue to explore. *An Imaginary Life* comes out of a different place altogether, which is an extension of poetry. Almost all its questions come from Ovid's poetry, ideas of transformation and language. After those first two books, people said, "These hardly seem like works of the same writer." I knew that I wanted to continue writing books that were poetic in structure and were held together largely by metaphor or analogy but which dealt with historical situations. I don't think I ever planned to take on one historical situation after another. By the time I wrote *The Conversations at Curlow Creek*, it was clear that, without intending to, I had written about every twenty or thirty years of Australia since about 1827. The arc of my work presents a version of Australian history. But it's not a history of events. It's a history of feeling. It's a history of relationship with the landscape. On the whole, it's more mythological than historical, but it is ultimately about the matter of Australia, about the compelling nature of the continent.

Part of that compelling nature of Australia, you've said, is the fact that the spoken language did not arise naturally out of the landscape. Is that idea always at the back of your mind when you work?

Even when living in crowded cities, Australians believe that they're in big, open spaces. That's different from what you would think if you were living in Paris. Wherever you are in Australia, you know that space exists. The business of the language not fitting the landscape makes you extremely conscious of language as an artifact and of its being a manipulatable material for dealing with the world. You may be much more self-conscious about language in Australia than you would be if you were in a place where the language arose naturally. I think that may happen even when what you're attempting to describe are peculiar effects of light or weather, for instance. You're aware that the language has to be manipulated to present sensory qualities. Maybe all writers face this problem. But in a place where the language has been imported, you're more self-conscious about how that language must be forced and stretched.

The main thing about how landscape affects us as Australians is that in Europe and other places, man seems entirely in control of the landscape because he has been in it for so long. His shaping influence on the landscape is so absolutely present and obvious that in those places you take it for granted that man belongs naturally to the land. There, the landscape exists so that man can shape it to his needs, his dreams. The message you get very strongly from the Australian landscape, however, is that it exists independently of you. It does not need you. You can't change it. A metaphysical question then arises from this: How is man related to the world we actually find ourselves in?

You've said that writers must sometimes write certain books that are expected of them before they can write the books they want to write. What do you mean by this?

Everybody writes a first novel which is vaguely autobiographical, and sometimes what you're doing, without realizing it, is getting rid of that material so that you can be free of it. Of course, everything you write about will be autobiographical in some way because you've got to test everything against your experience. But fiction is fiction. A lot of modern writing never wants to make the leap into real fiction.

There's a certain point when you must do it, though. Getting rid of so much purely autobiographical material in the first book certainly frees you to make the rest of it up.

My case is different. By the time I had published *An Imaginary Life*, I didn't think of myself as having written two novels. I didn't know what to call *An Imaginary Life*. After it was published, I gave up my teaching job and moved to Italy. Only then did I sit down and say, "Now I'm going to try and write some books." That's when I wrote *Fly Away Peter*, *Child's Play*, *Harland's Half Acre*, and the stories in *Antipodes*—all of it in a rush, one after the other.

Child's Play and Fly Away Peter were both published in the same year, 1982.

I wrote them together, in Campagnatico, in the first half of 1981. I would turn from one and then continue work on the other one.

Am I wrong to see Child's Play as something outside the thematic realm of your body of work?

In some ways, it's the least characteristic of my books, but it's also the one that's closest to the writing self. I knew that as long as terrorism in Italy was a subject in the forefront of everyone's mind, *Child's Play* would be regarded as a book about terrorists. To me, though, it was always a book about a different kind of obsession. It's as much about the relationship of the young narrator to the writer and his work as it is about terrorism. What interested me about the terrorists was not that they were committing violent acts or that they had a political agenda, because in the case of the Red Brigades we have no idea what their political agenda actually was. A lot of the things I like best in *Child's Play* are times when the narrator behaves like a writer. His interest in the person he is to kill, the famous man of letters, is much like a reader's or critic's interest in getting inside the work and mind of the writer. In *Child's Play*, this happens to the point where the narrator believes he has been "accounted" for inside the writer's work.

Other than Child's Play and Fly Away Peter, were you working simultaneously on the other books in Italy, as well?

When *Child's Play* and *Fly Away Peter* were finished, my publisher and I decided when to publish them. *Child's Play* came out in June and

Fly Away Peter in October. By that time, I had written the first draft of *Harland's Half Acre*, in September and October 1982. I wrote some of the stories in *Antipodes* at the same time, and also the first essay in *12 Edmondstone Street*. All of those things were finished, but not necessarily ready for publication, by the end of 1983. Then I had to get the stories into a proper shape. I added a few pieces to *12 Edmondstone Street*, one about Italy and another about India. So, yes, I was writing all of that pretty much simultaneously between 1981 and 1983.

Leaving your teaching position at the University of Sydney freed you up, to say the least.

In Italy, I was locked up in a house twenty-four hours a day by myself, in a place where, mostly, I didn't see anybody. I did a lot of reading. But I also did a lot of writing. That was a concentrated period. Half of my output was written in those three or four years.

You've said that you write longhand for two hours each morning and then rework your pages in the afternoons and evening, a habit you began when writing Johnno *and which you've kept to this day. How do you edit your work? What's involved in the reworking process?*

In the mornings, I'll just write on. When I come back later in the day and look at it, I'll see that something more needs to be said. My drafts are always filled with caret marks and the word "inset" in the margins for more paragraphs to be included. I'll see that I may have come upon an interesting idea, but it's only hinted at. While walking or cooking or ironing, another paragraph will get itself written in my head, and I add it. Sometimes the work will be exactly as I left it in the morning, but more often it might expand to double its length in the rewriting I do in the afternoon. The work grows like that.

How do you rewrite or edit, on the level of the sentence?

The reader is more affected by the music and rhythm of the book than we take account of. Sometimes, I deal with sentences on a musical level. Also, certain ideas belong to the same, long, physical phrase or structure. I like sentences which have their own contradiction—not just qualification—but sentences that may begin in one place and seem to be saying one thing, but they go on to discover quite the opposite. That's the way the world works.

Flaubert said that the last pages of *Madame Bovary* already existed as music before he had words for them. A lot of things in my books come as snapshots, or visions. I'll see a scene or a character doing something, and the images will tell me what's going to happen. In the actual writing, I'm certainly aware of the music of the sentence and paragraph. I frequently put down a notation of long and short stresses for a phrase or an adverb or adjective in a sentence when I can't yet think of the words. I'll know the rhythm, though.

Did you know you would return to Australia when you went away as a young man?

Not necessarily. But everything that mattered to me, I'd never left. Almost all of my work is written out of strong memories that had already been laid down by then. If I hadn't come back to Australia in 1968, it may well be that my writing would be no different.

What do you hope readers see when they read your body of work?

I want to provide a recognition of the inner life and inner dialogue that goes on in people's heads. The level of this dialogue has nothing to do with the way people are educated or how sophisticated they are. Even if an entire world of apprehensions is not necessarily capable of being articulated, there is, nevertheless, a glimmering at the edge of people's consciousness. I'm interested in what it's like to have those apprehensions, what they're about. That's largely what the fabric of my books is made of. Readers are liberated by seeing their own experiences written objectively on the page. Too often, however, no writer gives that to them.

That's also something that recurs throughout your work. Only when something is consigned to paper does it become real.

I think people are moved by recognizing their own involvement with the world. They may recognize this as being their own, but they have never been able to show it to anybody and, therefore, wouldn't know how to prove it. The writer can validate this for them. There are some specific things I do that I wouldn't necessarily know about except that readers tell me about them. Women readers tell me about the world of men they find in my novels. Australian men are extraordinarily romantic, though not *boyish* in the way American men sometimes are, especially in fiction. Much of what goes on in my books is a sort of secret male business. It's about an openness to experience and vulnerability that men can't otherwise show. I've always been interested in the secret codes of men's worlds. One of the things that may be stronger in Australia than some other places—it's what we think of as being the mateship tradition, which presents a range of feelings that is expressible only because it's so highly coded—is that men work and play and depend on one another; they have to provide all sorts of comfort for one another. And all of that has to be coded in such a way that it won't be mistaken for overt or even latent sexuality. Men, especially in the way these codes work in Australia, have created a kind of possibility for the strongest forms of feeling to be there and for them to be relied upon without our ever mistaking the emotion that drives them. It's the kind of thing that made it possible for men to survive the WWII prisoner of war camps I was writing about in *The Great World.*

What still intrigues you about writing?

Several things remain peculiar for the writer. We don't always recognize our own habits, thoughts, and obsessions. It often takes a reader to recognize them and tell us what they are. We also don't know why the reader returns to us. Writers don't always recognize the deeper patterns in their books. Because we're so close to a book, we sometimes know less about it than an attentive reader, because so many of the connections are unconscious. These things will remain unconscious even when the writer reads the book, whereas a great reader coming from outside will see clearly all the book's patterns. Different readers see different things. Presumably, if the work is rich enough, if it is complex and varied and contradictory enough, then it's not only that different readers will like different books, but they'll recognize you as one kind of writer rather than another kind of writer. That's good. It takes proper account of what you're presenting in the writing, all the things you've felt but which you are not necessarily aware of and often not fully responsible for.

Kevin Rabalais is co-editor of *Novel Voices* (Writer's Digest Books), conversations with award-winning American novelists.

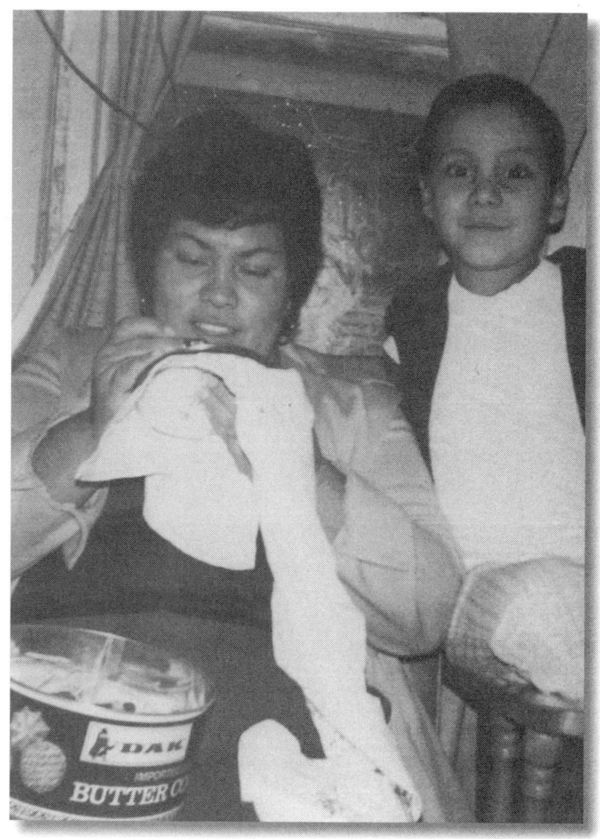

As a six year old with my mami, Esmeralda, circa 1978. Freshly showered and wearing my favorite plaid pants, it was a calculation to win her attention from the evening telenovela. It worked—it's one of her beloved photos.

Manuel Muñoz is the author of a short-story collection (*Zigzagger*, Northwestern University Press, 2003) and the recipient of an NEA fellowship for 2006. His work has appeared in many journals, including *Swink*, *Epoch*, and *Boston Review*, and has aired on National Public Radio's *Selected Shorts*. Algonquin Books of Chapel Hill will publish his second collection in early 2007. A native of California, he now lives in New York City.

BRING BRANG BRUNG

Manuel Muñoz

Lincoln School, on the good side of town, on the north side without a single railroad track in sight, is where Martín enrolled Adán for kindergarten. When Martín was growing up, Lincoln was the rich-kid school, and, by default, better. When his mother drove the back way home from Thrifty's after an ice-cream cone, you could see how much bigger the Lincoln playing fields were, and the blacktops still without the basketball nets ripped down. Nowadays, Martín wasn't so sure how good the school was, but when he moved back from San Francisco, he looked to rent first on this side of town, even though the places were too big for just him and Adán. There was Roosevelt School over on the west side in a newly incorporated part of town, brand-new buildings and landscaped fields resurrected from fallow orchards. Or Grand View, where all the farmers' kids went, a tiny school a few miles out of town springing up out of the grape vineyards, teachers always yelling at the children during recess when they cornered a gopher snake and threw rocks at it. Wilson and Jefferson he struck out immediately, both of them on the south side of town where he had grown up and now home mostly to kids struggling with two languages. It hadn't been so bad when he was growing up, but later, when he was in high school, he would drive by those schools and wonder about their disrepair, their inadequacy, even the lagoons gathering at the bus stops during rainstorms, the kids haphazardly jumping across them, trying

Glimmer Train Stories, Issue 59, Summer 2006

not to get their shoes wet. But he settled on Lincoln because of how he remembered that particular side of town and its clean streets and sidewalks and wide lawns. There was never mud on that side of town, never a flooded street or a sewage leak. The north side was pristine.

At the front office, painted in the clinical, soothing light-green he remembered from Jefferson, Martín held Adán's hand. The boy quietly watched as Martín set down the pile of identifications: Adán's birth certificate, his inoculation records, his preschool report cards. It took him a moment to recognize the woman at the desk, who had smiled wanly at him when he entered, unsure of how to approach him: she turned out to be Candi Leal, a girl he'd gone to high school with and a good friend of his younger sister Perla. He had never liked Perla's friends, a whole brood of mean, belligerent girls whose troublemaking began with skipping school and ended up with pregnancies by the tenth grade, the father-boys nowhere to be found. But here was Candi, who had had her own kid, if Martín recalled correctly, sometime in the eighth grade, and now a grown woman in a respectable job at the very elementary school she had attended.

When he stated his business, without really saying hello to her, Candi slid him some forms and a pen, glancing down at Adán, who stood on the other side of the counter as if waiting for questions. Martín ignored her, deliberate in writing out the usual information: child's name; parental contact information; emergency phone numbers. He pressed hard through the triplicate, lifting the sheets just to check if the marks had gone down all the way to the goldenrod at the bottom. When he got to the section about Adán's mother, Martín casually slashed a large *X* across it.

"So when did you move back?" Candi asked. Her tone wasn't innocent and it wasn't oblivious: Martín knew she had already heard from Perla.

"Last month," he answered, as Candi skipped her fingers down the information on the forms.

"San Francisco's tough," she said. "Expensive, too." She reached the section he had slashed out and paused on it for a very brief moment, as if she had expected to learn something.

"How's your kid?" Martín asked her. "He must be in junior high by now."

"Eighth grade," Candi replied, but didn't say anything more. She gave Martín his goldenrod copy and told him when Adán should report to school. He tried to get her to look him in the eye the whole time, knowing he had the upper hand, the way people would be prying and wanting to know. People had made their mistakes a long time ago, when they were young and hadn't known better, and he was perfectly willing to remind them if it came to that.

On the school documents where Candi stopped her fingers, in the space slashed out with pen, was a small town just south of Orlando, Florida, and a burial in a torrid heat, tropical humidity searing through Martín's suit. Missing from that document was a name—Andy—and a car accident outside the airport at Denver, Colorado during a business trip, a family in Florida who had barely acknowledged Martín and offered no comfort. What Candi wanted to know, when she asked Perla, was more about who Andy was and what had happened, but Perla had no way of knowing about any of it. Martín had kept Andy close and offered little; not even the accident would change that. No one but he would know about the uncomfortable trip to Orlando for the funeral, or about the cousin, Priscilla, who was cordial, but whose cowed silence, in the end, meant Martín would have no ally in Andy's greater family. No one—not even Adán, who was too young to be able to remember it fully later—would know about the cheap, pink-walled motel room where they had spent the night, a heavy breakfast of eggs and hash browns the next morning before the flight back to San Francisco, Martín staring out the taxi window at the pastel colors of Florida, knowing he would never see it again. If his sister Perla had been with him, maybe her defensive, angry way of seeing the world would have prepared him for the legalities and the long, fruitless contesting of beneficiary money from the accident. Perla would have said he hadn't fought hard enough, that you get only what you fight for, and whatever he lost to Andy's family was the result of his own stupidity. Perla would have said this if she had known the whole story—but it was almost as if she knew the undercurrent of it when Martín announced that he had to move away from San Francisco and come back to town. "Is that right?" she had said, over the telephone, her voice coming over, he thought, with barely disguised triumph. "You can stay with us if you have to," she had offered, meaning with her now-teenaged son, but Martín had politely refused.

Before long, though, it was humbling to face what was happening with his finances, and, for once, admit that circumstances could overwhelm a person. Always, Martín had been a person who believed that choices governed one's road: you had to look past the crumbling downtown and imagine something better. You had to count the pregnant teen-aged girls and swear not to get involved in anything like that. You had to think of the orange groves nestled on the brink of the foothills and look past the deep green leaves for the meth labs hidden there. The Valley was a mess of lack, of descending into dust, of utter failure, and he had learned that long, long ago. But in the San Francisco apartment, opening the letters from the Florida lawyers and reading the documents that allowed Andy's family to siphon away what little had been left behind, Martín finally came face-to-face with failing. He thought of the helplessness of his sister when she had had her baby, the decisions she had to make as a teenager, and he thought of the girls who had done the same, what little they could do in family courts, in lawyers' offices, at juvenile detention centers where the father-boys served out a month or two. He thought of the cruelty of Andy's family saying nothing about wanting to gain custody of Adán for themselves and bring him to Florida. In the end, he was the same as those girls in retreating back to the Valley. He would have to make do.

In his honesty with himself, Martín would never call himself arrogant, but he knew his sister Perla would. And she would call him hypocritical, insensitive, unforgiving, judgmental, quick tempered, and mean spirited. She could very well have reveled in his struggle. Still, on the day that he had made the move to the new place in his old hometown, Martín had finished the long trip from San Francisco with Adán sleeping the entire way, and there was Perla on the sidewalk. She knocked on the passenger window, waking Adán, and waved a stuffed purple elephant at him in greeting. Adán had rolled down the window, smiling for the first time in many weeks as Martín parked the car.

"Look what your aunt Pearl has for you," she said to Adán. As for Martín, she greeted him cautiously, a hug that felt more like letting go.

In the late dark of the new house, in the rooms that echoed with their emptiness, by the wide windows that still had no curtains and let in the streetlight, Martín was the one who could not sleep for nights on end. Grief would come like a ghost at the foot of the bed, just as he was sleeping, and the curve of Andy's face would ask why he was trying to forget.

He ignored the grief as best he could and fretted endlessly over the new circumstances, trying not to toss in bed because Adán slept soundly next to him. Despite having his own room, Adán refused to sleep alone—this the only indication in his behavior that something was amiss. In the first few days in town, Martín not yet prepared to look for a job and running daily errands to get their house in order, Adán had fidgeted and scrambled at every line Martín had to wait in. If Adán wasn't playing with another child in line, he distracted himself with the simplest of things: a pebble in an empty plastic bottle, a nickel deposited over and over in a payphone. Misbehavior, if Martín read all of the faces around him correctly, but he paid them no mind. All the more to exhaust Adán and not have to battle with him at bedtime, leaving Martín the night hours to go over what needed to be done.

In the dark, he owned up to how he felt about Adán: this was not his child. All along, it had been Andy's idea; it had been Andy who had spoken plainly and honestly with a woman he'd been friends with for years—Holly, a chubby white girl from way back when in Orlando. Martín had gone along with the idea, perhaps not fully grasping the responsibility, but appeased by Andy's enthusiasm. Andy would be the one to raise him, and he would be the one earning the money, too: a sales job took him up all around the western states, commissions rolling in, Martín maybe too self-satisfied with a no-nonsense accounting job he had in Oakland. The mistake was colossal. He had never considered what it would require to be the sole guardian. In the dark, he had to raise himself quietly from the bed, careful not to wake up Adán, and pace in the kitchen, wondering how he would ever admit something like this to Perla.

What plagued him most was the repetition, the continuance of a cycle he thought he would never be part of. One afternoon in town, stopping at the post office to mail off documents to yet another lawyer in Florida, Martín had caught a glimpse of Perla's son, Matthew. He hadn't seen Matthew except in pictures, and even those were of his nephew when he had been nine or ten. Martín knew it was him, though, because he looked every bit like the skinny white boy who was his father, a troublemaker who disappeared long before Perla even knew she was pregnant. Martín had gone to school with that guy, only a year ahead of him before the guy had dropped out, and yet he still remembered his slouch, his dirty-blond hair, the way his eyes always looked bruised and damaged underneath. His nephew looked enough like that guy for Martín to do a double take, and that's when the sadness of the situation hit him deeply. His nephew was fifteen, a walking mirror of his absent father, the same darkness under his eyes, and it was all Martín had to see to understand why Perla never brought him over to the house.

To be in a house with only one parent: look how it had turned out for Perla. Their mother had fought with her repeatedly, pointing to her older brother as an example, but Martín had set an impossible standard out of sheer distaste for his sister's belligerence, her selfishness, her disrespect, and her stupidity. He went to church even though he didn't like it, just to pull one more thing over her. Perla fought against rules, leaving the house in the middle of the night, sometimes the car that came to pick her up shamelessly idling right in front of the house to wake up their mother. Such rebellion—it scared Martín now, alone, even though the prospect was years away with Adán.

In the dark of the kitchen, sitting at the kitchen table that had only two chairs, he poured himself a glass of milk. He would never dare ask Perla to discuss their mother these days, how she truly felt about her. They did not speak to each other. But surely Perla knew that their mother had also stopped speaking to him after he had moved in with Andy. Both of her children, then, cut off: a monumental anger she had with them for having failed her.

This is how he thought at night, starting with simple, solvable problems like the electricity bill and a doctor's appointment. Grief summoned itself, impossible to release, Andy insisting himself back to life—he had to ignore it to keep from being overwhelmed. Then his eyes stayed open in the dark as a wave of guilt swept over him for a love he couldn't summon completely for either Adán or his sister. He would sit in the kitchen until sunrise, asking himself questions that were impossible to answer. What would make him happy, satisfied? How would his mother have answered that question? Perla? Had their mother favored him more because he looked like her and Perla looked like her father? Did Matthew know that he looked like his father and that Perla saw it every time she looked at him? Is it possible to will yourself to love someone? If it isn't love, then what is it?

By the beginning of October, Adán a few weeks into kindergarten, everything eased some when Martín found a job at a small accounting office in Fresno. The job wasn't the best of circumstances: the building was on the south side, the more dangerous part of the city after dark, and the office was situated in a converted warehouse, the false ceiling perfect for tossing up sharpened pencils to see if they would stick. Drafts of the hot afternoon air somehow snaked past the warehouse's corrugated paneling and into the core offices, which were nothing more than walls of sheetrock; in the mornings, the drafts were chilly enough to force Martín to a third cup of coffee. Every Friday afternoon, the secretary would come around with the paychecks, personally signed by the company owner, and Martín would decide not to complain about the ten minutes he'd be docked if he had been late.

Perla mercifully made it easy for him. She kept her phone calls cautious and intermittent, but when he had told her that he had found a job, she had been the one to volunteer to care for Adán after school. "I'll pick him up and bring him to your house or mine, whichever," she had said. What, then, was she doing for work, Martín wanted to know, especially with a teenager at home, but he felt too ashamed to pry when he himself was in need. "My house," he had told her, and gave her a set of keys.

Most days, after he came home from work, Perla wouldn't linger more than a few minutes before she excused herself to leave, touching Adán gently on the shoulder. Neither he nor Perla would bring up the subject of money, but it was on Martín's mind once a few paychecks came his way. He knew it was costing her something, and he knew her willingness to help was rooted in a desire to move past their differences. Somewhere along the line, like her friend Candi Leal at the front office of the elementary school, she had eased into a forgiveness of the world at large, and that included him. One Friday night, he came home to Perla cutting a roast chicken from the grocery store, Adán busy folding paper towels for the table. "I bought dinner," she said. "I hope you don't mind. Matthew fends for himself most times anyway." In helping her set the table, he took a peek at the receipt in the bag to see how much she had laid out for the containers of macaroni salad and wild rice, the rolls. She had bought beer, too, but that would be for later, apparently. When they were ready to eat, he insisted she take one of the two chairs and he ate leaning against the kitchen counter.

When bedtime came for Adán, Perla helped get him into pajamas and cajoled him into sleeping in his own room. "Here," she said to him, handing him the purple elephant. "Me and your dad will be in the kitchen, so no monsters can come, okay?" Martín, putting away the dishes they had washed, could hear the murmur of protest, but Perla's voice was gentle in its command and patience. "I'll leave the door open a little bit, but be a big boy and go to sleep," she said, and made her way down the hallway to the kitchen.

She pulled two cans of beer from the refrigerator and handed him one. "I went to the school today," she said, sitting at the table.

"Yeah? Why?"

"The school pictures they took the first week? The money? A kid in the fourth grade took the check you gave Adán."

"That was weeks ago," he said, thinking of the morning he had given in to Adán's pestering to wear his favorite sweatshirt—a purple one with a green dragon on it. "I forgot all about it. He never said anything."

"Did you expect him to?" She took the tiniest sip of beer from the can, licking her lips a little, and it occurred to Martín that he had never actually seen her drink. She was almost demure about it, and it reminded him of one of the first times he'd gone out to dinner with Andy, at a restaurant with thick tablecloths, and the careful way he had to handle the wine glasses. He tried to picture his sister at such a place.

"He got beat up that day," Perla added. "Or shoved around. You know how kids exaggerate a little. I don't think he really got hurt."

"Who was the kid?"

"Just some older boy. Probably the older brother of some kid in his class."

He took a deep drink from the can, the beer watery and cheap, but it was from her courtesy and generosity. "You should have called me. I would've come down and taken care of it."

"What was there to take care of? You can't be bothered at work right now. Not with you just starting and everything. I know how bosses can be."

"So what did they do? Did they punish the kid?"

"Well, the principal—do you remember Roberta Beltrán?—she was three years ahead of you or something like that? That really fat girl? She's the principal there, if you can believe it, and she had that boy in tears in no time. He still has the check, and he has to bring it to the school on Monday."

"For what?"

"To apologize. He's supposed to write a letter," she laughed, shaking her head. "Can you believe it? That's the punishment. We would've gotten a lot worse back in the day."

He laughed with her, but he felt he forced it, and he took another drink of his beer, Perla looking down at the lip of the can as if she had remembered suddenly what it had been like for her as a teenager, as if she had become lost in pinpointing where the trouble had started, how young she had actually been.

"You know, I hate to ask you, but I gave them some of the money for the pictures. I told them you'd bring the rest on Monday."

"Oh, yeah?" he said, putting down his beer. He reached into his back pocket for his wallet.

"I had twelve dollars on me. So you owe them thirteen," she said, getting up from the chair. She went into the living room and reached behind the couch, where she had hidden the pictures. "I wanted to bring them to you as a surprise, so you wouldn't have to wait 'til Monday."

He pulled a twenty from his wallet, this being payday. Then he pulled two more and put the bills on the table as Perla made her way back.

"It was just twelve, Martín."

"Yeah, I know, but you've been doing a lot for me. It's just a little bit." He reached for the pictures and pretended to study them closely. Only the head of the green dragon on Adán's sweatshirt was visible, a cartoon dragon with bubble eyes and a little tongue upturned as if in thought or effort. Adán was smiling in the photograph, as if nothing had happened that particular day. All the pictures were the same, but he slid them out for inspection so Perla could reach to the table and fold the bills quietly in her hand.

"Who does he look like?" she asked him as Martín returned the pictures to the envelope.

"More and more like his father," he nodded. "Andy was Cuban. Dark hair, a little wavy," he said, "dark eyes."

"He's kind of light-skinned."

"His mother was white. A friend of Andy's." She had never seen a picture of Andy, and he thought for a moment that she might ask. He didn't know if he would show her or not, and, if he did, where he would begin the story. Maybe from the beginning, which was the end. When he moved into the new place, he had left pictures of Andy packed in their boxes, hoping Adán wouldn't say anything about them.

Perla went to the refrigerator to get another beer, and she turned to wiggle a can at him in invitation. He nodded, and she brought them back, popping hers open with relish and taking a longer drink this time. "In the car," she said, "on the way home... he told me that he looked like you."

Martín almost snorted and ran his fingers through his hair. "Oh, Jesus," he sighed. "The things I'm going to have to explain to that kid..."

"Well, you know, I'm here to help you," Perla said, tapping her fingernails nervously against her beer can. "You're my brother," she said.

"Yeah," he agreed, but couldn't add much more. Part of him felt ashamed of Perla's attempt to bring their slow reconciliation out in the open, felt ashamed of how little he was trying to meet her halfway.

"I've learned a lot trying to raise Matthew," she said. "I made a lot of stupid mistakes. So did some of my friends, the ones who had their own kids. It's hard, Martín. It's harder than you think."

He looked at the picture of Adán, the joyful color of his purple sweatshirt and the cartoon dragon, and found it hard to imagine a point when Adán would fully form into his own person. The fourth-grade boy couldn't have been more than ten years old, and already he had discovered the value of things by how they were acquired. You could bully your way through this world if you wanted. You didn't have to follow the rules.

"Perla," he asked, "what do you do for work? For money?"

"I clean houses," she replied. "Mostly here, but sometimes over in Reedley or in Visalia. A lot in Visalia. There's people moving there from the Bay Area. Lot of money."

"Not me."

She laughed slightly. "Normal situations, I mean. People who had money to throw around to begin with, so they buy land and build these really huge houses to live in and then rent tiny apartments in San Francisco so they have that when they need it."

"Is it enough? The money you make?"

She sighed and put her chin in her hand. Her hair was pulled back and knotted up almost haphazardly, and though Martín knew it was as long and black as he remembered it, the sheen was a little dull, as if her hair were somehow thinking of shading gray. It was hair pulled back out of necessity, to keep it out of the way, of hurrying in the morning, not like she wore it in high school. Combed razor-straight like the other girls, her eyeliner heavy, and her lips glossy with a deep blackberry. "Money comes and goes," Perla said. "I work hard only for myself now. I used to do for Matthew, used to do a lot, but he's just a real angry kid. He's got a lot inside him that I can't get to."

"He looks like his father. That kid..."

"Well," she interrupted, "that's the problem, I think. Every time he looks in the mirror... the things he says to me sometimes." When she put her hand to her mouth, the way she did that, he thought of their mother and her regretting. "I'm almost thirty years old, you know? I did what I could and the rest is up to him. If he wants to come home, well, then he comes home. And if he stays at a friend's house, that's none of my business anymore. You can't control that if they don't want to let you."

When she began crying, as he expected her to, Martín sat quietly and watched his younger sister's resolve shimmer through the helplessness. One hand was still on the beer can, and, because he looked closely now, because he paid attention, he saw that she wore no nail polish and the two rings were simple, unadorned silver. Rings she must have picked out for herself, shopping alone at one of the malls in Visalia, studying the velvet display boxes intently, not bothering to worry over the price, thinking of herself for once. But it wasn't selfishness—Martín understood that. It wasn't like the way he thought of himself, of deserving and wanting, the self-satisfaction and the near greed of having, after years of not-having. Instead, it was a containment and a self-knowledge, a forgiveness for her own part in her unhappiness, a releasing.

"Do you want another beer?" he asked her. "Finish off the pack?"

"I have to drive home," Perla said, dabbing at her eyes gently with a knuckle.

"Sleep on the couch," he told her. When she didn't answer, he rose to the refrigerator and brought back the last two cans. Perla popped hers open as if with effort, grinning a little, and, before she took a drink, she raised her beer as if in toast. They tapped cans, the aluminum sounding as sincere as glass.

Monday morning, he called in sick to work, and though the secretary quizzed him unnecessarily, Martín held his resolve over the phone and promised to be better by the next day. The principal had asked to see him at ten o'clock, and he arrived at Lincoln School fifteen minutes early. Candi Leal, busy with the phones and a string of kids slumped in plastic chairs against the wall, nodded knowingly at him, raising her wrist to tap at her watch: she'd get to him soon. On the way over, Martín had imagined himself speaking to Candi at her desk, prompting an exchange that he should have engaged in weeks ago when he had registered Adán. She was too busy to do that now, and he regretted how he might have misread her before, her initial spark of forgiveness, of new possibilities, of growing and maturing, and how he had wiped it away by not returning her grace.

Almost on the dot, the door to the principal's office opened and Roberta Beltrán came over to shake his hand. "Good morning," she said, good naturedly. "It's nice to see you again." If anything, she had gained more weight, always a large girl, but now it gave her a commanding presence that Martín had always associated with both principals and mean teachers. "Jesse," she said, crooking a finger at a boy in a Raiders jacket. "In my office, please," she ordered, and turned to hold the door for them.

"We'll make this quick," Roberta said, sitting at her desk and clasping her hands. "Jesse, do you have something for Mr. Grijalva, like I asked you on Friday?"

"Yes," Jesse answered in a half-groan and dug into the pockets of his Raiders jacket.

"Sit up straight, please," Roberta ordered, as Jesse took his time finding a piece of paper that he then unfolded. "Speak clearly."

Jesse read from the paper, his voice flat-footed despite his sincerity. "Dear Mister Grijalva, I am sorry that I stole the money from Adam, and that I brang the money to my house. I am sorry that Adam did not get his pictures because of me, and I am sorry that I hurt his feelings. Sincerely, Jesse Leal." Finished, he handed the letter to Martín.

"And where is the check?" asked Roberta.

Jesse fished in the other pocket and drew out the check, folded tiny in a triangular shape, its edges smoothed down and worn.

"Unfold it," Roberta said. "Is that how you took it from Adán?"

"No," he answered. His fingers seemed confused by the folds, but he unraveled the check and smoothed it against his leg before handing it to Martín.

"Thank you," Martín said, taking it.

"What do we say?"

Jesse turned to her, confused, but Roberta only tilted her head down at him, as if looking over the brim of glasses. "We need to apologize."

"But I did...," he protested.

"You read the letter. You also need to say it like you mean it. Look him in the eye."

Jesse Leal turned to look at him, and though he said he was sorry, he drawled it. Martín nodded his head as if in acceptance, but he thought of the battle Jesse Leal would turn into, a ten year old who had somehow already managed to convince his parents to buy him an expensive Raiders jacket. "Fine," he said to Jesse Leal. "Just don't do it again."

"You're excused," Roberta said, and Jesse turned abruptly to the door. "Get a pass from Ms. Leal to get back to your room," she called out after him.

When the door closed, Martín reached for his wallet and pulled out the money he still owed for the pictures. "Was it twelve or thirteen?"

"Thirteen, I think. But Candi knows for sure. Why don't you give the money to her?"

"Okay," he said, but before he walked to the door, he asked Roberta quietly, "That wasn't her kid, right? Candi's?"

Roberta shook her head and reached for the phone. "Oh no," she said, dialing. "Maybe a cousin of some kind, but not her kid. She had her own problems long ago." She waved goodbye to him as she waited for her call to go through.

Since he had the rest of the day off, Martín went to the Kmart that had opened in town when he had been in high school, but was now losing out to some of the newer chains of the broadened strip mall. He found a large frame for Adán's picture and then bought a smaller one to give to Perla.

Waiting in line to buy them, he pulled out the check and the handwritten letter from Jesse Leal. When Jesse had read it, there had been no way to imagine how lousy all aspects of the note would actually be: the lone emphatic period, circled dark and certain when there were clearly two sentences. The misspelling of every name except his own. The crabbed penmanship. Martín bristled at the blatant *brang*. He thought of Roberta Beltrán and Candi Leal and any of the people he might have grown up with who were teachers now, all of their night-training at the local colleges, their effort to push books and paper in front of kids like Jesse Leal. Somewhere along the line, they knew when the right time would come to correct these errors, before they became bad habits, worse in speech: these were the smallest of a whole string of corrections, and Martín multiplied it by the numbers of kids in the office this morning, of the kids waiting in the classrooms, the enormity of the task. It had failed Perla. It had failed his mother: that day he remembered, when he was a teenager, when he had opened the envelope from the adult-training center in town, the application that his mother had put in, the handwriting scratchy and uncertain, the information inaccurate or missing because his mother had not understood the questions. Her application for job training had been denied. He had thrown it away before she even saw it. Diction, syntax, grammar, basic math, conceptual thinking. Symmetries, the logic of sympathy, the order of gratitude, empathy, concern, the rigor of understanding, the faulty equation of grief and anger. It had failed him, too, somewhere along the line. He handed the money for the picture frames to the woman at the register, her arms bare, thick and dark, and her red smock rumpled from a long early-morning shift. He thanked her aloud when she handed him his change.

At the house, he put Adán's picture in the large frame and hung it in the living room. For a brief moment, Martín considered putting it in the hallway, just as it had been done in their house when he and Perla were growing up. Their individual year-by-year school pictures, Perla in her glasses and barrettes until she changed into the girl with the razor-straight hair in eighth grade. Pictures of him and Perla when they were both very young, their mother with them, standing behind proudly, and even a picture with all of them: Martín, Perla, their mother, their father, the tint of the photograph so old it had washed out in an odd red hue. But the living room it would be, just Adán's photograph above the couch. There would be time enough for others.

Later, he left a message at Perla's to come for dinner, and after he picked up Adán from kindergarten, they went to the grocery store where Adán helped select the dinner items for his aunt Pearl. He let Adán call her whatever he wanted and didn't correct him. Though he had no reason to be, Martín felt exhausted, but there was dinner to make. There were many days ahead. Still, when they got back to the house and before he started dinner, he fished in one of the boxes that he had stashed away in his own bedroom and found a picture of himself and Andy. He loosened it from the turns and turns of plastic he had wrapped around it, Andy coming back to light. His mother, upset, would say she could feel a knot in her throat, but the Spanish word meant more: un nudo—and then the gesture toward the neck as if to ward off the noose doing the damage. Martín gave the frame a quick swipe with his hem of his shirt, and set it on a little table in the living room.

On the day of Andy's plane trip to Denver, Colorado, the morning had brought a hard rain to San Francisco. The two of them had shuffled quietly around the apartment, packing Andy's suitcase. Andy would return on Monday night if there were no delays—Denver meant the possibility of snow. Adán slept with a raging fever, and, for a rare time, it would be Martín taking complete care of him. There would be no driving to the airport, no goodbyes with tickets in hand.

That rainy morning, the apartment sat dark. The windows let in a feeble, weak light. Adán didn't budge in his sleep, though his pajama top soaked damp with sweat and his face flushed. There was a sticky pink medicine that smelled like citrus.

Martín spent all day in Adán's room with the apartment quiet. He spent the day looking out the window at Coit Tower in the distance, and fell into a well of doubt. Andy was a good man, but he was all his own, and not fully Martín's to love. There was a young child here, but he was Andy's, not Martín's. After years of wishing for a relationship, here it was, but with it came a certain boredom and an isolation—Martín found himself longing for something to change in his life. He thought, for the first time in years, of his father, and in the quiet of the apartment, Martín let himself inch toward understanding him.

Adán's fever broke, but he remained sleeping. The daylight stayed the same gray—it was impossible to guess the hour. Martín flipped through four magazines and tried to read a book, until finally the call came from the Denver airport, Andy's tired voice telling him that he had landed safely. Martín wasn't up for much talk; he wanted to go back to the warm, quiet room of just thinking, of solitude, so they chatted for a minute at most. Monday would come soon enough.

All day it rained. Nothing changed. It rained all day. 

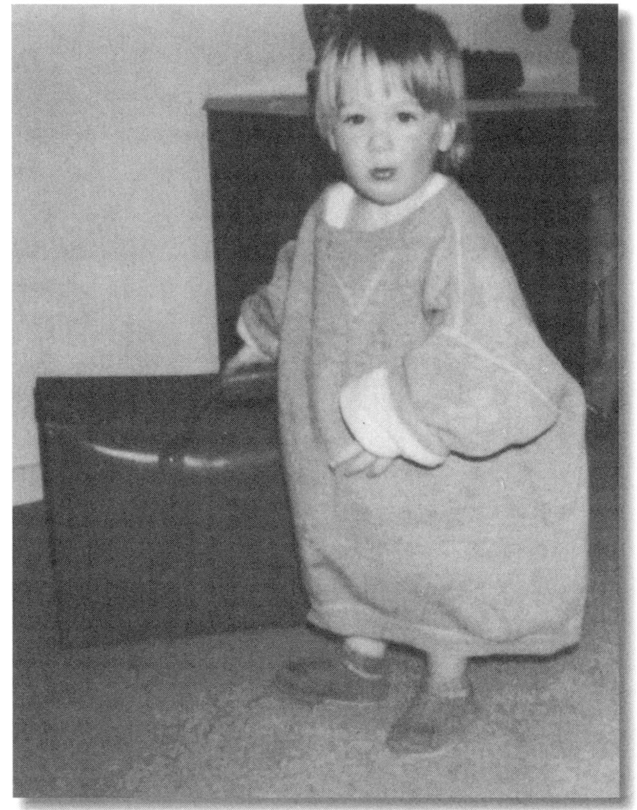

Here I am, off to work. Long day, long sweatshirt.

Justin M. Kramon is a recent graduate of the Iowa Writers' Workshop. Originally from Baltimore, Maryland, he attended Swarthmore College, where he played keyboard and harmonica in a garage band called The Wandering Warriors. He lives in Long Island.

SHEL

Justin M. Kramon

After she washed her face she looked at the spot in the bathroom mirror again, a little brown bump just below her eye. It seemed out of place, like a tear or a piece of food that had gotten stuck there. She ran her finger over it, as if to wipe it off, and saw it disappear under her fingernail, then reappear again on the other side. It was smoother than it looked, which gave Shel the uncomfortable feeling that it wouldn't move easily. The spot was hardly distinguishable from a hundred other moles and specks and freckles scattered up and down her body. Only maybe a bit lighter in color, or maybe not, maybe just a tad larger. But also maybe not. It had seemed different—that's why she wanted to tell her husband about it—but now she wasn't even sure about that. She had looked at it so many times and for so long that she'd begun to question what she saw.

Her husband was a doctor, a neurologist. He worked in a hospital in Brooklyn. She showed him the spot that night after she was done washing up. He was in bed, reading, as he did now that they didn't make love anymore. Leonard was fifteen years older than Shel, and he seemed happier with his books than he ever had during sex, which had always been brief and perfunctory. *Sexless*, she had once told a girlfriend: "The sex is completely sexless." He would roll on top of her and they would wiggle around for a minute or two, until he was satisfied that something had been done, and then he would slide off and go to sleep with his back to her. There had been a conversation she'd started with him about what she referred to as their "sex life," although it quickly became clear how foolish the term was. So the talk ended with him saying something to the effect of, "What's the point?" And she couldn't help but agree.

Now they just read at night. Leonard turned pages for hours without talking. The lamp by his face shone on his bald head. He read things with titles like *Aristotle's Theory of the Virtues* and *Living in a Kingdom of Ends* and *The Good Life*. He loved moral philosophy. He had studied it in college, and he told her that if he had it to do over again he would almost certainly be a philosopher.

"It's the purest kind of knowledge," he said. "There are no complications. There's no messiness. Only truth."

She laughed when he said *truth*.

Sometimes he would read her a line he liked from one of his books. He wouldn't introduce it or say anything after. They'd be lying there reading in bed for over an hour and all of a sudden he'd just pop out with it. He offered it the way you would throw a peanut to a dog, without asking if it's hungry. "It is impossible to think of anything at all in the world, or indeed even beyond it, that could be considered good without limitation except a good will." Or: "The rules of good manners or politeness have been introduced in order to facilitate the intercourse of minds and an undisturbed commerce and conversation." Then he would go on reading in silence.

And there were other times when he laughed at something in the book, or smiled privately to himself. This made her angry. She would try to find a funny part in her own book to laugh at, or else she would go to the bathroom and wash her face and come back to tell him she was tired and she wanted to go to sleep.

"Okay," he would say, and focus his bedside lamp more closely on the pages so the light wouldn't bother her. "I'll be here."

They lived on the East Side, a few blocks from the river. Every Sunday morning, when the weather was okay, Shel put on a T-shirt and some shiny pants that stretched over her thighs. She wore headphones and ran uptown on the promenade by the water. People passed her on both sides, shirtless men and kids on bikes and women toddling on skates. They wove and dodged each other. She got lost in the people, dazed by the busyness of it, the criss-cross and confusion of so many lives. She tried to avoid knocking into people. She said *excuse me* and *sorry* a lot. It was impossible not to jostle and to get jostled along the way.

Leonard told her never to go into Harlem.

"It's dangerous," he said.

"Lots of things are dangerous," Shel said.

"But this is *really* dangerous."

"So is driving," she said. "You do that every day."

"But I have to for my work. I can't avoid it. You can avoid this. You can lead your life exactly the same way and do everything that is important to you and still not go to Harlem. There's no reason for you to go there."

Impeccable logic. It sounded like a quotation from one of his books.

"You don't know what they'd do," he said.

She tried to think of something to say back, but he really was right. She didn't know what they would do.

Once, she had been running for a while and she got caught up in thinking about something. It had rained earlier, and the sky was a milky gray color, making it hard to see far in it. Only a few people were out on the promenade, mostly holding umbrellas or walking with their hands in their pockets. It was summer and she could smell the heat rising off the wet pavement. A large boat pushed along beside her, dragging a rippled *V* of water with it. She liked that, the way the boat looked in the clouds by itself, its slow crawl toward somewhere she couldn't see. It made her think, and then she forgot how long she'd been going. She saw a man casting a fishing line into the river. He had a boy with him. He handed the rod to the boy once the line was in the water, and they pulled at it together for a while. They paid no attention to Shel. But as she passed them she heard the boy say the word *agua*. Then she realized she was in Harlem and got scared and turned back.

Shel taught kindergarten part-time. She had been an elementary-school teacher for a while after she got out of college, and it gave her something to do with her days. She went in to fix the snacks and read stories and watch the kids during recess. They called her Ms. Shelly. She liked helping them with their little chores, with picking clovers or tightening their shoe laces. They did it all so earnestly. She and Leonard had no children. He was too old by the time they got married. "It's too late for me to be a father," he said. "I should be a grandfather by now." Truthfully, he was a little young to be a grandfather, and Shel was a little old to be a mother. She was in her thirties when they married. She didn't protest when Leonard said the thing about being too old for children. She had wanted kids, but the idea made her terribly afraid, depressed even. This took the pressure off.

"Leonard, what do you think it is?" she said to him from the bathroom the night she showed him the spot.

"How could I know?" he said. "I haven't even seen it."

"I just described it to you. It's a big brown bump that wasn't there before."

"Let me see it," he said. "Come here and let me see it."

She sat down next to him on his side of the bed. It felt strange because she had never been on his right side in bed before. He was still lying down, his shoulders propped on some pillows, but he had closed his book and placed it on her side of the bed.

"Come here," he said.

She moved her face near his. He examined her with his reading glasses slid to the tip of his nose and his mouth slightly open, focusing the lamplight on her skin. It was warm. He brushed her hair aside with the backs of his fingernails, and she shivered from the contact. He pressed his thumbs into her cheek, trying to get a good angle. His breath came short and fast from his mouth, and she felt it on her forehead. He smelled like toothpaste and aftershave. There was something awkward about it, about the way he touched her, something unexpected. She almost thought it would come to something.

"You should have that checked out," he said.

She pulled away, cold. "That's all? I should have it checked out? That's what I thought I was doing."

"You need a dermatologist."

"I need something," she said.

"What does that mean?"

"I don't know, Leonard. Maybe you should tell me."

"Look, I don't get what you're talking about. All I said is that I think you should get it checked out. It's not my area. I'm sure it's nothing to worry about. But when you have a chance, I think you should get it checked out by someone who knows how to look at that kind of thing."

"It's not your area."

"Right."

"What *is* your area, Leonard?" She pushed the lamp away and got up off the bed. She didn't know where to go, so she just stood there in the middle of the room.

"I'm missing something here," he said.

She had started out life as Cheryl. Her mom called her that, or sometimes Sherry, if she was feeling affectionate. She called her Sherry the day her father died.

"Sherry, I need to talk to you about something," she said.

Shel was at the dining-room table with her homework. Her older sister had been talking quietly for a few minutes with her mother in the kitchen, but then she had left the apartment without saying anything to Shel. When her mother called her, Shel was copying out a line she needed to know for a test. *In sooth I know not why*, she had written.

"Come talk to me for a minute, sweetheart," her mother said.

Shel recognized the way her mother was talking, a sort of high, breathy tone she used to say things like, "Your father won't be eating with us tonight. He's not feeling so well." She said that a lot. And when he did come out it was as if he weren't really there anyway. He watched the dishes passing across the table in front of him like it was a television with the sound turned off. He had the look of a sick man, drawn and hunched over his plate. Shel would watch him sometimes while her mother and sister talked. He wore black wire-frame glasses that looked like they were made out of a stronger stuff than him. His eyes moved behind them, or else they just stared at the table in a way that made Shel think he wasn't looking at the table at all. This could go on for minutes at a time. He always had a silk handkerchief tied around his neck, and for years Shel thought this was about fashion. Later, after he died, her sister told her it was to hide where the cancer treatments had disfigured him.

At the table her mother talked and talked the way people do when they're afraid of silence. She told them everything she did during the day, and everything she wished she had done but didn't get a chance to. She talked about thoughts that popped into her head out of nowhere, and often the conversation became so disjointed and the connections so unclear that her mother would simply stop in mid-sentence and ask who wanted more to eat or whether they were in the mood for dessert. It was as if she were pointing at things around them, and each time they looked she would point at something else so they couldn't get a focus on anything. She was fast and loud, and even as a child Shel knew she was trying to cause a distraction. She asked questions the way doctors do, to get you to look away from whatever awful thing they're sticking in you.

Sometimes she would ask Shel's father if he wanted anything and he would simply say, "No." Never anything more. He would answer before she had finished asking. Almost like a whisper he said it, like a parting word at a late hour, without looking at anyone or gesturing or shaking his head or smiling, as if he were just trying to walk off somewhere by himself. It didn't matter what she was going to say. That was his answer. No.

Shel's sister, Susan, answered most of the questions from her mother. She was good at that, at anticipating those quick turns her mother liked to take. Listening to them talk it almost sounded like the questions made sense and followed from each other. Each time her mother changed the subject Susan would narrow her eyes a little, then when she realized where she was going Susan would lean forward and grin and nod her head as if her mother had said exactly what was on her mind. She caught everything and threw responses back with skill. If her mother held up a bowl and asked if anyone wanted more meat or some beans or applesauce, Susan always took it out of her hand and helped herself and started saying how wonderful the food was. She got very heavy in her teens, and even heavier as an adult. She became a smoker in college, and developed a rough voice and a cough.

Once, long after they had both moved out of their parents' apartment, Shel had been talking to Susan on the phone and she asked her how she could have enjoyed those dinners so much.

"I mean, they were close to torture," Shel said. "Mom was manic. She sounded like she was on something."

"It was pretty bad," Susan said.

"*Pretty bad*? It was an asylum. Mom was a crazy woman. I thought I had been committed as an infant. Sometimes I sat up in my bed at night and yelled, 'Guard! Guard!' "

Susan laughed. She was always very generous.

"I know," Susan said. "I can understand that. Mom had a way of making people nervous."

"And I didn't even know what to be nervous about. I was a kid. I felt like any minute someone was gonna tell me to hit the deck and I'd have to grab my weapon and duck and roll for the nearest cover."

"Was it really like that?"

Shel was about to say something, but she paused. The danger was never really like that. It was something softer, sadder than the talk, something quiet and persistent beneath all the craziness. She used to look out the window behind where her parents sat at dinner, past the buildings to where the sun hung ripe with color. They ate at a gray time of evening, when the street looked empty and cold. It was still enough that you could hear it if someone shouted from a long way off.

"Close," Shel said. "Almost like that."

One time, while Shel was sleeping, she heard some voices out in the hall, some men, and then there was some clanking around. It all had the lazy, unreal feeling of a dream, like they were talking underwater. After a while Shel separated the sounds into two voices. One man would say things like, "This way," or, "Turn him on his side," and then there would be some more clanking, or else the other man would say things like, "No chance," or, "Are you crazy?" When he said things like that his voice got louder and the clanking would stop, then the first would say, "Okay, all right, what do *you* think?" This went on for a while and Shel had the feeling that she wasn't supposed to hear it, that this was the kind of thing her mother was afraid she'd hear if the talking stopped.

She was going to stay in bed, figuring the voices would get softer, passing the way things do. Getting involved always caused more trouble than it was worth, and more often than not people didn't want any help in the first place. This was an attitude Shel would take with her into the world, this reluctance. She kept her distance in life, offering the people who felt closest to her no more than some nervous gestures of affection. Then she'd start in with the excuses, the not returning calls, the backing off without reason. More than once it had cost her a friend. Once it cost her a man she loved. It was all very sad and confusing, and Shel couldn't explain it any better than the people she had ended up hurting.

There was some pounding on her door. One of the men said something, but she couldn't understand it. She sat up in the bed. The pounding started again. It sounded like they were banging into her door with whatever had been clanking around before. She felt the kind of disbelief she would feel on waking up with a cold, swallowing again and again to convince herself that it was a mistake. And she wanted just as much as at those times to fall back asleep. She heard her mother now, too, saying something to the men. It was hard to hear over the banging, but it sounded like, "She's Cheryl."

Shel got up and went to the door, but then it opened on its own and she found herself being pushed back into the room. Susan was in front of her, blocking her view. She hardly saw anything out in the hall. There was no time. If someone asked her now, she couldn't say anything about the men who were carrying her father, or the stretcher that must have been too wide for their narrow hallway. All she remembered was Susan pushing her back, her hands on Shel's shoulders, stepping with her slowly, holding her off, sitting her down on the bed.

And one more thing. There's one more thing Shel thought she remembered, but it all happened so long ago she could hardly say whether she didn't just make it up. Over Susan's shoulder, for the briefest second, she thought she saw her mother. And she was looking right at Shel. Staring right at her. Her mother didn't say anything or turn away or smile. She made no move to comfort. She just looked Shel in the face with the kind of look her father had at the dinner table, like she wasn't really looking at what was in front of her. And it was as if she were saying, *This is it, Sherry. Now you know. This is it.*

So when her mother called her in that sweet, high voice and said, "Sherry, I need to talk to you about something," Shel knew what it was. She knew her father had been dying, even though no one ever said it. Death was in the apartment, like some voices whispering just outside her door, or a kind of dullness in the light. There was nothing terrible about it. No flashy surprises. It was nothing like the way she later described it to Susan. Instead, there was a kind of obviousness to it, like a phone call she had been waiting for all night. *Your father has had some complications.* She knew the words before her mother said them. *He won't be with us anymore.*

There was some talk about how their lives were going to change. Shel's mother would take a job as a school teacher. They would have enough to keep living where they were until Susan finished school. She would graduate in the spring. Then Shel would go to a boarding school in Massachusetts and her mother would move to a smaller apartment on the West Side.

When Shel got up from the table she couldn't think of what she should do, so she went back to do her homework. She had not cried about her father and would not for a long time. She had a feeling that was nothing like what she thought it would feel like to know he was dead. There was no splash of emotions, no thrill of loss, only a tired sort of calm, like a great sheet had been spread out and laid over everything.

She sat down at the table and finished out the line she had been copying: *I am so sad.*

• • •

The doctor was running late. Shel had been in the waiting room for over an hour. She had gotten there early, but still this was too much. For a while she had read a magazine, an article about a crippled woman who climbed a mountain. There were pictures of her hanging off rocks and sitting on the edge of a cliff. It was almost funny. The photos made the mountain look so dramatic and terrifying that it was hard to imagine anyone getting up it, let alone this woman. And it was hard to imagine why anyone would *want* to. "It was the happiest moment of my life when I reached the top," the woman said in the article. She was short and husky. Not attractive. She had red hair and some braces on her legs. Her legs were the problem. "I am so thankful for this," she said. "Life throws a lot of stuff at you, but you can't let it get in the way."

After that Shel stopped reading. Her mind was running too fast and she couldn't concentrate on the words for long enough to get what they meant. She let the magazine rest on her lap. It was open to an advertisement with a picture of a blond-haired model. She had a face like a doll's, smooth and white as soap. Shel had split open the flap on the side of the ad, and now the scent of perfume rose from the pages like a cloud, thick and sweet and slightly repulsive.

She looked around at things in the room, bouncing from one to another the way her mother used to change subjects at the dinner table. There was a fish tank in the middle of the room. Some exotic-looking fish glided through a hollow city of rocks and tiny caves. The rocks had holes in them that looked like windows, and there was a fake pirate ship wedged in the pebbles at the bottom. The fish wound through it like it was just another rock. One of the fish was black and orange and had some scaly ridges across its body. Another had cheeks that blew out like bubbles on the sides of its face. Shel thought they looked like examples of skin disorders, a prop the doctor stuck there to make people feel better about their own maladies. *Maybe they're patients*, she imagined saying, if she'd had someone with her.

The others in the room didn't look like they'd appreciate the joke. There was an old couple across from Shel, both as creased and spotted as aging fruit. The man had his hands on his knees and he kept looking all around the room, making a face like he was smiling, and then letting his mouth fall slack. He seemed to be greeting empty spaces as if they were people. The woman had some knitting in her lap, and she worked the yarn automatically, her speckled hands turning in tight circles while she watched the floor. Neither said a word or looked at the other. Their relationship must have been as automatic as the knitting. Shel couldn't tell which one was the patient. But she had the idea that at this point it was probably the same thing either way.

The only other person in the room, besides the receptionist, was a girl with a giant rash on her face. She was sitting on Shel's right, a few seats down, staring into the fish tank. Shel could get a good look at her, pretending she was watching the fish. The rash on the girl's face was remarkable. It was red, but it had these tiny ridges and shadings in it, as if it had nothing to do with her face at all. It looked like a strange map attached to her skin. The girl would have been average looking without it, but it made her stand out. Not completely in a bad way, Shel thought. It gave her a kind of importance she wouldn't have had if she were just average. She was exotic, like the fish.

The receptionist called Shel. "Cheryl Himmel," she said. Shel thought it was funny that the name wasn't even hers. She had taken Leonard's when they got married because it seemed like the reasonable thing to do. Since then she hardly thought about it, except once in a while when she would see it on a letter or a paper at school and it would take her a moment to realize it was her they were talking about.

She closed the magazine and followed the woman into the exam room. The receptionist wore her hair in tight, shiny curls that looked like they had been sprayed on her head. *Do you think the doctor might be able to help you with that?* Shel imagined joking to a friend.

"Doctor will be with you in just a minute," the woman said, and closed the door on Shel.

In the room there was an exam table and two folding chairs. Shel sat on one of the chairs. She touched the spot again to make sure it was still there. It slid under her finger, like usual, with just a bit of texture. There was a poster near the door that read "Skin Cancer Warning

Signs" across the top. Then there was a list with a photograph of each warning sign. "Irregular Border" was one. "Uneven Coloring" was another. Her spot had none of these features. It was just a plain brown bump. She thought she should tell the doctor this. Maybe it would be enough to call the whole thing off.

The room made her feel helpless. It was a trap, really. She couldn't go home until the doctor said so, and only then under whatever conditions were chosen. If it was cancer, she would have to agree to that before she left. She couldn't say, *No, I won't take it*, or, *Let me shop around and see if I can find a better deal.*

The doctor came in and introduced herself. Shel stood up to greet her.

"Cheryl?" the doctor said. "Dr. Ferrer."

She held out her hand and they shook.

"Shel's fine," Shel said.

"Shel," Dr. Ferrer said. "Nice to meet you."

She was much taller than Shel, younger too. She had a pretty face and a slender figure, and she smiled in a glassy way. Like a woman who was used to flirting, Shel thought, the kind who always knows something. She wore make-up and she carried a clipboard.

"Can you tell me a little bit about what brings you here today?" Dr. Ferrer said while she was sitting down in one of the chairs. Then she must have noticed that Shel was still standing because she looked up and said, "Oh, the table's fine. Why don't you have a seat up there."

Shel hoisted herself onto the table clumsily, trying to think how to start.

Then she said, "It's this bump on my face."

She started going by Shelly when she went off to boarding school. It made sense. She was a new person, or at least she wanted to shake off all the traces of that old life. It clung to her, Shel thought, like the smell of some dingy place she shouldn't have been. She bought new clothes and cut her hair short. She would have liked to be free of all the old ties, to have left her childhood like a burning building, watching it dissolve into the smoke. But she did owe her mother something. She had pulled it together, found work, gotten Shel into a good school and Susan into college. She had not dissolved in the smoke.

At the boarding school Shel shared a symmetrical room with a girl who smoked marijuana in the stairwell at night. Her name was Beth. She wore a necklace of beads and sea shells, and she dated college boys from the schools nearby. They took her to parties and bought her presents, which she arranged around her side of the room. Glass swans and candles shaped like flowers decorated Beth's desk and her window sill. Shel didn't think Beth was beautiful, but she could see the appeal. It was a way Beth had of giving herself over, of letting you know that she wanted more than anything to go somewhere else and you were the only one who could take her.

Shel saw it when Beth would stand at her window, waiting for the boys to come pick her up for a movie. There was a certain eagerness, an excitement, almost a childish wonder about it, as if she had no idea what the world had in store. Beth would stand there, sometimes for an hour, pretending she was fixing little things with her swans or just enjoying the way the night looked. Then they would come up the drive with their headlights bouncing and she would say a quick goodbye and run out the back stairs so the monitors wouldn't see.

These nights Shel would lie on her bed and look out her own window. The school was nested in some trees, and in the fall the branches would lose their leaves, and you could see their black skeletons crossing each other against the sky. Beyond the branches the sky became a silver-blue lake, expansive and flecked with the light of stars. Looking at it, Shel had the feeling one gets at the edge of water that extends further than the eye can see. There is a peace in that, in knowing that it goes further than you can see.

It would be quiet at this hour. At least there would be no more human sounds. They were given up to the swishing and chirping of the woods, the music of the world without us, before us, after. There was a smell of salt and pine and something like ashes. Sometimes a breeze would start up and the trees would shake their slow limbs overhead. Birds flew between the branches in short, definite paths. Everything that moved was a black shape, flickering on the surface of the night like a reflection. In this light objects took on a magical significance, the way silence does in the normal course of things. A gesture, a cry, any motion put you at the center of the world. And beneath it all there was a hollowness, maybe a kind of loneliness, but calmer, deeper than any longing, something like the steady hush of wind or the empty sound of water.

She cried once, lying on her bed that way, watching the night. It was a dreadful, abject sobbing, the way men cry when they resign themselves to crying. Each breath rises with the hope of finding something to catch it, a voice or some headlights in this bounding darkness, and dissolves again into an endless silence. She didn't understand until much later, until she had lost a man she truly and honestly loved with all her heart, that she was crying for her father. Loss always touched her this way, in a tender place at a late hour. And this is how she knew it had been with her all along, that the silence is always there and it's only when we're alone that we ever hear it.

Days were noisy and fast. Shel was good in her classes, and she played sports in every season. She made some friends, enough that she would look back on the school with fondness. She had classes with boys and girls, but she lived only with the girls. Most of her friends were on the same floor with her in the dorm. They were shy, studious girls who missed their parents. They baked brownies for fun and always made curfew. At night they sat in circles and gossiped to each other about boys or the girls they didn't know. Shel had no trouble leaving them.

Once Shel walked in on Beth with one of her boyfriends. They weren't doing anything. No kissing or rustling of clothes. But when she opened the door Beth put her hand on her mouth. It wasn't because she was afraid of getting caught. She snuck boys in all the time, and she knew how to explain it away to the monitors, sleepy old women who would take a good excuse over a punishment any day. The reason Beth put her hand on her mouth was that she was talking about Shel. Shel had experienced that before, that hush when she came in a room, and it gave her a feeling on her skin, like a layer of dust was settled there, something she should have brushed off a long time ago. All she heard was Beth saying, "You should get a look at the whole bunch of them. It's a good thing they found each other." Then the laughing, then the silence when she came in the room.

In college Shel lived in a studio apartment by herself. She wanted the space, and it turned out to be cheaper anyway. She went to school in Philadelphia. The freedom was extraordinary. She ate meals at odd hours, slept during the day, saw movies by herself. She used to walk out of her apartment at night and over a few blocks into Rittenhouse Square. During the warm weather, families gathered on blankets in the grass with picnics or board games. Children dashed across the lawn. Couples held each other on the park benches and kissed or looked up at the trees. This was a time in her life when loneliness was exciting, when the evening air was a promise of things to come, and she enjoyed the tension of holding herself away for a little while. The kids screamed and the couples necked under the stars, and she liked being a part of it all.

There were boyfriends. One she met in her classes, one in the bookstore where she worked, another on the subway, and another on one of her walks in the park. She was good at teasing them, at making them think she wasn't interested, then smiling or looking down at just the right moment, so they knew they could get something from her. They went to the museum, ate in restaurants, had some brief conversations, and made out incessantly. They would find little nooks and alleyways to duck into, shadowy corners in stores to sneak a kiss. She brought them back to her apartment if she liked them enough, and she slept with a few. She didn't see why it should be such a big deal. It didn't feel like a big deal. The first time she did it she remembered thinking how simple it was the way another body felt, and how the whole thing was so much sillier than she'd imagined. *Oops*, she thought when he slid into her, *there goes that.*

The bookstore she worked in was called Kinsley's Rare and Used Books, and that was all they sold. It was a small, dusty-smelling place on a side street. The people who came in were mostly older, scholarly looking people, with thick glasses and ill-fitting clothes. Shel was a cashier and she stocked the shelves when the orders arrived. The woman who owned the store, Myrna Kinsley, was gray and frail looking. She was unmarried, and never mentioned anything about any husbands. She liked to come in at odd hours, greeting friends and falling into some excited conversation about a dead author or a recent production of an old play. From what Shel gathered, Ms. Kinsley didn't think that much useful had been done in the last fifty years. But she was always pleasant to Shel, and she paid more than the bigger stores, so Shel stayed on working for her all four years she was in school, and then kept the job after she had graduated.

Sometimes the customers tried to talk to her about a book, and Shel would find ways of avoiding that. She didn't know anything about the books they sold. She read magazines and mystery novels, and she had developed a definite distrust of the sort of truth you could find in a book. She was waiting for life and the knowledge living brings, and that was somewhere else, in a cold night or a lover's room. The customers at Kinsley's had missed that. They missed living, she thought, and now they were trying to make up for it. So when they asked her if she had read this or that, or what she thought of his or her writing, Shel pretended she was busy organizing some papers, or else she shrugged her shoulders and scrunched up her face as if to say, *Don't ask me. I wouldn't have a clue in the world about those things.*

She got to know Matthew because their paths home crossed. They would usually meet by a statue of a Revolutionary War hero, if the timing was right, and then there was a space of a few blocks where they would walk together until they had to part at the corner where Shel lived. She knew when he usually got there, and she tried to time her walk so she would run into him and he could say something a little forced like, "Fancy meeting you," or, "Care for a walk?" She liked that formality, that touch of anxiety she sensed in him, as if she were worth being nervous about. He had dark hair and he parted it sharply on the side in a way that looked like it took him time. His voice was a little high, a little light for his size. He was over six feet, and broad, but he spoke with a practiced gentleness, a kind of apology for the space he took up.

The first time they walked together was the winter after Shel had graduated. Matthew was wearing a sweater but no coat, and he had his hands in his pockets. It was windy and his face was red from the cold. They had passed each other a number of times before, but this time Shel decided to smile at him. He looked surprised. Then he waved back at her. She was close to him by this point and she noticed that his hand quivered when he took it out of his pocket.

They introduced themselves and he shook her hand. He offered to carry her bag for her.

"It's no trouble. Really," he said when she refused.

"Maybe not for you," Shel said.

She had gotten fast with men.

"Okay," he said. "Whatever you want."

She had expected him to come back with something. They usually did. That was how it started, with that playfulness, just the slightest edge that let her know she was being tested. Then maybe she would slap him on the arm, or give him a little shove, and things would go from there.

But he just said, *Okay*. He said, *Whatever you want.* She had never been with a man who didn't push back.

On the days when she got to the corner where they usually met and he wasn't there, Shel would keep walking without him. She never waited. She didn't want him to think that their walks were any more than a convenience, although she counted on them and found herself in a rotten mood when they didn't happen. She would walk around her apartment with an unsettled feeling, like she had left something at work. Later, after they had been lovers for some time and Matthew felt comfortable telling her about all of the feelings he'd had in those early walks, all of the excesses and foolish dreams, he once mentioned that he used to hide behind the statue of the soldier and wait for her. He knew she got there at the same time every day, and he would look at his watch and peak out when he thought she'd be coming. Then when he saw her he would walk out like he had just arrived.

"So you stalked me," Shel said when he told her.

"Not stalked. Followed. I was taken with you."

Shel was thinking of telling him that she timed her walks home, too, but she decided to keep it to herself.

"Call it what you want," she said. "It sounds like stalking to me."

Then he surprised her. "I think I've loved you very much and for a very long time," he said.

Shel thought she would pass out when the doctor told her it was cancer.

"Not the life-threatening kind," Dr. Ferrer said. "Nothing like that at all. But not entirely superficial either. It does need to be taken care of right away."

"I can't believe this," Shel said. And then she kept saying it. "I just can't believe it. I can't believe this is happening."

"I can refer you to a good oncologist who treats this sort of thing all the time with very good results," Dr. Ferrer said.

Shel started to cry. She tried to stay focused on the doctor, but she had the terrible feeling that her life was running away from her. Her eyes filled and her breath began to come in spurts.

The doctor stood there with the clipboard, staring. She had the look of a child who'd just broken something, like she was the one in need of comforting.

She gave Shel an awkward hug.

"I know, I know," Dr. Ferrer said.

Shel wanted to say something smart about what the doctor knew, but there was no one to laugh at it.

Matthew didn't laugh so much at Shel's jokes, and this put her in an odd position. Her jokes pointed and said, *Look at that!* while Shel was sneaking out the door. There were times when men had become serious about her. They'd tell her she was beautiful. They'd buy her something with her name on it. They'd look at her in a prying way that let her know they wanted more out of her than ever before. When they'd start in on the looks and the compliments, Shel would turn cold, as if the faintest curtain had fallen between her and the world. Then she would begin with the jokes. She repeated words that were funny, or else she would twist up what they had said into some kind of bizarre shape and pass it back to them. They hardly knew what to do with it, so they laughed, too, and then Shel would ease back into the room.

Once, after she had slept with a man, he told her that he wouldn't mind it if that was the last thing he did in his life.

"I like a man with aspirations," she said.

Then he kissed her and said, "I was aspiring to be romantic."

"But it's disappointing when they always fall short of them."

It was meaner than she had intended, but it did the trick. He said something almost witty back to her, but his voice was flat, and it was clear that he was hurt and that he had begun to inch away like her. She wanted to tell him that it was just a joke, but that would make even more out of it. So she just told another one.

Shel stayed in Philadelphia after college. She began teaching in an elementary school part-time, while keeping her job in the bookstore. The kids liked her. They appreciated her sense of humor, and how she used the same tone of voice with them as with adults. She had a book of jokes and she read them one every day. One of her favorites was: *How many feet does a king have? One, if he's a ruler.* She laughed at that one longer than any of the children. When they made excuses about their homework or told her stories to get out of a test she said things like, "Nice try, buddy." Then, if the kid was nice enough, he would usually smile, and Shel would, too.

They made her a full-time teacher at the end of the year, and Shel stopped working at the bookstore. She was dating Matthew, and he spent a lot of nights at her apartment. He had wanted to move in with her at the end of the summer, but she told him to keep his own place. He had started graduate school and was studying to be a social worker, like his mother. Sometimes at night he would call his mother and tell her about his life. Shel would watch him reporting things to her, then waiting for her to tell him what she thought.

Matthew had a work placement in a school for children with emotional problems. They were normal most of the time, he said, but sometimes they would just lose it. One kid threw a desk at the teacher. Another would start screaming strings of curses when he couldn't do a math problem. Some of them were brilliant, Matthew told Shel. They wrote plays and made up beautiful songs on the piano. But they were very mixed up. A story Shel would always remember was about a girl who hugged Matthew and was about to say, "I love you," but for some reason the words came out wrong and she said "beat" instead of "love." Then there was some silence, and the girl finally said, "*Love*. I meant, *love*." Shel thought that was so sad.

After Matthew said the line about loving her very much for a very long time, Shel was at a loss for words. They were in her apartment and he had just come out of the shower. He was wearing a T-shirt and his hair was uncombed. He had said things like that before, and she had always tried to slip out of it. He said that he couldn't think of a person he'd rather be with, and she asked him if he knew many people. He told her he could marry her, and she said that she was sure he would be a faithful and dedicated husband, but that she could never share a bathroom with him. And all of these times Matthew would look right at her and say, "I mean it." It was paralyzing. At first Shel had thought he was slow, that he didn't get it, or that he had a bad sense of humor. But then she realized that he was looking through that curtain she had raised, and that behind it she was alone and truly scared.

So when he said the thing about loving her very much she almost laughed. She almost told him to take a colder shower next time, or that she had already gotten the Hallmark card it came from, or something else that would make him feel her distance, some sorry line she would remember when she was old and sore from her memories. She imagined his reaction, that patient stare, those words. *I mean it.* This was a moment Shel would recall much later, long after Matthew had died, and she would think of it as the saddest and the most beautiful in her life. It was both things. Later she would come to see each moment of love as a moment of loss, because it buried itself in memory, along with the awareness that it would never come again. The things on this earth, the people she loved most in this world, were like reflections on water, catching the light for just long enough to reveal themselves, then passing without a trace, and with little understanding, into evening.

She held his hand and she kissed him. She didn't say anything because she didn't need to. He pulled her close, and when she reached under his shirt she could feel the heat of him. He smelled like soap. He touched her face and brushed back some hair with his fingernails. She knew even then that all of these details would play themselves again, often, in her mind, that they were already running like water into her thoughts, sinking into the tiny splits and caverns she would only discover later, when she was alone. Yet she let herself live, this once.

Another thing she would always remember was the way he looked at her when they made love that time. She was used to men closing their eyes or staring off somewhere. Then the breathing, then the moaning, then the rest of it. It was easier for her that way, because it made her unimportant. She was part of that, but it could have just as easily been someone else. Matthew held her in his eyes the whole time. She would close her eyes for a while, and then she would open them, and he would be there, with that soft look and that tender half-smile, like he wanted to keep her there, like he was bringing her again and again back to that place, back to life.

That night he said her name, softly, as she was drifting off to sleep, and it startled her back into the room. "Shelly, I want to marry you. I think we should get married."

"No you don't," she said.

"I know that we should," he said, and even though he didn't have a ring, even though he had never mentioned a word about marriage to her before, she knew he meant it.

She kept her eyes closed. "Let's just go to sleep now," she said.

"I want to talk about it with you."

"I'm too tired to think. I couldn't talk about it now."

"Then tomorrow," he said. "I have this feeling. I know it's the right time to talk about it."

"We will," she said. "We will."

But the next morning Matthew was crowding her side of the bed. He had his arm over her when she woke up, and she pushed it off. It was too hot in the room, and his closeness agitated her. He was breathing too noisily. She left the apartment before he woke up.

Later, when she thought back on that night they spent together, she would recall how she already felt his absence in the middle of everything, how she missed him most when he was inside of her. This was not a presentiment of his death, which came to her as shocking, horrifying news. The missing was part of the way Shel loved, and she could never learn to separate the two. After she left Matthew sleeping in the apartment that morning, the distance had already set in for her. She sensed it like that slightest curtain she had raised before. When she came back later that day—after eating breakfast by herself in a diner and browsing through a bookstore—his body seemed far away, and when he talked it was like those voices she had heard outside her room when she was a child, carrying her father off somewhere she would never see.

He asked her where she had gone.

"I was hungry," she said. "And I needed to get out."

"Where'd you go?" he said. His voice was pressing her, and when she answered it was like she was shoving him off her again.

"Just out. To a restaurant. Why?"

"It felt strange waking up without you there and everything being so quiet."

"I'm sorry," she said, and she meant it.

He didn't bring up marriage. He sensed her mood well enough to know it wasn't the right time. That night he stayed over again at her place. She watched him sleep next to her, across what felt like miles of space, and she thought of that line she had copied out years ago, after her mother had called her Sherry and told her that her father was dead. *In sooth I know not why I am so sad.*

It was a few months before the relationship ended. There was no fight, no crying, no dramatic or painful finale, only a gradual fading away, like a radio losing its battery. They would eat together, go for walks, make love, everything as they used to, but it was all missing something. Shel felt as if she were watching herself do it all from the other side of a window. And he must have noticed it, too, in the pauses after he spoke, the silence at the end of a meal. It was in the room with them, that constant hush, that slowness of bodies moving in water.

If someone asked how it ended she said things like, *My heart wasn't in it*, or, *I just couldn't see us together in the long run.* Matthew took all of his stuff out of her apartment. Not in boxes, nothing as decisive as that. He would just take a few things back with him—a comb, a shirt, his toothbrush—every time he came over. He knew what was happening and he prepared for it the way people do during the progressive illness of a loved one, with a kind of subtle, deliberate cleaning.

They had no talks about it, because he must have understood what she would say. Nothing. He could see that she had made up her mind. And if he pressed her the way he did those times when he told her all the things he felt and said, "I mean it," it wouldn't turn out the same. This was different somehow, deeper than before, and Shel would not let herself be pressed. She had given all she could. That was it.

Shel moved back to New York after living in Philadelphia for almost ten years, teaching school and making a life for herself. She had dated a few more men and things always went wrong at one point or another. Then she just decided to leave. Her mother was still in New York, and Shel realized that there was absolutely nothing tying her to Philadelphia. She had a job and some friends, but nothing she couldn't have anywhere else. It was funny to think that you could spend ten years in a place and not have any reason to stay there.

She found a job teaching in one of the city schools and got lucky with the rent on an apartment in the Village. The streets at night made her feel young. She started taking walks like she had in college. She passed by crowds of tattooed street punks and dope dealers bowed over their merchandise with clients, and none of it scared her. It wasn't that she didn't think they would hurt her. It was something else, just a feeling she had about the world, that things weren't as heavy as before. The feeling was different than the one she'd had on those evening walks in Philadelphia. It was like she had passed by a giant building that was blocking the sun, and now she could see everything in a kind of gray light that bothered her eyes.

She began going by Shel instead of Shelly. It was simpler, and she liked the sound of it. No frills. It fit with how she thought of herself.

She had cut her hair short again, even shorter than when she had gone off to boarding school. The cut was almost boyish, but it looked right for the way her face was now, she thought. "I've been pared down," she liked to tell people.

Shel's mother lived uptown. She had gotten a master's degree and taught at a private school, where she met her second husband, the father of one of the children she taught. He was an investment banker who had been divorced, and Shel only knew him from her occasional visits with her mother. Richard Alman was his name. He gave strong handshakes to men and big bear hugs to women. He always kissed Shel on the cheek in a forceful way that made her cringe. He had a weekend home in Long Island where he took Shel's mother, and sometimes they would invite Shel out to sip daiquiris on their deck and watch the sun set over the bay.

Both he and Shel's mother had grown fat. They sunk into their deck chairs and stared out at the water, smiling. The sun would roll down the sky, spilling its colors onto the water. Then Shel's mother would take a deep breath and say how beautiful it all was. She said it in a mechanical, uninterested way, like a child reciting her prayers at bedtime. Sometimes boats would ride past and Richard would yell at them if they went too fast or got too close to the shore. "You have to protect your peace and quiet," he'd say when he was done yelling. After a while Richard would ask Shel's mom to fix them up another round of drinks, and when she brought them out they would all sit there in the dark with smiles on their faces and nothing to say.

Susan lived upstate now. She'd had some bad marriages, so she stopped doing that. She lived alone and worked as a drug counselor for young adults. Shel talked with her on the phone once a week and they told stories about their lives and remembered things from when they were kids. Talking on the phone with Susan, Shel felt close to her. There was a connection, something about what they lived through together, or the way their lives had gone from there.

Susan liked to refer to the people she worked with as "my junkies," and Shel told her she used to call her students that, but the parents didn't like it.

"I can't imagine why," Susan said.

"I think it had something to do with the dope I was giving them."

Susan laughed into the phone in the wheezy way she had developed, and then she coughed a little and cleared her throat.

"I don't know where you got a sense of humor from," Susan said.

"Why?" Shel said. "Our house was a laugh *factory*. Most people pay for that kind of entertainment."

"Seriously, Sher, was it all bad memories for you?"

"No, not all."

Shel stopped for a second. Once, before he got so sick, her father had lifted her on his shoulders and carried her around the house. He was a stiff, uneasy man, who must have known by then that he had a disease that would kill him. So it was an event. Her mother came to the door of their bedroom and watched. They galloped around the apartment for a while, and he told her he was a race horse. Shel remembered the way he had loosened that day with her on his shoulders, how his strides became a little easier, like he had forgotten about the things that troubled him. When he put her down they were laughing.

Shel was going to tell Susan about it on the phone, but she remembered how her father had started wearing the handkerchief soon after that.

So instead she said, "I especially liked the dinners."

Shel started dating Leonard after she'd been back in New York for a few years. She got set up with him through Richard Alman, who had done some investments for him. Leonard was already established by then at the hospital in Brooklyn. He commuted every day from the apartment on the Upper East Side where he had lived with his first wife, who had left him. He never talked about her, except once in a while to set the context when he was telling Shel a story. "Diane and I were living in Queens then," he'd say, or something like that. And that was all. He'd just go on with the story. Shel never really asked much about it, or even why Diane had left him. She had the idea that it was for another man, and she spared them both the trouble of having to hear about that.

There were no surprises. Leonard was everything she had expected him to be. He was very kind to her, and their dates were agreeably predictable. He took her to restaurants and theater, held doors, talked about his work, asked her about hers. He always picked up the check. The sex was unremarkable, or remarkably average. Everything about it was normal. He lay on top, never sped up or went harder, always kissed her once on the cheek at the end. It was an ugly, smacking kiss that made her think his mind was already somewhere else, that she had become a part of his delicate routine. But that was such a small thing. At that time Shel didn't think she needed any more than Leonard gave her. She'd had the other stuff and she was ready to settle down, for things to get calm.

He took her to concerts at Carnegie Hall. There was one where they performed a Shostakovich symphony, and the loud, brassy crescendos had disturbed Shel. The piece dragged on through its peaks and valleys, and she couldn't wait for it to end. Her head hurt. She wanted to walk when it was done, but Leonard told her he had a horse carriage waiting to take them through the park. They sat in the velvety seat, he with his arm around her, she looking up at the sky, trying not to get sick from the smell of the horse.

"Isn't this nice?" he said.

"Lovely," Shel said. She meant it to sound honest, but the word came out like a punch line to one of her jokes.

Leonard didn't seem to notice. He was digging around in the seat for something. Shel thought he had lost his keys.

"What?" she said. "What is it?"

After a minute he pulled out the little box with the ring in it. Shel screamed. She didn't hug him or start crying. She just screamed like he was holding a giant bug at her. The carriage driver turned around in his seat. Then she stopped and she and Leonard just looked at each other. Neither one of them said anything.

"You startled me," Shel said, even though she knew it had been coming to this for a while. And this is exactly how it would happen with Leonard, in a horse carriage under the stars. Predictable.

"I'm going to need to think about this," Shel said. "This is a lot. I'm just going to need to think."

He was still looking at her, holding the ring. This was the first time she hadn't done what she was supposed to. He seemed like he didn't know what to say now that he couldn't say his line. He stayed quiet for the rest of the ride.

The next morning Shel received a letter that she took to be a sign. It was written in tight script on a sheet of white stationery with a plain blue border. "Dear Shelly," it began,

> It has taken me a long time to find your address. I know that you were a very good friend of Matthew's, my son, and so you may have already heard that he is no longer with us. Since the funeral and the memorial service have already passed, I thought that you would like to know the circumstances of his death.
>
> As you know, Matthew had been working for several years as a dedicated social worker. He counseled many emotionally troubled children. He was a wonderful friend to them and they loved him. He had drawers of cards they had made for him and pictures they had drawn for him.
>
> He had taken an interest in one particularly angry boy. For a while Matthew believed he was coming around, but you never can tell with people. One afternoon the boy asked Matthew to come on a walk with him in his neighborhood. He took him to an alley where his friends were waiting to rob Matthew. They only wanted to take his money. But Matthew tried to talk with them. He always wanted to get through to people. One of the boys shot him.
>
> I know that Matthew felt very close to you, Shelly. He talked about you up until the end, and I am sure that he took his love for you and all of us with him to a better place. I offer this news only so that you have the opportunity to make your final peace with him, as we all have had to do in recent months. I wish you the best in your life and in coming to terms with the enormous loss we have all had to face.
>
> Sincerely,
> Elizabeth Stedford

Shel folded the letter and put it back in the envelope. Then she took it out and read it again. She read it ten times, and each time she finished she felt as if she had missed something. The whole story seemed impossible. She stared at the lines and waited for something to change. She refused to cry. If she cried she would be admitting that it all happened—not just the things in the letter, but all of it. That would be too much, to think of everything. Shel could sense the weight of those memories without lifting them. So she held herself back, stayed on the surface of it, did all she could to move on.

She looked at the last lines of the letter one more time. *His love for you. Final peace. Coming to terms with the enormous loss.* It was impossible.

That night she called Leonard and told him she would marry him.

She had a choice. She could have it removed in an operation, which had some risks because the cancer was so close to her eye. It might affect her vision, the oncologist had told her. His name was Dr. Mahaffey, but he introduced himself as Jim. He was fleshy and kind looking. He had a moustache that moved when he talked.

"The risk is small," he said. "But it *is* something to think about. The advantage is it would be over and done with and you could walk out of here and right back into your life."

"You're assuming that's an advantage," Shel said.

He laughed. He touched her shoulder.

"I am," he said.

The other option was radiation, a low dose every day for a couple weeks.

"I only like to use very low doses," he said. "I think it's gentler that way."

"I wouldn't mind gentle," Shel said.

"The risk there is that it's harder to predict the long-term effect. Also, there are some side effects. You have to think about what would make you more comfortable, both now and in the future."

She chose the radiation.

"So I have to do this every day?" she said.

"Well, not the weekends," he said.

"Good. I wouldn't want my social life to suffer."

"That's the last thing we'd want."

They made a mask for Shel out of a material like papier mâché. She thought it was like one of the art projects she did with her students. When they took the plaster off her face she examined it, ran her fingers over the features—a crude reflection of her own. The face on the mask looked like a younger version of her. There was a hole where the spot was on Shel's face. Dr. Mahaffey had explained that they needed to do this because the spot was next to her eye and he didn't want any of the radiation to get there. It was an idea he had thought up himself.

"The kids at school would love this," Shel said to him after she'd felt the mask. "It's really a lovely idea. Maybe you could come in later for art class."

She had the radiation every morning before she went to work. It didn't take long. Even with the waiting she was always out of there in less than an hour. Dr. Mahaffey supervised sometimes. The technician would fix the giant machine over Shel's head and then he would slip out of the door into the next room, where he and Dr. Mahaffey would watch Shel through a window. She couldn't see anything because of the mask. She just heard them adjusting things, then the door click shut. Dr. Mahaffey would talk to her through a speaker in the machine. The first time he did it Shel was horrified.

"Relax," he said. His voice crackled in the speaker. It was completely dark beneath the mask, and Shel closed her eyes anyway just to make sure.

"Breathe a little," he said. "It'll be over before you know it."

For a minute she lay in the dark and smelled plaster, listening to the sound of the machine's motor.

After the first time he asked her how it was.

"Like a coffin," she said. "Only cozier."

"I know it's not a pleasant experience," he said.

"But hey, that's not what I signed up for."

He smiled at her in a concerned way. "Still," he said, "I know it can be hard."

She didn't go into work that first day she had the radiation. She had called and told them she was getting treatment for a skin problem and that she might be tired. They would have a substitute to help out with recess and with the snacks.

She went home. She turned off the lights in her bedroom and slept. It was fall and the days were getting shorter. When she woke the light was already dim outside. The afternoon was quiet. Cars passed below, and she heard them like breezes through her window. Some birds twittered outside. Their shadows passed over the window. There was a stillness, a dullness in the air that was not yet pain. She had the anxious feeling that she had lost time. Next to her on the mattress was one of Leonard's books. Shel switched on his bedside lamp. She opened the book to an essay called "Morality and the Sentiments." She read a passage:

> It seems, then, that an emotion is not like a strong gust of wind, pushing us this way or that without reason. This is why we say that emotions have objects. I love *someone*. You fear *something*. Emotions have an aboutness that is not captured by the non-reasoning forces account. Furthermore, our emotions involve values and judgments about the world. To be sad for the death of a loved one is to *value* that person's presence, and to *judge* that he will no longer be a part of one's life. In this way we can see...

She put down the book. Leonard wouldn't get home until late, and then he was on call through the night. They could phone him any time, and his little black box would beep, and then he'd go running out the door. Sometimes Shel didn't even wake up. She'd look over in the morning and see the sheets tossed off where he went to sleep. Then she would fix them like he was still sleeping there. It didn't matter. She would eat breakfast by herself and watch the news with the sound off. She had a feeling that if she turned on the sound it would disturb something. And she just wanted to look at it anyway.

She could never say all the things she felt in a day. There was so much. There were so many shocks and eruptions, and feelings that were like that view from her window in the boarding school, stretching on and on, past where she could see. She clutched onto those feelings, as if they would take her along with them, beyond the borders. More than anything she wanted to know where it would all go; what happened to the millions of images on the lake at nightfall. Were they ever there? That thought would always hold her in wonder, that idea of the things we can never see.

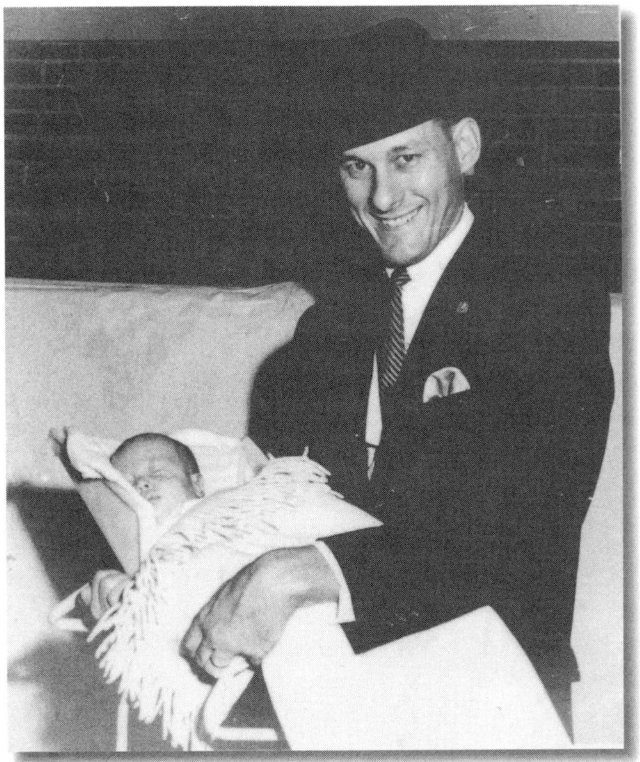

This photo was taken on September 16, 1966. That's me in the basket, seven weeks old. The man in the jaunty hat is my father.

Clark E. Knowles lives in Portsmouth, New Hampshire with his wife Gail and his daughter Grace. He teaches writing at the University of New Hampshire. His fiction has appeared in *Black Warrior Review*, *Scribner's Best of the Fiction Workshops 1999*, the *Flying Horse Review*, and *Red Rock Review*. This is his second appearance in *Glimmer Train*. He is currently working on his MFA in writing at Bennington College.

DO YOU THINK IT MIGHT BE THE TOFU?

Clark E. Knowles

Larry has to duck coming through the door to his classroom. He looms over his students, has to stretch downwards to scrawl on the board. For years, he has been short—or short enough that people didn't notice him—now, his head scrapes the flaky ceiling tiles. The gigantic desk at the front of the room, behind which he normally conducts his class, is today as tiny as a child's play thing. He can feel the growth in his toes and his calves and his joints—he feels he might explode all over the room. He should have noticed something earlier in the day when he could not get his sweater over his giant head. He puts his hands to his ears and is surprised by the circumference of his skull. It is the size of a watermelon—or even larger. As he begins to speak—about the indiscretions of Henry Wilcox with a working-class woman in *Howard's End*, and how the ramifications of such a thing are insurmountable—he wonders if his neck can sustain the pressure.

Mr. Dack? one of his students says. Are you okay?

He wakes drenched in sweat. He checks his hands, his feet, his neck, the shape of his head. He's wrapped in the sheets. Denise, his wife, is showering. The dog, Oliver, is standing next to him, waiting, just like always, for his morning walk. It was all a dream, he knows, although he did feel deeply distant from his class the previous day.

He kept drifting off, they said, looking out the window. He hadn't the heart to tell them that he was remarkably saddened by their lack of involvement with the readings he had chosen. They had acted a bit concerned for his well being, one of them even going to get him a cup of water. For a period of about five minutes, he had remained almost totally silent.

But the dream was vivid. His heart is pounding irrationally inside his chest. He's relieved to not be growing uncontrollably. He reaches up and feels his head. It almost feels normal. Almost. After the reality of his dream-state, watermelon-sized head, his normal head feels too small, awkwardly so. Perhaps, he thinks, I am shrinking.

The bed, this morning, is much bigger than he remembers—far bigger than when he went to sleep. In fact, the room is expanding—the walls moving out and away. The ceiling is a thousand feet above him. The open closet door seems an entrance to a dark and hostile cavity. If he yells, he suspects his voice will be but a small peep that will float off and disappear into the incalculable universe. He becomes less and less whole on a daily basis.

Later this day, his son will be arriving, family in tow, for their annual holiday week. Larry is slightly afraid of Jimmy's wife, Candy. For starters, she has a stripper name, and he feels uncomfortable saying it aloud; it sounds as though he should be asking her for a table dance, or a lap dance. Also, she doesn't understand personal space, and always stands too close, presses into him when they talk. When these thoughts begin, he concentrates on the size and shape of the bed, wallows in the mist of imagination.

After her shower, Denise will come back and sit on him. She couldn't be expected to see such an infinitesimal dot in a vast ocean of off-white cotton bedding. There will be nothing he can do, nothing he can say, to stop the slow and inevitable lowering of her ass to the mattress. He wonders if death will come via immediate crushing weight, or by a slower suffocation. They have been married for so long, and she has been distant recently, occupied by new endeavors while he remains stagnant, teaching the same books to the same bored students in the same prep-school classroom.

Oliver, man's best friend, slobbers and licks his lips. As soon as Larry is the size of a liver-snack, the dog will pounce. Ungrateful beast. Larry knows that this is the end. He is doomed.

Larry, Denise says. Get up. You're going to be late.

In the car, he notices that Henson, the science teacher, is wearing cologne. Perhaps Grey Flannel? Henson is recently divorced and there are rumors that he's sleeping with Sarah Toluene, from the French department.

So, Larry says, got a hot date today?

Henson looks at him. Are you gaining weight? he says.

Larry looks down at his stomach. It is true. He has been packing it on lately, but he isn't sure how he let himself go so far. He really is a lard butt. He should exercise some, cut down on the pastries. Another inch or so and he won't be able to ride in the car. He'll have to sit on the trunk, or the luggage rack, ride to work like a piece of furniture.

I guess so, he says. But what about you? What's with the cologne?

Me? Henson says. I don't know, I just want to smell good.

There's a rumor, Larry says, that you are sleeping with Sarah.

It isn't a rumor, Henson says. We've been going out for a few months.

You never mentioned it.

Well, Henson says, you've been a little removed lately.

So you've been dating for a few months? Larry says.

I know it's quick, Henson says, but I think I might be in love.

Henson has a mole under his left eye. Larry imagines Sarah kissing the mole, finding it attractive in some way, the way some people are attracted to birth defects, inefficient genetics.

Love? Larry says.

The question hangs in the air as Henson turns left onto Route One.

That afternoon, Larry has a doctor's appointment. He has been worried about his cholesterol. He tries to explain the new sensations to Dr. Simpson, his doctor for over ten years.

He says, I feel like I'm in a time warp. I'm flying all over the place.

That's sort of vague, Dr. Simpson says.

I never know what's coming, Larry says.

Is it an anxiety that you can place? Dr. Simpson says.

I don't know if it is an anxiety, Larry says. I feel like I'm floating away.

Floating away? Dr. Simpson says.

Yes, like I'm a balloon, like I'm a feather.

How long has this been going on?

My whole life? I don't know.

I mean this particular feeling, this particular feeling of flight.

Well, probably since I came through the door. Sometimes it is like the ceiling is the only thing holding me down.

Is it like that now, like the ceiling is keeping you in the room?

Yes, yes it is.

I think we need to run some tests.

Have you ever heard of anything like this before?

Only in people with chemical imbalances.

When Dr. Simpson says this, his back is turned, and Larry cannot tell if he should take it as a joke.

Do you think I'm unbalanced?

I don't know. Have you changed your diet recently because of the cholesterol?

I've started eating tofu. Do you think it might be the tofu?

I've never heard of tofu causing the sensation of floating.

But it could, right?

Maybe. It doesn't sound like a food thing, but you never know.

Later, in the car on the way home, Larry feels the exact opposite of a balloon. He's a rock, a cement chunk. It is all he can do not to lay his head on the steering wheel. It is as though every part of his body is slowly being dragged to the ground, the weight of all these lives so unbearable. He sinks lower and lower in the seat, his feet are like lead weights. When it becomes time to slow the car down, he's unsure if his own body will allow it. He thinks he might have to die like this, a large rock in the car, a large weight that no one wants around.

All his life, he has been afraid of missing something important; the thought of missing out keeps him alive when nothing else does. There's Denise's graduation from law school. There's no way he could miss that. She went back when she was forty-seven. She was almost through. Just the bar exam and then she would be doing lawyerly things. It might be nice to have a wife who understood the legality of things, in case he wasn't around, in case something happened. He derived a bit of comfort knowing that she would be fine without him, better perhaps. He would certainly miss the joy in her eyes; he wanted so bad to see that look, that mischievous little glimmer absent for so long. Or perhaps it had been there—Henson had told him he was removed—perhaps it has been that way at home, too. Perhaps Denise's eyes had been glowing all along.

And of course, if he weren't here, he would miss his son coming home with his family. They would be there when he got home, Jimmy, his skinny little wife with the stripper name, their kids Lorrie, Joseph, all of them here for the holidays. The kids were always excited about the presents—he and Denise always went crazy, bought far too much, far more than anyone needed. Who were they kidding? Did they think they could just buy love like that? How could he not be there for that? Candy would touch his arm, make him think about things normally under lock and key—but not only sexual things—it was more than that—his own inadequacies—the immense light of his personal failures—his writing career—the plans he had for a manly and rugged life.

They'd go and buy a big tree tomorrow. The kids liked that, too: the singing, the lights. He hates Christmas, really. He feels lost during the celebrations. He wonders what ol' Jesus thinks of the trees and the drunken faculty parties where men put their hands on female coworker asses. What would Jesus think about those coworkers who didn't remove those lecherous hands, but let them rest or let them squeeze ever so lightly? What would the Son of God think of that? Merry Christmas, one and all. He supposes that is one of the reasons he's so flummoxed. How can he pretend to be merry for yet another year? He decides he doesn't have to be merry on the inside, that he can put on a merry face while they get going started with the Christmas spirit. There is no time to waste. Get that tree up and ready and twinkling for the kids. The pine scent made him sneeze. He longed for a time when there were no Christmases to worry about. But there were other things, most certainly, other things to keep him here, alive.

Oh, how he would miss all the things he was supposed to love.

But if he's a solid mass of concrete, there would be no need for him. He might as well lean his head against the steering wheel and let the car go where it may. He would crush his grandchildren anyway—eventually—he could never love them the way they needed love. People always needed more love than he expected. And love was such an active thing, like blood running through veins. Those needing love could never withstand the force of dead weight. He would be like the foot standing on a garden hose—no love could flow past his oblivious sole.

He grows heavier and heavier. But he's something mightier than concrete. He is lead, mercury. Soon he is slithering out of the bottom of the car, breaking through the floorboards. His body crunches and crackles on the asphalt.

At a light, a man in a phone-company truck leans out his window and shouts, What are you? Drunk or something? Sit up, you fucking freak.

The man's voice follows Larry all the way to the Food King, all the way down the frozen-foods aisle, back to the bakery, clear up to the cashier. The market loudspeaker system is blasting "Deck the Halls." The cashier has bright pink hair. She whips the food across the scanner so fast it makes him dizzy.

He lifts the bags of groceries out of the trunk of his car and carries them inside. The thin plastic handles on the bags cut into his skin. By the time he gets to the kitchen, they have sliced his palms open. He drops the bags and looks at his hands. They are hanging on by a thread. He moves his hands just a bit and the thread breaks and the tops of his hands just fall off, fall right to the floor, fingers wiggling there among the tomatoes and day-old muffins. He looks around for someone to mention this to, but what is the point really? What could anyone do?

Larry's son comes into the kitchen.

Look, Larry says. Look at what happened.

Jesus, Dad, what'd you do?

Things are the way they are, Larry says.

It looks like you just dropped the bags on the floor.

What am I supposed to do without the tops of my hands?

What are you talking about? Jimmy says.

Can you help me find my fingers?

Are you drunk? We've only been here a few hours and this is how you say hello?

I don't know, Larry says. He sticks his bloody stumps into his pockets and leans against the counter. The smell of Denise's lasagna coats the kitchen. He knows the others must be in the dining room, waiting for the loaf of Italian bread he brought home.

Mom said you were acting weird, Jimmy says. Are you having a mid-life thing?

Perhaps I'm falling apart, Larry says. Things like this never happened when I was young.

Let me help you pick up the groceries.

Your mother said I'm acting strange?

Are you depressed? Have you seen the doctor?

Dr. Simpson thinks it might be the change in my diet. He told me to watch the tofu. Stick with more traditional foods.

When Lorrie and Joseph are climbing over him as he lies on the big living-room carpet after supper, he is sure he is going to vomit. Not just puke, like when you have the flu, but serious vomiting. Like he might throw up his internal organs. He can feel them shifting inside of him, loosening, preparing themselves for expulsion. He puts his hand down near his liver and feels it pulse, and them raises it up to his stomach, his heart, his eyes. All of his organs roil beneath his skin.

I've got to go to the bathroom, he says.

He stands up and it feels as though his grandkids have adhered to his skin. When they let go, it is as though they are peeling it away, layer after layer, exposing all that internal mess. Of course, his skin is nothing but a sack for everything inside. A stretchy sack. That would explain the shrinking and the growing and the rising and falling. It is all about the sack of his body, and how the shape of the sack is ever-shifting. Perhaps it has been this way for a long time.

He smiles as he leaves the room. Candy leans over to pick up one of Joseph's trucks, and her shirt balloons away from her chest. Larry can see clear down her body, from her neck to her feet. She is wearing a red bra. He imagines diving down her shirt and never stopping—not even at the floor, but going right past her breasts and belly and thighs and ankles and crashing straight through the surface of the earth. He has never seen her exactly like this, so open, and when she lifts her face, she catches him staring at her. He's ashamed at first, but only for a second. She touches his arm and says, Thanks for having us up again. We all look forward to coming here.

Well, Candy, he says, isn't this what Christmas is all about? He puts his hand on hers, both of them resting on his arm, skin to skin.

Lord, he was happy to have an answer. His skin, his silly little skin. Holding him together and keeping him from losing himself—the largest organ of his body—the container of all his faults. If it wasn't for his skin, his guts would be all over the place, tossed like chum from a bucket.

You have a beautiful family, he says. You are both such wonderful parents.

In the bathroom, Larry thinks of Jimmy's wife with the stripper name and masturbates—he doesn't really picture her face or body so much as her name. The act itself is something tangible, and, as long as he is doing it, he feels almost normal. He wonders why her parents had named her Candice—and if they knew that men would automatically think of her as Candy. He wonders if her father hated the way her name could be shortened like that, to something that would cause men like Larry to run away from her and relieve himself this way—without much thought—for he hadn't thought of doing this as he was touching her; it was something he felt only as he moved down the hall, as if those two moments were a million years separated. It was only after he was away from her that he realized how close they had been. The act in the bathroom is something that happens seemingly without his attention. His penis is in his hand, and he is doing "it"—the same way he has been since he was twelve. As always, he feels fine until he is finished, and then he feels like an adolescent all over again.

He used to imagine Marilyn Monroe, or perhaps Jayne Mansfield, when he was that age. He had a secret place in his room where he hid their pictures. Then, before he really understood the attraction—only that it was and would ever be a divine thing—he imagined Marilyn and Jane trapped in a house, perhaps tied up by kidnappers. He would burst in at just the right moment and save them, untie their ropes, and they would pull him close and push his face into their bosoms.

This evening, there is no such fantasy. After he finishes, he thinks of Candy and her name and how disappointed he is for thinking the things he did—because that isn't him, not in the least. In fact, now that he is finished, he can't even imagine doing any of those things. He feels a longing to hold his wife. It was like a stranger had taken over his body for a few moments. She is his son's wife, after all. They have given him grandchildren. He feels as though he is looking over the edge of a large bowl. Not a pit, because he can see the curve of the bottom. He knows, however, if he steps into the bowl, the sides will be forever too slick for any exodus. He will be trapped in the curve, like a spider in a sink. After a few minutes, he looks into the bathroom mirror and sees the real Larry Dack, the fifty-five-year-old English teacher, gray skinned, balding, a bit paunchy, face rough with stubble, loose skin beneath his chin.

Once, when he was a child, after seeing *The Day the Earth Stood Still*, he pretended the world had stopped spinning for forty-seven minutes. He walked around and looked at everything in its stillness. Lying in bed, he imagines that stillness again. Of course, he has thought about killing himself before. That isn't the thing. He'd even called the

Samaritans once. He wanted to know what life would be like without him, and the person on the other end of the line had told him that it would be messy. He said that although it wouldn't be of any concern to Larry what the world was like once he was dead, he could safely say that existence would expand and contract in ways Larry could not understand—and if he killed himself, he never would understand. If he chose life, however, and peered deeper into himself, he might begin to find answers.

Why are you thinking along these lines? the man said.

I just feel like I'm falling apart, Larry had said. I don't know which way to turn.

Don't turn, the man said. Just stay the course. Ending your life is not a solution. Try to imagine the pain of those you would leave behind.

So that is what Larry does tonight. Denise, sleeping next to him, is a good wife. A loving mother and friend and member of the community. When he reaches for her, she is a million miles away, on shore, and he is drifting further out to sea. His bed is a raft in the middle of the ocean, and he can share with her none of the magic stillness.

You slept like a bag of snakes last night, Denise says from her side of the bed. I almost got up to leave at one point, but you finally calmed down.

I was dreaming about being still, he says. I was drifting away on a raft.

What's wrong with you recently?

I don't know, he says.

Is it Jimmy's visit? I know the kids can get on your nerves.

Did you know that Henson is sleeping with Sarah from the French department?

How would I know that?

Have you ever thought about sleeping with someone else?

The room swirls and swirls. The morning light comes through the window. Larry sits up. He looks over at his wife and is surprised to see her sitting there, quite calm and strong.

You aren't having an affair, are you? Denise says.

Jesus, no.

I know we haven't been too close recently, she says. I've just been preoccupied with school—but that is almost finished. She reaches over to him, touches his shoulder. Beneath his T-shirt, it feels as though his skin is jumping.

I don't want to sleep with anyone but you, he says.

Then why would you think I'd want to?

I don't know, Larry says. I've been having weird dreams.

Maybe you should see the doctor again? Did you tell him about the dreams?

He wants to do some tests.

Does he think it's the cholesterol?

I've been having the strangest sensations, Larry says. I've been dreaming almost all the time. The other day my students had to ask me if I needed help. I just couldn't breathe. I was standing in front of the class—and I felt like I was going to burst through the ceiling but I couldn't move.

Does Doctor Simpson think it might be a physical problem?

He doesn't know. What do you think you would do without me? Larry says.

At breakfast Larry runs his fingers through his hair. His hair is coming out in clumps. He begins to move through the room as though he is on a conveyor belt; the children and Jimmy and Candy are sitting still and he is gliding past, and he wonders if they can see him. He is ashamed to look at Candy. He thinks of her lips, of how she kisses his Jimmy, and is immediately repulsed by his own train of thought. He wants to say goodbye to each of them, but they appear like balloons in a distant sky. He glides to the door and out of the door without saying anything. He's bald now, and even his eyebrows are gone, vanished.

He thinks that if his eyebrows fell off in complete pieces, like Groucho Marx's tape, then they might be on his suit, might be lurking on his shoulder like caterpillars, or millipedes. When Jimmy was younger, he had a Vietnamese millipede as a pet. He had wanted a spider, a tarantula, but Larry had refused to share his house with a tarantula—it was another fear he could not explain, another fear that lessened his own opinion of himself. The four-inch millipede was a concession.

Over the course of a few months, while the thing was still alive, Larry had grown to appreciate it, its quick and decisive movements. He thinks that it would be a nice surprise to look down and see that freaky insect clinging on his shoulder. Perhaps it had been with him all along, sitting there, examining the world from its perch.

He glides all the way to the curb where Henson waits in his car. Inside, Henson smells sweet, like he bathed in cologne.

Jesus, Larry says. Did you spill a bottle of English Leather in here or something?

How's life? Henson says.

Life? Larry says. I think I'm sick.

Yeah, Henson says, you don't look so good.

It's my hair, Larry says.

Henson looks over at him.

No, he says. Your hair is fine. Looks like you didn't comb it though. You look like hell.

All day, he fights thoughts of spiders and bugs in the classroom. He wants the students to understand the plight of the poor in the midst of the industrial age. He has them reading Charles Dickens's *Hard Times*. He speaks slowly about the poor. His own father had been poor, he knows, but he never tells his students anything like this. His father had worked as a laborer all his life. He never remembered seeing his father when he wasn't covered in some sort of dust: drywall, brick, mortar, plaster, grain. During the summers, he worked on a road crew, and the smell of warm asphalt hung in the air around him, even after he showered. Larry knows that without his father's sacrifices, he never would be here in class teaching these kids about literary poverty.

Later in the year, he will teach *The Great Gatsby*.

Today, thinking about the decadence of not only the characters in that book, but of the author himself, Larry feels sick to his stomach. From deep inside, he feels the bugs coming up, crawling up his windpipe.

Pushing through his mouth. Climbing out of his nose. The class sits in front of him. They are bored and hate the book. No one notices that he is crawling with insects, or that he is bald, or that he cannot control how gravity affects his skin, or that he jerks off to thoughts of his son's wife, or that he cannot love his grandchildren in the way he wants, with all his heart, or that he can't summon up the energy to enjoy a few simple hours with his family, or that he reached out and squeezed Janet Golminiski's ass at the faculty party four days ago.

Look at me, he wants to yell. Can't you see these goddamn bugs?

Once, right after he married Denise, they went on vacation to a lake resort. He almost drowned the morning of their second day. During his lunch, he thinks about this while he eats his sandwich in the teacher's lounge. Sarah Toluene comes in, and she is as radiant as Henson was in the car. She smells like she has bathed in perfume as well—something lavender—but faint, like a mist rather than Henson's downpour. He wonders if they stood side by side and applied their odors. Her hair is long down her back, and Larry cannot help but picture her and Henson together. He sees them walking along the shore of the lake, and right out into the water, fearless.

Maybe he just needs a vacation.

Hey Larry, Sarah says. Can I sit with you?

Sure, Larry says. I was just thinking about vacation.

Two more days, she says. Are you ready for Christmas?

No, he says. I'm never ready. I mean a real vacation. Getting away, going up to the lake or something.

That must be nice, Sarah says. So how are you, Larry?

Me? Larry says.

He's drowning again, thinking about those early days in his marriage when he thought he could do anything, that life was something to be wrestled into place. In the lake, he gulped water and he couldn't help himself—saw himself rising up and then falling back down below, his arms extending above the water, but useless. Denise hadn't known what to do, and had resorted to just screaming from the dock. He could see her face frantic and distorted by the layer of water as he sank lower and lower. Eventually, the lifeguard pulled him out and tossed him onto the floating deck and sucked the water out of his lungs.

It was the first of the big failures in his married life. For months afterwards, he was surprised Denise still looked at him. And still he is surprised, surprised at how much mercy can be showered upon a man like him, who deserves so little.

Larry, Sarah says, we're worried about you. You aren't yourself. Henson says you barely talk on the way to school. He said he saw you crying in the parking lot.

I didn't even know you and Henson were seeing each other, Larry says. I had no idea.

Well, Sarah says, we didn't keep it a secret. We're in love.

That's wonderful, Larry says. Absolutely wonderful.

Larry can't bear the thought of seeing his son and his daughter-in-law and the grandkids, so he tells Henson that he needs to stay after school to prepare for the week after break. Henson shrugs. I guess that's just me, Larry says, always over-prepared. I know I've been slacking off a bit. Time to get back on the horse. I want to be ready, so I don't have to worry about it over break.

Sounds good. See you tomorrow morning?

Same time, same place, Larry says. He winks a bit, to let Henson know he's okay.

When the school is almost empty, he sneaks through the hallways like he's doing something wrong, and walks all the way down by the art rooms and out the back door. He cuts across the fields—both the upper field, with its coat of green turf, and over to the lower fields, the practice fields, which are dotted with hard dirt and crabgrass—at this time of year, the whole place brown anyway, no leaves, no cover. He feels naked out there, exposed. Part of him wants to believe he is naked—streaking across the fields—but the hallucinations are a bit too much for him at this point. He knows he isn't growing or shrinking or dying or bloody. He can't fool himself any longer.

What he does know is this: there isn't one reason to want to be alive. It has come to this. It has come to this. It has come to this. He thinks it as he walks over the fields. He knows this is the right answer. He's surprised that it took him so long to get there. Perhaps it is the crisp air, the lightness of the winter atmosphere. Part of him wants to go right back to the school, to somehow hang himself in the gym—and this is the first time he thinks of this—the real way it might happen—his death—although he thinks of dying often—this is the first time he thinks of how he might do it himself—not by turning to rock, or getting crushed by his wife, or by slicing away the tops of his hands and bleeding to death—but by walking back up to the gym and somehow getting the big A-frame ladder out onto the gym floor and finding a rope—perhaps from the weight room—a jump rope or even a wound-up volleyball net—and climbing up the ladder to the ceiling and throwing the rope over the top and looping it around his neck and just doing it.

Why hasn't he thought of this before?

There is no stillness now, though all around him is still. He's walking fast, thinking, hands stuck into his pockets, to where there is a hole in the fence. When he gets to the fence, he ducks through and walks along the dirt path and the stream. He follows the stream for fifteen minutes or so. He has heard his students talk about this path. It is how they sneak into football games, or how they sneak out of football games to smoke joints or drink beers. He's a bit afraid that he might run into one of them here, that they might be doing something he doesn't want to know about—and how they might ask him what he is doing; and he doesn't know if he has the capability to form the words. Everything comes to him in a rush, and he can't see much beyond his own skin. He might stammer and stutter, and the students might follow him for a while, or perhaps they might taunt him for some reason. What could he do? Report them? How could he explain walking along the stream? He couldn't. Perhaps these students could just kill him. Wouldn't that be convenient?

He's running now, pushing the branches out of his way, slipping here, falling, sinking. He thinks for a moment that he is falling into the center of the earth, but he is just sliding down a hill, and then he is on the bottom and running again, running for no particular reason except that the light is dying and he is in the woods. How is he going to explain this to anyone—the cuts, the scrapes, the muddy shoes, the fact that he lusts after Candy, that he is certain he will shrink to nothing while he sleeps, or expand like a balloon while he teaches, that he is the sort of failed man who cannot love his family, that he is, more than anything, the most horrible cliché of middle-aged manhood, cold and distant and fond of tinkering in his work shed and discussing working-class mores in twentieth-century literature? How can he explain that he is running to avoid thinking of the gym, the reality of his body hanging there, his torso hanging just about even with those enormous fluorescent scoop lights in the rafters? How can he explain to his family when he gets home that if he has to go and buy a tree, he will end up killing himself before the purchase? Perhaps before they leave the house? How can he tell anyone about slipping into the bowl, and not being able to climb up the sides? Even his voice, calling out for help, even that will echo and echo until it is nothing in the wind.

He does finally get home—dirty, cold, wet a bit—but not as bedraggled as he thought he might be. Everyone is in the kitchen decorating cookies, and he stands across the street next to a post box. His shoes are dirty and he doesn't know what to do. Eventually, Jimmy sees him standing there and comes outside. Larry knows he cannot talk to his son—but he does not know why. The feelings converge and separate inside of him, so he starts to run. But his shoes are muddy, and his son is fast. Together they run down the street. Jimmy calls to him as he runs. The lights from the Christmas decorations throw colorful shadows across the lawns. Larry's loafers slap against the pavement. He tries to turn on the corner of his street, even uses the stop sign to anchor his swing, but his shoes can't bear the pressure, and he slips and slides underneath a row of bushes along the edge of the sidewalk.

Jimmy comes running up behind him, and Larry looks at him as he charges up the sidewalk. To Larry, he appears upside-down, his feet clomping on the ceiling of the universe.

What the fuck, Dad? Jimmy says. What's wrong with you?

I've slipped, Larry says.

What the hell were you running for? Are you on drugs?

No, I'm just losing my mind. I don't know what I'm doing.

Get out from under the bush, Dad.

Jimmy leans down and puts his face close to Larry's. How had Jimmy grown so much? He is heavy, too, and more than likely has high cholesterol. He knows for a fact that Jimmy doesn't exercise. He sits at that desk all day eating chocolates. Even in his son, Larry has failed. He had always wanted Jimmy to be a great mind, and now here he is twenty-seven, working as a bookkeeper for a paint store.

Where did I go wrong with you? Larry says.

Here we go again. Look, Dad, I'm fine. You're the one under a bush.

Jimmy, Larry says, I almost didn't come home tonight.

Jimmy looks up and down the street. Remarkably, Larry notes, there seems to have been no witnesses to their little event. They are as alone as one could ever hope to be.

So, Jimmy says, maybe we should just get back before anyone sees us. Mom wants to go get the tree tonight. Can you shake this off? I mean, you're probably just having one of those days. We all get crazy, right?

The mud is seeping through Larry's jacket and pants.

Can you help me?

Take my hand, Dad.

Jimmy extends his hand. Larry takes it, pulls against it. It reminds him of the moment Jimmy was born, how he reached out his little arms. Even then, Larry had been stunned by love, by how quickly he had loved Jimmy, and how he instantaneously knew he would never be good enough for his baby boy.

I want to go home now, Larry says.

So is this what I have to look forward to? Jimmy says. Freaking out when I'm fifty-five?

I think I'm having a breakdown, Larry says.

Maybe you should buy a Porsche.

Maybe.

First, Jimmy says, let's go home. Let's get cleaned up. Let's get some dinner in you. And then let's go downtown and buy a damn Christmas tree.

Later that evening, they all go together to the Dairy Queen parking lot, where the Elks are selling trees. Larry knows the head Elk, a man named Quince who lost his wife in a fire about seven years ago. They have known each other since high school. Quince plows Larry's driveway. Hey, Larry, Quince says. How's it going?

Oh, you know, Larry says. Same old same old.

Lot of nice trees this year.

Yup. Looking for a big one? Little one? Fat one? Tall one? We got them all.

Denise and Jimmy walk down one aisle of trees. Candy and the kids down another. The Elks keep the largest lot of trees in town. As his family wanders off, it is easy for Larry to imagine them moving into some primeval forest, or disappearing into a Christmas fairy tale. Bright white lights are strung ten feet overhead, up and down each aisle—it appears as though it might be a runway of sorts. The glare is spectacular, and Larry is disoriented, but it feels real, as though all the other hallucinations have been mere preparation for this. He tries to conjure thoughts of floating or growing or sinking, but there are no images available.

Those lights are bright, he says.

Yeah, Quince says. Got to light up the season, you know.

How do you get through it all, Larry says.

Me? Quince says. I just do it. Same as yesterday, same as today. What about you?

I haven't been doing so good, Larry says.

Christmas will fix you, Quince says. It's the best part of the year.

He's touching his cash box while he talks, his breath coming out in little puffs.

Here, at the tree lot, Larry feels years away from the moment in front of the house when he looked in and saw Jimmy and Candy and Denise and the kids all sitting around the kitchen table making cookies. What he felt right before Jimmy walked out was something new—something better than the thoughts of death—but more disturbing. He felt then a swell of love such as he had never felt before. He did not know if he could contain the love, let alone express it. He did not know if there were even any words for what he was feeling—or if anyone else had ever felt these same things. It was a love that cleared away all the wreckage of his life, his failures and his presumed failures; it was a love that shined down from heaven, although he did not know what that meant, exactly. For a few moments his eyes weren't aching with visions of hanging from the gym rafters.

When they returned back inside, no one said anything about his appearance. He said hello to everyone and walked to the bathroom and stripped off his clothes and looked at his ridiculous body—ridiculous, but normal—just the body of a normal man with normal problems. Even his thoughts of Candy seemed a minor and silly thing—nothing to be so ashamed of. He stood in the shower and let the water run over him and down the drain. When he came downstairs, they were all ready to go and buy the tree, but they waited for him to eat a piece of chicken. The children stood around him and asked him questions about Santa Claus.

And it all ends up here, Larry thinks, in a tree lot run by Quince the Elk.

He hears Candy talking to her kids, and he knows he cannot talk to them, because he might start crying; he might fall to the ground and beg them for forgiveness. He slips in between the two big trees leaning against a fence. He pushes back into the chain links and pulls the branches up and around his face

Candy and the kids walk by, Denise and Jimmy close behind.

Dad! Jimmy shouts.

Larry! Denise shouts. We found the one we want.

Grandpa! Candy and the kids shout. We want the big fat one!

Yo, Larry! Quince shouts. Want me to tie it up? I can put it over by the car.

And there he is, holding the branches—a green veil—in front of his face. The pine needles tickle his skin—he can feel a sneeze building, but keeps it under control. He feels the sticky sap against his fingers and he knows it will be tough to get out of his clothes. He wants to call out to his family, his loved ones, those he has failed in so many ways—those who extend love in return for failure. But he isn't quite ready. He lifts his hands to his mouth and breathes onto them, warming his fingers a bit. There will be plenty of time to call out later, all the time in the world, but not yet, not quite.

The Last Pages

Baby Susan and Grandma Burmeister, and big sisters Dabby and Linda, 1960.

This is Lesson 15 from my father's first reader, *Little Pets Linen ABC*, published by McLoughlin Bros. Notice the misuse of a period instead of a question mark in the fifth paragraph. Maybe this explains why my father was a declarative sort of man, always charging ahead rather than stopping to question.

—*Lee Martin*

LESSON 15.

Do you go by the sea? yes, I do.

I saw a man, was he an old man?

No, he was a big man.

He had a net, and the net was wet.

How did the net get wet.

In the sea, but the man can dry it in the sun.

I spent the summer of 2004 in Malawi (southeast Africa) delivering medicines to rural villages. It strikes me that this photo represents what I try to do in fiction as well as in "real" life. Make a commitment. Strive for balance. Don't take yourself more seriously than is required. In "A Fine Father," I was interested in the opportunities Maxwell's desperation created for him, as well as in the ways he managed his vulnerabilities. Balance is always illusory. Things change. But we try. That's what I like about Maxwell—and about this photo.

—*Jean Colgan Gould*

I composed the first two paragraphs of "Ascension" while walking on the bluffs in Mendocino, California after reading Stacey Richter's magnificent story "The Cavemen in the Hedges." Her story thrilled me. It jerked me out of a rut I had been in and inspired me to experiment a little. My own work is generally very realistic; this particular story came out of a self-imposed exercise to see if I could inject a little of the fantastic into the realistic world. It started as something of a rip-off and then became its own story. I'm a big fan of copying and stealing; it's the best way to learn.

—*Samantha Schoech*

This photo was taken the morning of my first day at R. Dean Kilby Elementary School in Woodbridge, Virginia. I think I look pretty sharp in my patterned shirt, polka-dot tie, yellow pants, and black socks. In my right hand, I'm holding a Hot Wheels lunch box. In my left, a book bag. A great deal of the memories of my early childhood have this stretch of sidewalk as a platform. From footraces to the stop sign, to my first skateboarding accident, to dusky games of freeze tag, and hours of firefly collection—I must have traversed the street thousands and thousands of times. Later, I moved off the sidewalk and onto the asphalt. My friends and I played touch football and foursquare and rode rickety go-carts up and down Pinetree Drive until we were too old to do such things. Beyond the house in the center of the cul-de-sac were woods that seemed as vast as Yosemite. In reality, it was only about a quarter-mile stretch that bordered Interstate 95.

—*Clark E. Knowles*

Usually a story comes to me nearly whole, but this one came in two tiny pieces. First was the title. My job involves a lot of proofreading. Sometimes I'll run across a word I *know* is incorrect, but find myself puzzling over it, even saying it aloud. Brang? The wrong conjugation had a nice sound. The second piece was the simple inversion of the final sentences: I found something appealing in transposing the order. I thank my proofreading job for that, as well as my immersion in poetry. I am consistently moved by poets' finesse with words in the service of so many callings: Adrienne Rich, A. R. Ammons, Louise Glück, and many others. Poetry teaches me how language, fine-tuned and honed, is a marvelous way of understanding others.

The sentence inversion started the story, and I worked backward, discovering Martín's situation and believing he would hold all the answers to the story's arc. But the key to the story was Perla. Her forgiveness and ability to love others allowed Martín to recognize his self-pity and accept the responsibility of being a loving parent. I owe much of this understanding to my oldest sister, Sylvia: a single mother, she's raised her son—my nephew—with such grace and resilience that I can only marvel. She's been equally supportive of me. I thank her with this story.

—Manuel Muñoz

For any writer, I'd imagine, one of the most astonishing pleasures must be the moment your child begs you to read "just one more book!" My two-and-one-half-year-old daughter Sophia has conned us into an elaborate nighttime reading ritual. "Two books," she says. "Big books! I get it." She peruses her jumbled shelf, pulls out the longest volumes: *The Collected Mother Goose*, *The Collected Dr. Seuss*, or *Aesop's Fables* in Greek that only Daddy can read. It's not just about delaying sleep. It's her love of story, of the way words come together, imagining a world beyond the pages and pictures. Her lips mimic mine as I trail a finger beneath what is to her for the moment a hodgepodge of *A*'s and *O*'s and *I*'s. When Sophia hears me say, "Thank you, thank you, Sam I am!" she knows it's time to move from the rocking chair to the crib. So then she pleads, "Three books in bed!" I choose the shortest ones (the babyish board books) because my arms go numb hanging over the crib bars. Finally, when we say, *Goodnight! Don't let the bedbugs bite!* I crouch outside her closed door and listen as she tells stories to her three bunnies, Hoppy 1, Hoppy 2, and Hoppy 3. Though the narrative follows no logical arc (at least, none apparent to any adult), it always includes a wonderful muddle of new words:

dolphin sandcastle
cheese grater shit shit shit
now go to sleep, baby!!

—*Kerry Neville Bakken*

In this photo, taken at a party outside my former apartment in Iowa City, I am the one to the right of the snack table. I am holding my hand up, I believe, in order to bring more attention to the snack table. This is about as far as you would ever find me from the food at any party, which means that I was probably comfortable, and even more than that, hungry.

—Justin M. Kramon

Like so many things I've written lately, "Fire" is an attempt to understand the relation of the physical and the spiritual in the context of institutional religion—a dichotomy that continues to fascinate and confuse me, as much today as it did the day of my confirmation in 1966. At the time, I had hoped for illumination the moment the bishop of Los Angeles touched my head, but the only gift I received was the Seabury *Book of Common Prayer*, which I'm holding with much more optimism than my parents seem to possess. After the service, my uncle told me that I was now fit to partake of beer and crackers like the rest of the family. Such is the magic of faith.

Less magical is the memory of many years later when my yearning for confirmation of a spiritual reality led me to a small church and an altar call where I strained to speak in tongues. I tried desperately. I even tried to mutter something that might have been mistaken for a Phoenician dialect, but the message was all too dismal and clear: they also serve who only stand and wait, and in my case I was also supposed to be very, very quiet.

—*David Borofka*

I shot this in Paris, obviously, in December 1972. Surprisingly, after more than three decades, I seem to have become the man in the picture.

—Ken Kaye

"Fag Killer" was a difficult story to write, at least initially. I had all these doubts and don'ts firing through my mind. Don't let the story get too long or no one will publish it! Don't switch points of view in a short story! Didn't you learn anything in graduate-school workshop? The more gay characters you have, the more you'll limit your audience, brainiac. What, Eddie is going to put on his mother's dress? Stop, are you insane? And you're going to title the story *what*?

There, now you've pretty much offended everyone! Are you happy?

The story really began to reach critical mass for me once I grew stubborn enough to push aside all the doubts and don'ts and just let myself loose on the story, or, more accurately, let the story loose and did my best not to hold it back with concerns about audience or how the story might be judged. So the writing of "Fag Killer" became sort of a battle against inhibition, that human tendency to want to "fit in," to not cause controversy or break the rules, to charm rather than to stir or provoke. As I'm constantly reminded, the tendency to flock toward the "normal" will kill a good piece of writing... and it can also kill a good life if you're not careful.

—*Robert Schirmer*

A picture of me with Estelle Schirmer, my grandmother.

Cousins Elise Meier and Henry J. Burmeister, circa 1992.

COMING SOON

"While you're here, we need to go through some things."

"Papers?"

"No, things." Another yawn. "You need to know who's who in the pictures. And the tablecloths—tomorrow I'm going to show you all the old tablecloths, and tell you who embroidered them."

from "Almost" by Joan Wickersham

In all of one's life, you might harbor one real secret, and here was hers to hold like his own.

from "Honeymoon" by Evan Shopper

She kept having to adjust her pace so that she didn't leave Bo behind. She thought it was strange how having the arm amputated made him *walk* slower, but she didn't mention it.

from "Good News for a Hard Time" by Belle Boggs

Ten minutes sometimes makes a difference in the ER, but not as often as you would think.

from "Bonsai" by Mark Sindecuse

"Ha," my husband says. He manages to say it without sounding insincere. That is his greatest gift—an almost ridiculous capacity for sincerity.

from "The Boulevard of Heroes" by Michelle Richmond